"Hey, come here, I got
something for you."

Joel Brogan paused and turned around. The girl was blonde and as she smiled at him, she arched her back, her body straining against the cheap knit dress.

"I got a sale on," she said. "Two for the price of one."

She couldn't even be out of her teens, Joel thought, but she was all woman. He shook his head slowly and walked on, her laughter taunting him.

This was Reno Street, and he was back —but on his own terms, he vowed, not those of The Street.

A strikingly realistic novel
of a big city sin-street
and the man—and his woman—
who changed it.

BY BOB BRISTOW

SIN STREET

WILDSIDE PRESS

INTRODUCTION

Sin Street—credited at the time of publication to "Bob Bristow:"—is the work of Robert O'Neil Bristow (1926–2018), an American novelist best known for depicting the lives of Black Americans in small town South Carolina during the years surrounding desegregation. This early, sensationalistic crime novel is a far cry from his later works, such as *Time for Glory* (1968), which received the University of Oklahoma award for literary excellence and was designated as recommended reading by the Black Panther Party and the Christian Book List.

Mysteries, however, were an integral part of his early writing. He published at least 135 short stories in the 1950s and 1960s, the bulk of them with mystery themes in such markets as *Alfred Hitchcock's Mystery Magazine*, *Manhunt*, *Trapped Detective Magazine*, and he also broke into more mainstream publications, such as *Adventure* and *Redbook*. He also published in the (quite well paying) "men's magazines" such as *Rogue* and in the western genre.

Bristow received a master's degree in journalism from the University of Oklahoma in 1960. For his master's thesis, he conducted interviews about story outcomes and demonstrated that people will choose the morally right outcome versus the morally wrong outcome regardless of their personal choices to partake in illegal activities such as prostitution. This divergence between "cash-register honesty" and "emotional honesty" lay the groundwork for the characters and plots in his fiction.

Bristow moved to Rock Hill, South Carolina, in 1961, where he became writer-in-residence and professor in the Dept. of Communications at Winthrop University until he retired in 1987. Little wonder, with mainstream acceptance of his work, that he began to leave his more sensational crime-fiction credits off of his bibliography. But connoiseurs of mystery and crime still enjoy his work, such as *Sin Street*, which lays the literary groundwork for all that was to follow.

—John Betancourt
Cabin John, Maryland

1

The 9:05 bus was due, but it would not be on time, as it had not been on time yesterday or the day before or as long as anybody could remember.

It did not matter to the townspeople of Toyah, Oklahoma, but it mattered to the Reverend Joel Brogan who stood alone, conspicuously alone, in front of the drugstore, a worn leather bag at his side, his ticket in hand.

He let his body slump, looked at the cracked sidewalk and wished the bus had been on time. He waited in silence, aware that from the windows they secretly watched him. What did these people see?

A tall, unco-ordinated, thin body. Black-brown eyes bearing an expression of frustration. There were lines in his face. Above the eyebrows the unmistakable wrinkles of anxiety, of fear, of countless pains. Because of these lines he looked considerably older than his thirty-one years.

The narrow face, the high cheekbones hinted of privation. His nose, once a straight, proud nose, had been crushed by the butt of a rifle in a long ago battle. The result gave this tragic face a touch of humor. Flat and crooked, and at times unsightly.

The jaws were set tensely. From tensions that had begun when he stole his first bicycle, had grown when he faced his first police lineup, etching narrow lines

5

about his mouth. For each line there had been worries, hates, angers, sadnesses and shames.

His were the eyes of a man who had known death and fear, humiliation and misery, hunger and desperation. And a measure of love.

He saw the roof of the bus reflecting sunlight as it completed the curve a half mile away. He watched it grow, then reduce speed as it neared the stop.

The exhaust filled the air with an acrid odor. As the door of the bus opened, he methodically took the first step. He looked up to see an old woman wearing a shawl coming out.

"Out, please," the bus driver said quite loudly, impatiently.

The Reverend Joel Brogan moved back apologetically as the old-lady laboriously made her way down the three steps. She brushed past him.

A man with an unlighted cigar in his mouth followed. He stepped down. "Toyah, Oklahoma," he said. "Some dump."

Reverend Brogan looked at the man with the cigar and he felt the beginning of a smile pulling at his lips, but it died there quickly. The passageway was empty. Ticket in hand, he mounted the steps, found an empty seat and eased over to the window.

The man with the cigar waited outside the bus. He was very obviously amused at the small town. But it wasn't really a funny little town. It wasn't to the Reverend Joel Brogan.

The post office was located across the street in Mr. Maurice Bailey's drugstore. Mr. Bailey had a habit of taking the floor in session meetings, declaring how things should be done. Such as the time the elders discussed rumors of dissatisfaction with the pastor.

"It's my judgment," Mr. Bailey had pronounced

6

blandly, his balding head bobbing, his long thin neck moving like an old father crane, "that we should bring these things out in the open. I've had some experience with these matters and believe me, I know. We were having trouble with a preacher at Lone Fork once a few years back, and I told them folks that it'd be best if we brought it right out in the open and talked it over. But they didn't think much of my idea." At this point Mr. Bailey smiled supremely. "And you might well know, the church was split so bad they had to stop having meetings for a month or two. Lost nearly half the members to the Baptists." Of course, as it developed, Mr. Bailey was undeniably right.

Mr. Bailey's drugstore was now faded white, badly in need of paint. High upon the glass windows a sign had been pasted. It read: *Make Us Your Christmas Gift Headquarters.* It was June.

Two doors down the street, Mr. Hawks stood, his back to the window, busy at the cash register of the Toyah Food Market. Mr. Hawks was a very small, intense man, much overweight, quite red-faced. Mr. Hawks was an elder and spokesman for the congregation. In truth, being mayor, he was the spokesman for the entire town of Toyah.

Mr. Hawks had been wildly irritated at the minister of the First Presbyterian Church. His neck turned deep red and the veins in his forehead bulged when he talked of the minister. The fever of his anger swept like an electric shock to most of those who listened. Nearly everybody became angry at the preacher. Even the Baptists were mad at him.

"Now look here, preacher," Jess Hawkes had demanded that day in the study. "I like a preacher that gets in there and tells these people they'd better get in line." Jess Hawks had wiped his brow with a stained

7

sleeve. "You'll be all right if you just yell at them. You've got to treat some people different."

"You mean teach them the fear of God?" Joel offered.

"You've got it, son. That's exactly what I mean."

Joel Brogan had braced himself, considered retreat, then made the irrevocable decision that he could not abandon his belief. "I'm sorry," he had said evenly, "I don't preach fear. I preach love."

Jess Hawks had squinted, had spoken through his teeth. "Maybe you do," he had said.

"And forgiveness. I teach that, too."

"All right, son. I tried to help you. You'll just have to find out the hard way. You've got a lot to learn. You may not last very long here."

You don't have to be mad any more, Mr. Hawks. I didn't last very long after all.

Jess Hawks had been spokesman for the session that voted unanimously for his resignation. Joel had requested a vote of the entire congregation, as was his right. After the vote was taken, Mr. Hawks opened the study door, stood tight-lipped, his eyes glowing fiercely. As he spoke, he had to pause often for breath.

"Reverend Brogan, the congregation has voted," he said. In his hands, Mr. Hawks fumbled a piece of paper.

"What have they decided?" Joel asked, already knowing the result by the throbbing pulsation at Mr. Hawks' neck.

"They voted to have you leave. That's what they did."

"I'm fired."

"If you want to put it that way. You are just that."

It was difficult for Mr. Hawks to control the surging emotions that the vote had aroused.

"What was the vote?" Joel asked.

"It don't matter as I see it. They just voted for you to go." But as he spoke, Mr. Hawks raised his head so that he could see the trembling paper through his bifocals.

"A hundred and fifty-nine against you. And twenty-one for you."

"That leaves little doubt," Joel said.

And Mr. Hawkes, unable to suppress his feeling, had answered, "That's for sure."

"I can leave any time?"

"We didn't set no date. You can appeal to the Presbytery if you think it will do any good."

"No," he said. "The vote makes it plain enough. I'll leave as soon as possible."

Mr. Hawks had left the paper on his desk, had turned and closed the door behind him. A few came to tell him they were sorry. Then he was alone.

Joel bent over the desk and rested his head against his arms. When he looked up, he saw the face of Jesus Christ on the wall, glazed and distorted by tears.

The next morning he wrote the Dean at the Seminary informing him of the congregation's action, and asked for advice.

The Dean's answer had been prompt. It was consoling, but more formal than he had expected. *You failed in your first charge. We secured you another. Now you have failed again in your second.*

The letter explained that with this record, it would be nearly impossible for him to secure another church. The Presbytery would grant him a release from pastoral duties. *Wait a year. Or two years. Perhaps something will come along.*

The Dean asked him to take this time to discover what was wrong. Surely a man is not fired from two

9

churches in less than a year without reason. *What were you doing wrong? There was no evidence that either of the churches was torn with strife when you entered.*

And, quite gently, it suggested that if during this year he found something that more nearly suited him, then by all means he should take a stab at it. *After all, there are many ways that we can serve God. Being a minister is no greater in God's eyes than . . .*

Mr. Wiginton, the eighty-six-year-old custodian, had come this morning. For the last time he brought the pot of coffee from the church kitchen and knocked on the door softly.

"Come in."

The old man opened the door, took the cups from a tray, and poured the coffee. They sipped the coffee silently for a few minutes, knowing that tomorrow it would not be this way, that this was the last time.

"Well," the old man said smiling, "we got rid of you, didn't we?"

"Yes," Joel said, glad that Mr. Wiginton had not made a melancholy speech about how it had been and all. He didn't think he could stand any of that. Not on the last morning.

"I figured it was coming," Mr. Wiginton said. "But I was surprised at the vote. You didn't show well at all."

For the first time all day he was able to smile. "You're a diplomatic old cuss," he said.

The old man laughed and the laugh was good. It came from deep down and rolled out like a clap of distant thunder. "If I was a diplomat, I wouldn't be janitor," he said.

They smiled at each other, drank the coffee.

"You're all washed up, aren't you?" Mr. Wiginton

10

asked, his face growing soft, the lines melting almost to smoothness.

"I suppose so."

"I read that letter from the Dean. It was on your desk and I just nosed over there and read it."

"I'm glad you kept up with all the developments."

"There's no place for you to go."

"No."

"Said wait a few years. Maybe it'll come out all right. That sounded like a brush-off to me!"

"A kindly one."

Mr. Wiginton rubbed his chin. "It's a funny thing," he said. "I knew you was doomed to fail the day you got here. But I knew just as well when you carried that Bible up here that you loved God. I can tell."

"I'll get along," he said. He didn't want Mr. Wiginton to go into that business of a sad farewell. He just didn't think he could possibly stand it.

"No . . ." Mr. Wiginton said thoughtfully, "I doubt if you ever preach again. You'll never find out what's wrong with you."

"What is wrong with me?"

The old man smiled. "I don't know. I could tell you a thousand things that I see wrong, but that wouldn't tell you what was wrong. It's inside you. The best I could say was that you just never did fit. Like you was trying to put on a little boy's coat. It was impossible from the start."

He looked at his watch. It was time to be going. The bus would be along soon.

Mr. Wiginton placed the empty cups on the tray and stood aside.

Joel lifted his suitcase and stepped to the door. "Well," he said, "it's finished."

11

Mr. Wiginton did not speak. Great tears welled in his eyes and ran down his cheeks, falling into wrinkled gullies. He was smiling, a very small angelic man in overalls, crying and smiling, standing there in the doorway holding the tray with the pot and two cups that he would not need any more.

"Good-by," he said.

Joel carried his suitcase down the hall and opened the door. When he glanced back, the old man was still standing there.

The driver climbed aboard the bus, came down the aisle, and took his ticket. He handed Joel a baggage check and returned to the front. The thin-necked man with the cigar boarded the bus and sat down. The starter whined and the bus was moving. He looked a last time at Mr. Bailey's drugstore, Mr. Hawks' grocery. Mr. Hawks was standing in the doorway, his hands on his hips. He watched as the bus passed. Mr. Hawks was smiling.

The town of Toyah was falling behind the hungry wheels. Gone was the bench where the men gathered and sharpened their knives on the worn bricks and whittled in the shade of the afternoon. The same men who, on Sunday morning, sat in the church wearing a clean pair of overalls, a white shirt buttoned at the top, but no tie. Gone were the children whose faces were polished and bright, who squirmed and giggled through his sermons. The babe in arms whose mother covered the face of her child with a clean diaper while the child nursed noisily at her breast. Gone the tired men whose eyes closed at about eleven-fifteen, whose heads sagged and who sometimes snored until a neighbor nudged them in the ribs. There were the old men who could never quite hide the fact that they had a dip

12

of snuff tucked neatly in the lower lip and who immensely enjoyed this added pleasure during the service.

Did they know the terrible emptiness he felt when the vote was taken, when he was told that he was not wanted?

The last houses had vanished, replaced by rolling hillsides, magnificently green pastures spotted with cattle.

He tried to pray. It was useless. He had lost that, too.

Then he thought of his childhood days down on Reno Street in Oklahoma City, where he ran barefoot across the hot sidewalks. Where he had stolen, lied, cheated. He thought about how he had grown in the shadows, caring for an alcoholic mother. How he had been hurt and how he had learned not to show that hurt. The times he fought back rebelliously. The line-up at the police station. The cigarettes and beer when he was fifteen. The women. The whores. The things they had taught him.

The war. The injury, the chaplain. And then he was sent home . . . to Reno Street. When he arrived, he learned that his mother had died while he was in France. His Uncle Charlie had buried her.

He had gone to college and worked in a kitchen. Graduated. Enrolled in Austin Presbyterian Seminary. Then his GI Bill ran out and Uncle Charlie helped him with money. It was money that had trickled from whores' fingers for drink, money from drunks, pimps, riffraff from Reno Street.

But he had taken it. Maybe someday he'd have a church and be able to help a young girl over that problem, keep a boy from becoming an alcoholic, a thief.

Suddenly he was pastor of a church in a town of

fifteen thousand and he was making over five thousand dollars a year. Then it happened. Like Mr. Wiginton had said, perhaps he didn't fit. *Step down, boy. Down a little lower.*

That wasn't so bad. Lots of ministers were accepted at posts too large for them. Some labored, polished quickly and made it. Others were forced to take smaller churches. He had taken the step down gracefully. And it had been a long step. Down to Toyah, a town of 2,000. But he hadn't made it there either. Now the Dean was afraid to recommend him again. He was through. He was useless.

2

The bus entered Oklahoma City from the south, through the section called Capital Hill. A great deal of the tougher element circulated there, but the toughest belonged to Reno Street and California Street and Grand Avenue. These were the evil streets of the city, snuggled close under the shadows of the great skyscrapers.

The bus passed along the Avenue moving north through the salvage yard section. This was home. How many times had he stolen hub caps and spotlights from new cars and hustled them down to those yards for the change he could make? The first time he had brought a set of four hubs. He dropped them at the salvage owner's feet.

"How much?" he had asked. And when the offer was too low, he shouted, "Up your old lady's butt! Gimme a buck or no deal. These is real caps from a Cadillac, buster. I don't heist no caps from no Cad for no measly half buck!"

The salvage yard owner spat, and part of the tobacco juice ran down his shirt front and his eyes shifted like they were on ball bearings. "Six bits," he said. "That's all. Take the six bits or haul ass, kid."

"I can get a buck and a half down the street."

The man, heavy shouldered, twisted his neck like an old turtle. "Haul ass, kid."

Then he threw the caps down and spat just as

defiantly as the owner had done. "Gimme the damn six bits." He quickly pocketed the money and walked away with a swagger.

Even now as the bus passed, he saw two or three teen-aged boys walking around the salvage yards. Tough-looking kids. Kids that could get you a stick of marijuana as fast as a Coca Cola. They were wide awake.

The bus lumbered through the underpass, up and over. Along the street a few stands sold cold watermelon. There were several beer joints. A corner grocery. Dozens of run-down two-story apartments.

The bus swept past Reno and California and crossed Grand Avenue, turning into the bus station, creeping easily to the ramp. "Oklahoma City," the bus driver said. "Fifteen-minute rest stop."

He was feeling a weakness in his stomach. Did he eat breakfast? He couldn't remember. The coffee with Mr. Wiginton . . . that seemed a long time ago! No, he hadn't really eaten anything. He made his way down the aisle, left the bus and waited in line for his bag.

In a moment a red cap tossed his bag on the sidewalk, looked at the tag, stared impassively at the small group of passengers and shouted, "Reverend Joel Brogan?"

Joel stepped forward, slipped a quarter into the Negro's hand and lifted the bag. Once away from the crowd, he jerked the tag from the handle. Scribbled on the tag was his name . . . Reverend . . . Reverend . . . He tore it in four pieces and dropped them wearily on the sidewalk. Reverend of what?

"Cab, mister?" the driver asked, swinging open his door.

Joel ignored him.

16

"Take you anywhere . . . show you anything . . ."
the cabbie promised.

Joel moved down Grand Avenue. As he walked east,
respectability diminished. He recognized the front of
the burlesque house. A fat woman sat in the ticket
booth, her lips painted so high the red appeared to
almost touch her nose. Her face was puffy with bluish-
red lines on the cheeks. Joel knew her kind. Every ten
minutes she had to duck down out of sight and take a
little drink to keep going. *Don't they ever change?*
Why did he come back to this?

"How 'bout it . . . see the girls. Lots of pretty girls.
Real live flesh . . . and what flesh . . ."

He passed beyond her voice. A panhandler staggered
from the building. "My wife has a new baby and I
need . . ." His breath smelled like a Milwaukee
brewery.

Joel was angered. "You're drunk enough!" he said.

"Screw you," the man mumbled, moving away.

Joel turned south at the corner, headed over one
block, toward Reno. A Negro porter sat in the doorway of a small hotel. He wore a spotless white jacket.
He knew all he had to know to live. He knew the
names of five girls upstairs, a somewhat exaggerated
description of the attractiveness of each, and their
prices. He always recited them without looking up as
though it did not matter, that the law of averages
would take care of everything. It always had.

Joel had known it was going to be this way. Why
did he let it disturb him?

He swung around the corner, past a tavern, and
looked at Reno Street. On both sides of the street
representatives of society were leaning against the
buildings in the afternoon sunshine. Their eyes were

17

streaked with red. They did without haircuts, shaves, clothing, sometimes shelter, and often food, for a drink. It could be whisky, wine, beer, vanilla . . . it did not matter as long as it numbed the brain. Joel had seen them fall on their hands and knees and pray for God to send them another drink. When they reached this point, they were picked up and shipped out. One less. But another came to take his place. Work a few days pearl diving and then a big wet drunk. Then back to work. They were like snakes, sunning in the afternoon.

The panhandlers were more active on Reno. They didn't cry out a story about the wife having a baby. They walked up and shouldered against you. They were bitter and hardened and demanded help. "I gotta have a half buck, mac," they said. "C'mon. Let's not be rough on an old guy like me. Gimme the damn money." Joel moved through them.

Music throbbed from the bars and he heard the shouts of men and women. Four o'clock in the afternoon and they were already on a toot. But then they never really got off of one, did they?

The buildings were only two or three stories high here. Across the street a big blue sign read: *Cots—25c.* That's one thing that hadn't changed much. Cots were costing a quarter ten years ago in that same place. The price hadn't yielded to inflation. The bugs on the cots were probably the same.

He reached an open doorway. A blonde stood in the door wearing a knit blouse and a tight skirt. If she sneezed hard she'd be naked. When she saw Joel, she arched her back against the door, emphasizing her breasts. She smiled.

"Hey, boy . . . c'mere, boy. I've got something for you."

He paused. The girl was about nineteen. Her hair

18

was natural blond, but she had brown eyes. It occurred to him that she was actually a beautiful girl. Her eyes danced for him. "What is it?" he asked.

"I got a sale on," she said.

Joel hesitated, frowning. "Sale?"

"Yeah . . . two for the price of one. Any kinda date you like." *Nineteen years old.* Joel turned his head, still standing in front of the door holding the suitcase. "Ten bucks. It's a bargain, buster. Ask the man who's been there." She laughed, moving her shoulders enticingly.

Joel shook his head, turned in the hot sun and started away.

"Okay . . . I'll make you a deal."

He glanced back,

"Seven bucks," she said. "How 'bout that? Best seven dollar's worth in town."

"I'm a minister," Joel said softly.

The girl frowned, jerked her head away. "A damn do-gooder." He was passing out of range of her voice but he heard it ring after him. "I've had preachers before, buster."

At the corner, when the light had changed, he crossed the street. The big sign, even at four in the afternoon, was a glare of flashing neon. It read: *The Green Parrot Bar.* There was a black glass front and, painted on the glass, a large green parrot.

Joel stepped over the curbing and turned into the bar. The darkness was sudden. For a few moments he could see nothing but the gaudy bubbling juke box at the far end of the room. He dropped the suitcase and made out the bar, a beer sign flashing on and off. He saw old Viola White running a towel over a table.

At the center of the bar, opening two cans of beer, he saw the short, thin silhouette of Uncle Charlie, his

19

balding head glowing softly in the light of the beer sign. The odor of beer was strong.

He walked around the bar and sat on a stool in front of Uncle Charlie. Without looking up, Charlie asked, "What's for you?"

"Milk," Joel said.

"Who the hell serves milk in a . . ." and Charlie's stunned face contorted in surprise and embarrassment. "Joey!" he shouted. "Hey, look, Viola," he cried. "Look who's come slummin'." The old man reached across the bar and they shook hands. Old Viola White moved slowly toward him, squinting her eyes. Her eyes had been going bad for a long time. She seemed to make him out satisfactorily. She extended her hand and Joel pressed it warmly.

"Take over a while," Charlie said. "I gotta see the kid." Then, moving around the bar, he ran his hands over his thinning hair.

They reached a booth and Charlie sat down. He was thin . . . very thin. He didn't look right at all. But he was smiling, and it was obvious that he was pleased to have Joel there.

"Joey . . . I been meanin' to get down to Toyah to come to church, but when we close Saturday night, man, I'm bushed. I just don't have it like I used to. But I sure would like to see you up there in that pulpit. I wish your mom could take that one in, huh, Joey?"

Joel smiled at the little man who talked so fast that in his excitement he became difficult to understand. His face was long and narrow, only a few strands of gray hair sweeping back across his head. His cheeks were pitted with pockmarks. He looked like a carnival shell-game operator, a misleading appearance. He was a soft touch. He'd given many a whore money to buy a ticket out of town in the hope that the next place she

20

hit she'd get a better break. Some thought him foolish for this. But the street protects its own, and Charlie had done all right.

Joel studied his uncle's face, remembering the money he had received from him when he was at the seminary.

"How you doin', kid? I bet you got them cats all saved and in the side pocket for Jesus, ain't you?"

Joel shrugged. "I guess I lost more than I won," he said.

"How's that? Somebody give you a rough tussle?"

"They fired me," Joel said.

"The bastards," Uncle Charlie said quickly, then clamped a hand over his mouth. "I meant that . . ."

"It's all right," Joel said. "I'm afraid I'm not much of a minister."

"Aw crap! People down in that part of the country are so used to leanin' on a plow, they ain't got no appreciation of a real classy preacher."

"That first bunch didn't either."

Uncle Charlie poked his finger across the table. "That's why I never got mixed up with a church. There's always a bunch ready to pick a fight with another bunch. Just a mob of vultures. What you gonna do, boy?" He asked it, not raising his eyes, as though it didn't matter.

"The Dean said to wait a year or two and maybe he could line up another charge."

"A year?"

"Charlie, I've been fired twice. They can't force me on a congregation."

"All right, Joey. I was just thinkin' a year's a hell of a long wait."

"The Dean said if I found something else . . . to go ahead and forget being a minister. It happens more often than you'd think."

The old man straightened his skinny neck and squinted his eyes fiercely. "I'll tell 'em one thing. They ain't never been down here. Anybody that climbs out of it and studies all the way to be a preacher, he ain't made no mistake. God's got a place for him or He wouldn't of drug him out to start with."

"I had it figured that way too," Joel said.

"Yeah. What you supposed to do in the meantime? Pass a tin cup on Reno and Grand?"

Joel frowned and his uncle apologized with a smile.

"How d'ya like the place, Joey? I did some hammerin' and stuff. Looks pretty nifty, don't it?"

"It does look all right."

The room was not wide, about thirty feet, and about a hundred feet long. At the rear the lights of the juke box bubbled, changing colors. The rest rooms were on either side of the juke box. Booths were built against the walls. The middle provided a place to dance, not large, but enough. At the front was the bar. Uncle Charlie had built special racks for glasses. But most of the beer he sold came in cans. Not many on Reno drank out of glasses.

The bar was built on a half circle, done nicely in dark woods. An old chandelier glowed from the ceiling. Neon beer signs flashed behind the bar. The place looked clean, anyway clean for Reno.

Uncle Charlie leaned over the table. "Joey, you want a beer to make you feel better?"

"No," he said. "That wouldn't help."

"You tired?"

"A little."

"Tell you what. You go upstairs to your mother's old room. I never rented it and . . ."

Joel scrutinized his uncle.

"I just couldn't rent it. I even left the pictures on

the dresser and all. You want to stay there? I mean till you get a church or something?"

"Yes."

Uncle Charlie jerked a string of keys from his pocket and went through them. When he reached the right one, he took the key from the ring and handed it to Joel. "That's yours, Joey. I mean till you're through."

"Thanks," he said.

"Evita's got the room across, just like when you went to service. And down the hall, old Judge Hanson has still got his room."

"Evita?" Joel asked. "Is she still . . ."

"Yeah, but she don't hustle up there. She's got a call number and she don't ever take nobody up there."

"And Judge Hanson?"

"He still thinks he's a great lawyer. Imagines he's got a case comin' up before the Supreme Court."

"Broke?"

"He pays a little along. He's got the pension."

Joel knew that this was not quite true. Old Man Hanson had been behind in rent money for fifteen years. Uncle Charlie let him have the room against the possibility that if he ever needed a lawyer, he'd call Hanson, but he hadn't needed a lawyer in all these years. The Judge was seventy-five now, maybe more. He always wore a battered old Homburg and maintained the air of a court lawyer. He was incessantly busy. Busy with this and that. But he never did anything but drink beer.

Joel took the key, lifted his suitcase, and went outside. The stairway to the rooms was immediately to the left of the bar entrance.

At the top of the stairs, breathing hard, he realized how really tired he was. He moved wearily down the hallway, reached his mother's room, inserted the key and turned it. The door swung open. It was a small room, with one window. In the window stood a flower pot, bearing the shriveled remains of a long dead plant.

On top of the chest of drawers were two pictures. One was a faded picture of his mother and father. His father had got lost before Joel was born and hadn't been located yet. His mother appeared very young, very bright and happy. In the other frame was a picture of himself in his army uniform.

There was an iron bed covered with a tattered spread. The floor was linoleum covered. On a table by the bed was a pitcher and a glass, probably the same glass his mother had used to take her last drink. In a corner of the room stood an old cardboard wardrobe, one of the doors torn off. It was empty. Joel remembered the countless nights when he listened to his mother's sobbing. For a moment he wanted to close the door and leave. Where? He carried his suitcase and put it down by the wardrobe.

Where else was there?

He moved to the window and opened it.

"Hello, Joey."

He turned. Evita Cato stood in the doorway. She wore a robe pulled tightly about her, her hair combed neatly, her mouth tastefully made up. She was still a very attractive woman at thirty-five.

"Hello, Evita," he said.

"Mind if I come in?"

"No. Come in."

She sat in the straight-backed chair, carefully covering her legs with the robe. "Home for a visit?" she asked.

"No," he laughed almost bitterly, concealing a degree of pain.

Was it going to be this way always? How many

24

people would he have to tell that he'd been fired, that he had failed? Why did it matter? *What difference did it make to these people?* Where were *they* going?

"I got fired," he said bluntly. The room was hot. He removed his tie and sat on the bed.

She laughed.

"Is it funny?" he asked.

"Yeah, it's funny."

"Good. You have a big laugh over it."

"Look how far you had to go to get there. Then," she snapped her fingers, "they junk you."

"That's one way to look at it. I don't blame them for that part."

"So what do you do now?"

"I don't know. What about you? What are you doing?"

Evita's eyes were steady, very brown and even. "Same thing."

"Oh."

"I know what you're thinking."

He shook his head. "No, you don't. Nobody knows what I'm thinking."

"You're thinking I'm a rat and I'll always be a rat and that I'm going to hell for it."

"What *is* hell?" he asked.

She stared at him thoughtfully. "So let's don't talk about it. We been friends too long to start a bunch of silly crap."

"Okay."

"Do you know about Uncle Charlie?"

Joel frowned. Something *was* wrong. "No."

"Cancer."

"Evita, do you know that?"

"It's the talk."

"Just talk." He shrugged, not wanting to believe.

25

"Has the talk ever been wrong down here on the Street?"

He shook his head. "What kind of cancer?"

"Cancer of the stomach."

"How long has he known?"

Evita examined her nails. "Who knows? Maybe a long time. We've only known for a few months. He can't take it down there any more."

"Has he seen a doctor?"

"I haven't asked him. The word is he has."

"I'll get a specialist."

She shook her head. "He wouldn't go."

"Why do you say that?"

"It's plain. Uncle Charlie's tired. He's sick of Reno Street. He's sick of drunks and pimps and whores. We all get to feel like that after so long."

Joel sighed deeply.

"You're pooped."

He nodded.

Evita moved slowly to the door. "Sorry you got junked."

"Thanks, Evita."

"I mean it."

"So do I."

She closed the door. He wanted to say a prayer for Evita and for the girl in the knit blouse on the street, for Uncle Charlie who had helped so many in his lifetime, for the panhandlers, the addicts, the pimps, the prostitutes, the salesmen of pornography, the burlesque girls, for all of them . . . but it was like talking to a blank wall. God wasn't there.

He leaned back on the bed. His shoulders ached. The room was so hot he thought he would become nauseated. The faded flower designs on the wallpaper began to drift out of focus. *He was so tired.* He'd faced

26

the whole ordeal and now it was over and he wanted to sleep for a year until he could stand in a pulpit again.

The flowers of the wallpaper were gone and slowly, very slowly, he felt his body sinking into sleep. He began to dream. He heard a hymn swelling from the congregation, heard the boy soprano doing a solo in the choir loft behind him. And then the voices of the congregation began to shout at him. They cried out against him. They pointed their fingers and he saw hatred in their eyes. He cried back at them angrily. He grabbed a rifle and charged into the masses of them, ripping expertly to the left and to the right with the bayonet.

Then he jerked the hand grenade from his belt, pulled the pin with his teeth and sailed it into the midst of them. The blast killed hundreds of them at once. Men with snuff in their lips fell, and the woman who was nursing her baby lost it and she went about crying, her breast still exposed. He ran back. They were firing at him now. Someone was beside him. He turned. It was Corporal Benny English. "We got 'em on the run," English shouted. "Ain't nobody gonna get us, huh, Joey?"

One of them fired almost point-blank and the shot hit Benny in the face. He cried out in pain. "Joey! Oh, God, Joey, I'm dead and I ain't ready. Joey, I'm goin' to hell. I know it. Joey, tell God I don't mean to do wrong. Joey . . . Joey . . . I can't hear you . . . I can't hear you . . . say a prayer. . . ."

And the congregation stopped shouting and stood about because they knew that Corporal English was dying. Joel asked the congregation to say a prayer. "Our Father Who art in heaven. . . . Forgive us our debts . . . forgive us . . ." Then English was dead and

27

the congregation backed away. But one man whose neck muscles were twitching pointed his finger at Joel and shouted, "You're fired. You hear? You're fired. Everything is your fault."

Joel turned away and ran. He saw a light in the distance. It came closer and closer. It was a sign. It was the neon sign of the Green Parrot Bar, but the letters didn't read the Green Parrot . . . they read something different. He strained his eyes to read it, and two or three times he thought he wouldn't make it before he went far off to sleep, but finally he managed to read the letters. He spelled them out until he had them all. It read: *God's dead. God's dead!*

Suddenly he awoke, bathed in sweat, choked for breath. Joel staggered to the window. He leaned his hands on the sill until he was calm. Then he returned to the bed to wait for sleep.

3

The knocking seemed to come from far away. He listened to it groggily for a long time, until finally it began to mean something. He swung his legs over the bed. His head was thick and slow. It was still hot in the room, but now the shadows were falling to the west. He looked at his watch. It read eleven-thirty, but the second hand was motionless. He had forgotten to wind it. The knocking again.

"Come in," Joel said. "The door is open."

Uncle Charlie came in and peered down at him. "Boy, was you dead. I come up last night with a sandwich and you didn't move. I thought you was sick. You was sweatin' all over. You feel okay, Joey?"

Joel stretched. His eyes were swollen, puffy. "I really conked out, didn't I?"

"You was bushed."

"What time is it?"

"Nearly ten. I was on the way to open up the place. There'll be a few wet heads down there with the shakes. I thought I'd stop by."

"Thanks."

"What you gonna do today?" Charlie asked.

"I don't know."

"You need some money?"

"No."

"C'mon, Joey, you need a little geetus, don't you?"

"Charlie," Joel said standing, stretching again,

"when you're a minister, you don't see enough money to notice it's around. I wouldn't know what to do if I had any. No. That isn't right. I've got some. I've got four hundred dollars. They paid me off before I left."

"Yeah," Charlie said. "Well, c'mon down after while and I'll go out with you to get a cup of coffee."

"All right."

Charlie went to the door.

"Leave it open, Uncle Charlie."

"Okay."

Joel went to the small sink and filled it with water. It was cold. He opened his suitcase, found his razor and shaving cream, and lathered his face. He put a fresh blade in the razor and grimaced as he faced the small mirror. This was going to hurt!

He drew the razor across his cheek. The whiskers were stiff. He whistled low as he dipped the razor into the cold water. If the whiskers on the cheek hurt, what would it be when he got to his chin? Brother!

He had shaved only half of his face when he heard the loud thumping down the hallway, like some terribly old refrain of music that comes sweeping back from childhood. Joel recognized the rhythmical thumping of old Judge Hanson's cane on the hallway floor. The cane thumped closer until it reached the doorway, where it paused. Joel turned. Judge Hanson stood glaring into the room, pursing his lips in a question.

He had been a tall man, so very proud in the old days, but now his shoulders were stooped and his hands were unable to hold the cane steady. His face was wrinkled and pale. He wore the Homburg at a jaunty angle and, hot as it was, he had an old plaid muffler wrapped about his neck.

"Good morning," the Judge said.

His voice was still deep and surprisingly strong.

Joel wondered how hard it was for Judge Hanson to maintain this air of success. It fooled no one, perhaps because it is extremely hard to fool ex-convicts, whores, or pimps in their own environment. Judge Hanson had once been a good lawyer. Once he had been a giant in the courtroom. It was told that some of his cases had set precedent in the Supreme Court of the state.

But for many years he had been a failure. It happened after the fire. There were so many stories that one was never sure of the real truth, but the stories agreed that his wife and two children had burned to death, and from that day, Judge Hanson had taken to the bottle. Still, because of some strange desire for self-respect, he maintained the air of a busy, successful lawyer. Joel wondered if he really fooled himself.

The old man smiled, revealing a space in the front of his mouth where a tooth was missing. "I welcome you. I am Henry Hanson, attorney-at-law. If you ever are in need of professional services of that type," the Judge said gesturing as though it was of no great concern, "you can contact me down the hall. We are neighbors."

"Hello, Judge," Joel said.

At once the old man was taken aback. He twisted his face into a squint, fumbled for his glasses and tried to slip them on his nose without dropping them. It was a feat, considering how badly his hands were shaking.

The eyes loomed suddenly behind the thick glasses, owl-like, and the old man appeared to recognize Joel's face, but hesitated.

"I'm Joel Brogan."

"Mary's boy," the Judge said quickly. "Yes, how are you, boy?"

"Fine, sir. And you?"

"Never better," the deep voice responded. "Let's see. You've been away. What was it?"

"I'm a minister," Joel volunteered.

"Yes," Judge Hanson said, his face brightening. "Good to have you here. We need a little ministerial guidance. Not my field, you know, but I help those I can. I always try to offer my clients as great a service as I can. If we can save but one from the electric chair, by whatever means, we have accomplished a magnificent work."

"Yes, Judge."

The old man smacked his lips, straightened his shoulders proudly, almost losing his balance in the effort. He got his bearings, still chuckling to himself. "Render to Caesar that which is Caesar's and render to God that which is God's. Right boy. I'll handle Caesar's dues and you minister for God. There are some low derelicts about this section, you know."

"Yes."

"Well," the Judge said impatiently, "I must be going. I've got several legal matters to take care of. Too much crime these days," he said thoughtfully. "We simply can't do a thorough job any more. It's no wonder the penitentiaries are overflowing." He coughed into the muffler, started down the hallway. "Yes, I knew your mother well. Wonderful woman. Welcome home, my boy." Judge Hanson leaned against the rail of the stairway, pounding the cane fiercely to establish his footing.

Joel put his hand against his forehead, expecting the Judge to fall down the stairway. Victoriously the Judge pounded his way down.

Joel's lather had dried. He rubbed his face with cold water and tried to massage his beard. Then he smoothed lather over his face again and raked the whiskers away.

Rinsing his face in the cold water, he felt considerably better. He spread the suitcase on the bed and placed his clothes in the chest of drawers. These were the same tired drawers that had held his boyhood shirts and pants. His suits, two of them, he put in the wardrobe. One was the dark blue, for Sunday services, weddings, funerals. The other, a dark brown, for Wednesday night prayer meeting and church suppers. It also served for the Kiwanis and Lions Club luncheons when he was invited.

He put the ties in the wardrobe also. They were all plain colors, some grays to match the blue, some tans to match the brown, some dark solids the same shades as the suits. There were less than ten in the lot. He had four pairs of slacks, tans and grays to correspond with the coats of the suits for sport dress, but he hadn't worn them often, because they didn't wear such as that in Toyah. He would have been a great deal more acceptable in overalls.

You're here now. What are you going to do? Life is going on. Whether God needs you or not, life is going on.

He felt numb about it all. How was it the teaching went? You could run away from trouble, or you could refuse to acknowledge it, or you could accept it and do nothing, or you could fight it.

Joel remembered the girl, Susan Allbright . . . at Toyah. She had wanted to marry George Harris, a slow thinking, unambitious farmer boy. Carl Allbright, her father, had thrown a ninety-five-dollar-and-twenty-cent red-white-and-blue fit when he heard about it, because the old man had always wanted the girl to go to college. Susan had told him, tearfully as he recalled it,

33

that she loved George Harris. She said she knew that he was slow and plain and would never understand the finer things that culture brought into people's lives. But she loved him more than that. It didn't matter about college. It would have been nice, but it didn't matter. What she wanted was George Harris and a little house with room for four or five children. She wanted to sew and cook and come to town on Saturday. . . .

"You're a beautiful girl, Susan," Joel had said.

She blushed.

"You could do well in college, maybe marry somebody that would own a bank or be an engineer . . . something like that."

Her eyes clouded. "You don't understand either." She turned to leave.

"Wait, Susan."

"Yes?"

"You're sure about George? You've thought it over?"

"It's all I think about."

"And you are afraid of your father?"

"Yes. He refuses to even talk about it."

"You can run away and forget it. You can leave and start a new life without your father. He's just a man. He might never find you and George."

"Is that what you want me to do?" she asked hopefully.

"Or you can accept the fact that your father is against this marriage and go to college as he wishes."

"I can't," she refused.

"Or you can go into a world of pretend. You can pretend that everything is all right. It isn't, but you can pretend it is."

"But that's crazy."

He had smiled patiently. "Susan, you'd be surprised

34

to know how many people live in a world where they pretend. But you have one other choice. You can stand your ground and fight it. You can face it and win over it."

"You mean tell Father that I'm going to marry George, no matter what he does? And not run away? Is that it?"

"Well, that's fighting the thing. I'll say that. But you must be very sure that you know what you are doing."

The girl stared out the church window. "What does the Bible say about things like this?"

"It says, 'Honor thy father and thy mother that their days may be long.'" Susan's tense face turned briefly toward him. "And," Joel added, "in Ephesians it says something." He thumbed through the Bible. "Yes, here it is. It says, in chapter five," and he quoted, "'So ought men to love their wives as their own bodies. He that loveth his wife loveth himself. For no man ever yet hated his own flesh; but nourisheth and cherisheth it, even as the Lord the church: For we are members of his body, of his flesh, and of his bones. For this cause shall a man leave his father and mother and shall be joined unto his wife, and they two shall be one flesh.'"

When he finished, when he closed the book, there were tears in her eyes. She asked him to say a prayer. A month later Joel married them in his church. It was a small wedding. There were few guests. The bride trembled before him and the groom looked proudly down at his bride. They were so young, but so unafraid of life. Were they foolish? Or did they trust so much in God?

"Who giveth this woman?" he asked. The bride's older brother answered, for Carl Allbright had been stubborn to the end. He had neither given his blessing nor consented to attend the wedding. So it was.

From that day on, Carl Allbright was a tireless worker in the campaign to expel Reverend Brogan from the church, because when his Bible-quoting daughter had read to him from Ephesians, he knew . . . he knew! Carl Allbright's name headed the list urging his removal, even four months after his daughter had been married. Perhaps he was still trying to bring about a separation.

Joel straightened the sheets on the bed. Old Judge Hanson was the pretender. How long had he been pretending that everything was all right, that he was successful?

It seemed that there were so many people on Reno Street who were unable to face conflict. They ran away, they pretended, they denied a problem existed . . . denied like the countless drunks who kept telling themselves that they could stop drinking any time. "Sure, I drink too much . . . sure I ought to quit. Don't think I won't. I can quit in a minute. I've just been under a strain lately." The answer was ridiculous.

"You can't quit. You're an alcoholic."

"You're crazy. Me an alcoholic. Me?"

"Look at your hands. Go ahead, look at them. You're a drunk, and you can't quit by yourself."

"Don't make me laugh, buster. You make me sick. Hey, bartender? C'mon, bartender. How about a beer?"

"What kind?"

"Who cares. Just gimme a drink. Hustle, boy. . . ."

"Sure. You can stop."

Or you can fight. You can face it, hard as it may seem. Once you run, once you deny, once you try to escape, you are in trouble. Every backward step you

36

take makes it harder to face it. But you *can* fight it.

Okay, Joel, you failed. You practically destroyed two churches. That ought to be a pretty good sign. You thought God called you to teach His word. *You thought that.* You might have been suffering from one of the many guilt complexes the head shrinkers talk so much about. Perhaps a shame for your past life might have caused a great deception in your mind. Lots of soldiers promised God that if they got back alive, they would devote their lives to the ministry. But when it was over, they wisely found other jobs. You didn't. Maybe you were stupid.

It could have been the shame of your mother's terrible week-long drunks that tortured you. Were you trying to make up for all the punishment she made for herself by becoming a servant of God? Did you convince yourself that God reached down and tagged you on the shoulder and said, "I have chosen you"? *Or did God really choose you?* You've got to keep that possibility open. Sure, it's hard to figure that *He* chose you and then had no church for you. You've got to admit that's a little stupid. That you answered the call and nobody would have you. Reno Street painted all over you.

Did you ever think you fitted at the University of Oklahoma? Remember waiting on tables? Remember that morning Jerry Whitmore, the fraternity boy, was bragging about the broad he had laid down on Reno, how he had clubbed her with his fist and had taken thirty dollars from her purse? Thirty dollars that she had hustled from three different men. How he had said that she lived in some dump over the Green Parrot Bar. . . .

"You stupid ass," Joel had said.

Jerry Whitmore raised up from the table, as though

he had smelled an unpleasant odor. "You'd better watch your tongue," he said.

"I said you are a liar."

Jerry had stood, the veins in his forehead standing out, his face deepening in color. "Say that again," he demanded, his hands tight fists.

"Her name is Evita Cato. She's a stick of dynamite. She's got a switch-blade knife in her purse and she'd run it right through any Joe College that got smart. I've seen her flip that knife against the throats of tough hoods and, believe me, you didn't take any thirty bucks out of her purse. You're a liar. You went down there with your tail between your legs and you thought you were big time. You went to the hotel and paid her ten bucks for it. When you were through, she laughed in your face because you acted like you knew the score. That's the way it really was."

Jerry Whitmore had stalked angrily, but quite deflated, from the collecting crowd. But Joel was branded. It didn't matter. He'd have been branded anyway. His eyes weren't the eyes of a minister. They were the eyes of a kid who learned how to slip the hub caps off a parked car and get out of sight before he was picked up.

At the seminary there was Will Clarke; the fat kid from Tulsa, whose father was pastor of the largest church in town. Remember how he practiced sermons on how terrible sin was? About those horrid women of the street, about the confirmed alcoholics . . . the narcotic addicts? Somewhere today Will is making a fine salary in some fine church, and he may be using those sermons about sin . . . although like so many ministers, he knows nothing about those sins. He's never seen a drunk lying in an alley, unable to stand, unable to protect himself when his money, sometimes

38

even his shoes and his coat, are taken from his body. Will doesn't know how the whore turns to a bottle of gin to keep from going to pieces.

And it isn't easy to stand in front of the lights and do a bump and a grind at the burlesque theater while some mealy-mouthed sex deviate cries joyously. It isn't easy to keep abusing your body, throwing it to the wolves for a drink, for a few dollars, a cheap hotel, a far-off dream of luxury, or a home or love. It is murder to face that disillusionment. And there, in the dormitory room, young Will Clarke had preached against sin. Joel had listened until it became too impossible.

"Will," he said, "wait a minute, Will. . . . It just isn't that way."

Will's face flushed with color. "Well, I've never been . . . but I think I know what it's like. I've never been a thief or in jail, but I think I know . . ."

"Well, I have, and it isn't like you are saying."

The half dozen students in the room were electrified. Here, in Austin Seminary, a student was admitting that he had been a jailed thief. It was unprecedented. It was fantastic! And he was immediately branded.

"Look, Will. . . . You know about petty grievances, how people bear false witnesses, how they cut each other's throats with a pen and a contract around a business table. That's the kind of sinners you know. Why don't you talk about that? There's the sin that we are all guilty of . . . not loving each other. If you could get that across to the society matrons, you'll really have your hands full. But don't stand up there and tell us about stealing bicycles and beer. Will, it's like me trying to tell a doctor how to treat a disease I've never even heard of. It's that silly."

"You certainly have sinned," Will said. "You must

have a hard time not looking back on that experience with shame."

And another said, "What kind of a minister will you make?"

That day he knew all the answers. "I don't worry about it. I have been forgiven for those things. So I don't worry about how I will preach. Because there were dirty fishermen, uncouth people, and Christ called them. He called men who had been drunken and wild. They did all right." Joel was quite jaunty about it. But one student near the back of the dormitory room quipped, "And one of them betrayed Him."

Joel had looked away then. He knew no answer to that one. Then or now.

Was he betraying God? What did God want of him now? Did He want him to wait out the year and go back and try again? Or did He want him to do something else . . . become a carpenter or machinist? Joel felt abandoned, alone. For two days he had been unable to pray. There seemed to be such an emptiness, a Godlessness that he had not known since he was in the hospital in France.

Joel changed his shirt and left the room. A light was still burning in the hallway from last night, and there was the rank odor of garbage or vomit or something. He went down the stairs and entered the Green Parrot Bar.

Uncle Charlie was sitting on a stool behind the bar. He never used to sit down when he was working, but he did now. Old Viola, feeling her way about, caressed the bar with a rag. Four men and women were seated at the bar, glasses of beer in front of each. In a booth, Judge Hanson sat fumbling with some papers that he had taken from his briefcase. He sipped a glass of beer from time to time.

Uncle Charlie turned as Joel reached the bar. "You hungry?" he asked.

"Yes."

Uncle Charlie waved a finger. "Viola," he said, "I'll be back in a few minutes."

They left the Green Parrot and strolled along Reno.

"Place hasn't changed, has it?" Charlie asked.

"No. Not much."

"A street like this never does. Just the people. They change." His voice was almost sad.

They went into the Poor Guy Café and sat in a white booth with hard wooden seats. The place was twice as long as a Buick and about as wide.

A waitress with a pencil behind her ear shouted across the counter. "What say?" she asked.

"I want coffee, two over easy, and . . ."

"No breakfast. Are you nuts? Look at the clock."

"I'll have a bowl of soup then," Joel said.

"I got only vegetable. It's canned."

"All right. I'll take that. And toast."

The girl looked at Uncle Charlie. Her face mellowed. "Hi, Charlie. Milk?"

"Yeah . . ." he said. "I oughta get me a cow."

"Milk?" Joel asked.

"Yeah. I got to where I like the stuff."

"You used to hate it," Joel said.

"Stuff's good for what ails you," Uncle Charlie said, bobbing his head like a determined woodpecker.

"What *does* ail you, Uncle Charlie?"

Joel anticipated surprise. It didn't come. "Them meatballs is been yappin' at you, huh?"

Joel suppressed a grin. "What do you mean?"

"I mean about half the bums on this crummy street

41

has got me figured for a pine box any day now. I was never sick a day in my life."

"I heard some talk."

"Was this one the high blood-pressure talk, or the ulcer talk, or the . . ."

"Stomach cancer," Joel inserted.

Uncle Charlie whistled low. "A new one. I can't keep up with them." He shrugged his shoulders, pulled his ear, and for an instant looked like Jimmy Durante.

"Have you seen a doctor?" Joel asked.

"I don't mess with them guys. Everybody I know what messes around doctors' offices is always sick."

"Have you seen a doctor?" Joel asked again, patiently.

"Yeah. I seen one."

"What did he say?"

"He says I got gas."

The waitress brought the glass of milk and the soup and toast. "That'll be sixty cents."

Uncle Charlie had the money on the table before Joel could make a good effort at finding his pocket.

"It isn't easy," Joel said. "When you're a minister, you have to learn to slow down on everything."

"I been thinkin' about the crazy setup," Uncle Charlie said. "I been figurin' maybe it'd be good for you to volunteer for one of them African deals where you go out there and work with them natives as a missionary. Then after a year you come back and you got so much interestin' stuff you can have any church at all."

"Not a bad idea. They need help all right. But I've been thinking, too. I've been wondering if I should be a preacher at all."

"Aw, Joey . . . don't ever say that. Don't say that."

Joel was surprised at the intense tone of Charlie's

42

voice. "I know how you feel, Uncle Charlie, but something was wrong. Look at me. What do you see?" Joel asked.

The old man's face went soft. His voice was quiet as he spoke. "What do I see? I see this crazy little kid sneak down the sidewalk and pick up a cigarette butt and jam it in his mouth and he gets sick all over the crazy sidewalk. I see him get balled up with the cops and he scares hell outa his mama and everybody else because nobody on the street wants to see this kid go bad. Because you look in this kid's face and he's got somethin' real good. I see this medal he gets from the war. And Joey . . . honest to God, Joey, if a kid like you can come out of this crazy street and learn to be a preacher, then don't you ever get the idea that God ain't got no place for you to preach."

Joel began eating his soup. "What I meant was, I don't look like a preacher. You know how a general walks? He walks with his shoulders back and his head up and he swings his arms. You with me, Charlie? Do you see what I mean?"

"Yeah, I seen generals walk. In movies anyway."

"And you take off the uniform and put a suit on the same man and you can still tell that he's a general by the way he walks. He has a military bearing."

"Okay."

"Now what do I look like?"

"You don't look like no general, if that's what you're drivin' at."

Joel smiled. "No. I look like a kid that dodged around Reno Street all my life. I look like a guy that can spot the keys dangling in a parked car without turning my head toward the car. I don't look like a preacher. Uncle Charlie, I had to ask the janitor to tie my ties. Do you know that? I can't even tie a tie

43

right. When the congregation sat around after dinner at the church, they talked about politics and farming. Somebody asked me what I thought about the flea hoppers and the boll weevil situation. What did I say? I said, 'I don't know much about it.' And they excused me maybe, but after so many times, they knew they had a foreign idiot for a preacher. I can't mix. I can't talk. My sermons are unconnected. But there were bigger things. There was a woman there. Her name was Lorrie Dixon. She was a widow, but she wasn't a good widow. A real sexy type with hips that turned heads whether she meant to turn them or not. The truth was she had slept with about everything that happened along. And in a little town like Toyah, she was branded. The old scarlet letter. She had it."

"Scarlet what?" Uncle Charlie asked, frowning.

"Practically a whore. In Toyah everybody knew about her. But one day she came to my office, and Uncle Charlie . . . she broke down. So I told her we wanted to help her. As it happened, we had a big church social scheduled the next day. I invited Lorrie. I not only invited her, I went by and picked her up to make sure she didn't back out. I wish you could have seen it. I could have brought a leper and got off easier. Nobody would talk to her. Several of the men there had even had her. I knew that.

"She cried. Finally she left. After she was gone, they talked in little tight groups about her. The men who said the dirtiest things were the ones who had had her. Then I made my talk. I gave them both barrels. Do you think it made any difference?"

"Not a damned bit," Uncle Charlie said.

"Then there was the time one of the Negro families lost a child. This colored man came to my office. He told me that his family had been Presbyterians up

44

North. And his child was dead. He asked me if I would conduct a service for the child because there was no Negro church in town. I said I would. I'll never forget it. Uncle Charlie, everybody in town got mad. They called me a nigger-lover. They would hardly speak to me. So I made a sermon about it. I tried to tell them that Christ knew no color. Then they really got mad. I could feel it in the congregation. That made me hot. I gave them Scripture for everything I said. It just made it worse. Like a fool, I went overboard. I blasted the kind of Christian who had such a prejudiced attitude that they would not let me bury a Negro child, an innocent, even when it was not in the presence of whites. Verse by verse I proved the decency of it. They had to either buckle down or condemn me. I guess I didn't leave them any choice. I was considered a fanatic. I never fitted in with them. I didn't belong."

"Hell, Joey . . . everybody belongs some place."

"That's right. I guess I belong here. I can spot the drifters and the pimps no matter how they are dressed. There's no real escape from the Street. Evita was right."

"You make me sick."

Joel laughed bitterly. It had been a long time since he'd had that sort of feeling.

"I mean, you're feelin' sorry for yourself. How hard did you really try to make it? I ask you? Nuts! You're just like the rest of the kids these days. You went to school. So you want to start out on top. Look . . . Jesus? What happened to Jesus? Did He make it the first try?"

"Uncle Charlie . . . are you crazy?" Joel stopped eating.

"Well . . . lots of folks didn't go for the guy."

"Go on," Joel said.

45

"So He busts a gut to help 'em. He did, didn't He, Joey?"

"Yes."

"Then that day they thought He was the greatest. You know . . . I read about it once. He rode this donkey and everybody threw these palm leaves down and they said He was the greatest."

"Yes."

"Yeah! Then what did they do? They strung Him up like a dog. That was pretty soon after that, wasn't it, Joey? When they did that to Him?"

"Yes."

"They murdered the poor guy. Him, the guy who was the greatest a few days before. They nailed Him. So you're feelin' sorry for yourself. You got kicked downstairs and you think you'll never get off Reno. Boy, I'm tellin' you, for my half buck, Jesus was the one that got it in the teeth. And you ought to be able to take a little trouble. For my money, you can . . . Joey, are you cryin'? Now what the hell did I say?"

For a few moments Joel could not speak. "Would you like to know more about Jesus, Uncle Charlie?"

"Sure. I mean, I picked up what I could, but I never made it to church much. I went a few times, but they looked at me like I had the syph or somethin'."

"I'll tell you the story."

"That'd be okay. It'd keep you from gettin' too rusty, wouldn't it?"

"Yes. It would."

"See, boy . . . now it's all different. You don't think God tossed you on your can any more, do you?"

"No. I guess not."

"C'mon. I got to get back to the bar. Viola's so blind any more she takes nickels for quarters."

4

For Joel, these were hours of reflection. His heavy footsteps falling beyond count along the familiar landmarks of the Street in a fruitless search for understanding. For the time God remained a distant idea, a collection of past emotions so wracked by turmoil that they had no definite meaning. He examined singular thoughts lifted from the inner circles of his mind. Unconnected, single flashes which he pondered effortlessly as his feet trudged one after the other.

He remembered the fat woman who stamped her feet and slapped the Bible in the mission hall when he was a boy. Her fervor . . . a thing of fearful wonder. Joel had wondered if perhaps her voice might not even frighten God. Her theme had been that there are no atheists in foxholes. It was a good wartime subject. He wondered what mind had conceived this foolishness. How many men grown numb by the sound of war knew God? Robotlike creatures wallowing in filth, staring into the blank nothingness that was battleground. Joel saw these blank faces, and among them he saw his own. Heard the sound of the planes sweeping low, fire jutting from the wing tips, mud spouting like bubbling lava as the bullets sucked into the earth.

He saw these men staring without comprehension, too bone-tired to find cover, too drunk with fatigue to be afraid. An exhaustion so great that sleep, when it

47

came, was only a state of drugged wakefulness. They were corpses that breathed. A time when love was a word at the bottom of a letter, scrawled by a hand from another world, a word and nothing more.

His quiet footsteps brought him to the alley where he heard the boys shouting fiercely, circling the staggering thing in the center. He paused, awakened from his dream.

"C'mon, Pencils, show me how you fight." This from a tall boy, perhaps eighteen, a lean silhouette, dodging, weaving, until his arm shot out and his open palm slapped against the face of the creature. Pencils leaped convulsively toward the lean darting form. His face became streaked with the handprint.

He clawed back ineffectively. His hair was a mat of brown filth, more like a nest than hair. His back was twisted grotesquely, forcing him into a wrestler's crouch, even when he slept. His great head bobbed, his one eye crazily searching for his darting enemy. His mouth jerked into a loose-lipped sneer, from which came labored sounds of breathing. The teeth overlapped, oozing saliva. His voice made incoherent animal sounds.

At his feet, his pencils were broken, scattered about the alley. Pencils. His name, to man, to God. A creature conceived in unholy union, when a syphilitic womb had come in contact with fallen sperm. When the ovum became fertilized, adhering, starting the reproductive process that eventually brought into the world this thing. A senseless being, half blind, deformed.

The other boys taunted him, in and out like dogs nipping at his heels. Pencils groaned under the assault, staggering clumsily, and fell to the garbage-littered floor of the alley.

48

Joel moved quickly toward them. He raised his hands and shouted as the boys kicked at the fallen figure.

Pencils was on his hands and knees when the first sounds of the police siren reached the alley. Joel grabbed the first boy and pulled him back. They stood silent for an instant as the siren came closer.

"C'mon, beat it," the boy said.

Hurried footsteps as the boys retreated, disappearing into corners, shadows. Joel bent to lift the injured man to his feet.

Perhaps imagining Joel his enemy, Pencils reached his feet and his arm shot out in a wide arc. Joel saw it, sucked in his stomach, throwing his hips back in an automatic movement as the steel blade scraped against his belt buckle.

A police car lurched into the alley, the doors of the car opening before the vehicle stopped moving. The siren lingering, a dying sound.

"Pencils . . . they've gone. It's all right," Joel shouted.

A firm hand seized Joel's arm. "Get in the car," the cop said.

"Why?" Joel asked.

"We're going downtown." He was led to the car as the crowd from the bars closed in now.

"Put the knife down, Pencils," the other officer said.

Pencils backed away, pressing against the wall of a building, not understanding yet that his enemies had gone. Joel watched the officer move close, lunge, and pin the knife hand against the wall. Pencils bit the hand that held him.

"Damn you!" the officer said, betraying pain. Then the knife fell to the concrete.

The policeman slipped cuffs on Pencils and pushed

49

him toward the car. An old man wearing an apron appeared at the car window. "This ain't the guy," he said thumbing toward Joel. "I was the one what called. Them kids ran away. This guy was tryin' to stop 'em."

The officer turned to Joel, clucked his tongue against his teeth. "All right. Out of the car," he said.

Joel got out and turned to look at the now sagging, whimpering form of Pencils. "What are you going to do to him?" he asked.

The policeman shrugged, a line cutting across his brow, an expression of bored hopelessness in his eyes. "Lock him up."

"But he didn't do anything," Joel said.

"He had a knife," the officer said impassively.

"They were whipping him," Joel said.

"We'll lock him up."

"Then you can take me along. I'll talk to the Captain. I saw it."

The policeman hesitated, as if disgusted with the entire affair. "Okay. Get in," he said. "We'll probably turn him loose when you make a statement. Then he'll come back here in the morning. You know, citizen, he can't even feed himself. He spills most of it. I figured we could give him a few meals, a bath. But get in, mister. Maybe you've got an idea to feed him and wash him and give him some place to sleep besides the damn gutter."

The policeman opened the door for Joel, studied him angrily. Joel did not get in. The officer shut the door and waved a hand at the small crowd that had lingered. "Out of the way. Break it up."

The squad car backed out of the alley, as the spectators retreated. Joel was left alone. He saw the broken pencils on the pavement. Tossed to one side was a hat, streaked with stains, crumpled. A single unbroken pencil lay beside the hat. Joel bent and picked it up. He looked at it for a long moment, then dropped it and walked out of the alley again.

Did God supply a purpose in life for the congenital idiot? Or was this creature one of God's jokes on man? Perhaps the idiot had as much purpose in life as the president of a banking house. Or a film idol. Or a prostitute. Or a minister who was rejected. Joel walked on. He saw a woman standing in front of a bar. Her hair was streaked white, but it was mostly red, a bottled red, too bright, more like clotting blood. She had a large gold inlay that revealed her age even more than her wrinkled, powder-white face. She smiled and batted her eyelashes.

"Hello, honey," she said with a gold inlay smile.

Joel paused, noticed the brown sweater that pressed tightly against her sagging breasts, the wrinkled blue skirt, the scab-covered legs that were unshaved, and the red heels stained with street filth.

"Let's go up to your room," she said, moving closer. "I could be nice to a young one like you."

Joel searched for retreat, but she had moved around in front of him, angling him against the doorway of the bar. "No," he said, sickened.

"I could show you a good time for two bucks."

It was two dollars now. What had it been ten years, fifteen years ago?

"No . . ."

"Come on, honey. . . ." The eyes blinked. They were desperate eyes. They hungered for the past. They told him that today she had to find someone, anyone. That tomorrow it wouldn't matter. Only today.

Joel scooted against the door. It gave behind him. She saw him moving inside and her voice cried after him. "A dollar. A lousy dollar for the night."

51

He backed until the door slipped away and closed in her face. The room was dark and he heard laughter, was not aware for a long moment that the laughter was for him.

"Ol' Mol, she's hot tonight," the bartender said. It was hilarious. Joel examined the leering faces. The odor of spilled drink was strong.

"What you want to drink?" the bartender said.

Joel shook his head and opened the door again. He expected to see the old woman waiting. She was not there. When he was out on the street, he saw her an instant before she turned the corner. She shuffled along, her heels scraping against the sidewalk. Her shoulders were slumped, the flaming red hair tossing in the hot wind.

A man approached and she paused, held out a wrinkled hand to catch his sleeve, but he pulled away quickly. She watched after him briefly and mouthed an inaudible oath, turned the corner and was gone.

Joel walked on for a time, finding the street empty. At the corner he paused at a boarded-up theater. The posters from the closing feature were still stuck to the cases. A double feature. *The Price of Sin* in bold letters illustrated by a drawing of a man tearing away the brassière of a struggling girl, her face drawn in Hollywood-type anguish. And *Girls on the Town* in the same Gothic type, with an illustration of a girl on a bed, her legs suggestively posed, a bottle cradled against her breast. And beneath, in hand lettering, *Also, Mickey Mouse Cartoon.*

Two college boys, obvious by their sport coats and white buck shoes, rounded the corner, singing drunkenly. One wore a fraternity pin.

"It's National Nooky Night tonight," one of them laughed.

52

"All over the world," the other echoed.

Joel watched them swagger along the street. A girl stepped out of the doorway thirty feet away.

"Hello, baby," one of them said. They stopped.

"Did you know it's National Nooky Night?" the other asked.

She stepped closer, twisting her hips lustfully. A brunette with a peroxide streak above her forehead. A plain white blouse that was worn to attract eyes to the black brassière she wore beneath.

"You boys looking for a good time?" she asked suggestively.

The taller boy swayed and pinched her breast with one hand. She backed away.

"Don't handle the merchandise," she said, her fist making a tight ball at her side.

"It's National Nooky Night," the other boy said. "Did you know that?"

The girl's face showed impatience. "Ten bucks makes it National Nooky Night."

"You hear that?" the taller said.

The other did not answer. His eyes lingered on the transparent blouse. "You wouldn't take five, now, would you?" the taller said.

"Beat it," the girl said. "Your brains hang between your goddam legs."

This, oddly, they found amusing. The taller boy located his billfold. "Okay," he said, "brainwash me." This the other boy thought quite witty. He found a bill and held it out to examine it drunkenly. It disappeared in her hand and she turned back into the doorway. The boys followed, their laughter spilling down the stairway into the street.

Joel remembered the first time it had happened to him, right here, perhaps two blocks from where he was standing. He had been fifteen then. He had stolen a spotlight from a parked car. A junk dealer paid him three dollars for it. Joel had seven dollars and some change in his pocket. That day was no different than any other, except that at last his time had come. It was right.

He had gone through the motions of shaving that morning, even borrowed some of Uncle Charlie's after-shave to rub on his face. He was feeling big. When he left the room, his mother was sick, a half-finished bottle of bourbon on the table beside her bed. Joel walked along the street in the early darkness. The pimp had been standing in a doorway, unshaven, a cigarette hanging from his lips, moist from saliva around the end.

Perhaps he knew that it was time for the kid to learn, or that the kid was looking, perhaps thinking about it. "Hi, Joey," the pimp said.

Joel had shrugged a greeting, started on.

"Hey, Joey, you had any lately?"

Joel stopped and eyed the pimp coolly. He didn't want to say that he hadn't, but the snakelike smile on the pimp's face made it unnecessary for him to answer.

"You like girls?" the pimp asked.

Joel started to spit at the man's feet.

"Maybe you like the boys?" the pimp suggested.

The anger came quickly. Joel took a step toward the pimp.

"Ease off, Joey. I heard you like the girls all right. The word gets around. I hear you give 'em a hot time."

Joel shrugged agreeably, a bit too nonchalantly. He was not entirely displeased.

"You interested?"

"No," Joel said nervously.

54

"How 'bout that one across the street?"

Joel turned. But there was no girl across the street. When he looked back, the pimp was laughing.

"Come on up."

"I can get that a lot of places," Joel assured him.

"Sure . . ."

"And not pay for it either," Joel lied.

"Who can't? But you and me both know it ain't as good. Now tell me, is it or isn't it?"

"I guess not," Joel said uncomfortably. He wondered if the pimp knew the truth. He didn't think so.

"You got some money, Joey? I got a real doll upstairs."

"A little," Joel said.

"Since it's you, I'd make you a deal. Want a smoke?"

He took a cigarette, and the pimp flicked a match with a greasy thumbnail. Joel had been unaware that with this gesture he was committed. It was too late to walk away.

"New girl, too. You never seen her."

"Oh . . ."

"For you ten bucks."

"Nuts!"

The greasy hand touched his arm gently. "Like I say, she's a new girl. Since you know the guys, I might make it right. I mean you tell the guys how she is, and they take your word. They know you can tell. I need to get the doll some business."

"How much?"

"Well . . . ten's the price to start. Later she'll be worth twenty-five. You know, once it gets started."

"I ain't got ten bucks," Joel said, knowing he did not really care about the girl upstairs. Not really, he didn't.

"How much you got?"

"Seven," Joel said. Then immediately felt stupid. He should have said five.

"Well . . . seven. Okay. She's in the room on the left at the top of the stairs."

Joel pressed the bills into the pimp's hand. His heart drummed heavily as he climbed the stairs. He was breathless and afraid. At the top he looked down the stairway. The pimp was watching, the cigarette still hanging loosely from his lip.

There was no way out. He thought about all those things the older men had said about disease, and he wanted to go back down the stairs. His fingers turned cold as he stood outside the doorway. He knocked.

He heard footsteps and his face twitched with anxiety. The door opened as the girl pulled a robe tighter around her waist. She was just a young girl, hardly older than himself. But she was pretty. There were lots of high school girls just like her. The girl leaned out the doorway, glanced down the stairs. Joel followed her eyes. The pimp waved.

"Come in," she said.

Joel went inside and the girl closed the door. He had a tremendous urge to tell her they should just sit down and talk for a while. He didn't want to do it, didn't feel like it at all. He thought of the little brown-haired girl who sat next to him in biology class, the one with sultry eyes and the come-on smile. This girl looked so much like her. She shouldn't be doing this. Joel wanted to tell her. He glanced around the room, averting his eyes when he reached the bed, and noticed the blanket folded at the foot. At the end of the room was a window, the shade drawn, and an empty Coke bottle on the ledge. There were cigarette butts stuffed in the bottle.

It seemed as if he had been in the room for a terribly long while. He was trying to suggest they just talk for a few minutes, when the girl slipped the knot loose on her robe and let it fall from her shoulders.

She was wearing only panties and a bra. They were light blue. As long as he lived, he would never erase this sight from his brain. Finally, reaching her eyes, he saw that she was smiling at him. She moved toward him. His heart was beating so hard it choked him. Maybe he was going to be sick. Or maybe pass out. The girl put her hands on him and her fingers were like electric voltage. He let her pull his belt loose.

"I got to hurry," she said. "I mean, there's plenty of time for it, but you know, I can't fool around too much."

Joel agreed understandingly. She could have been the girl with the brown eyes in biology class. So innocent. He could not forget this. He let his shirt fall against a chair. She knelt and told him to step out of his trousers. She laughed as he did and bit his leg above the knee. He felt her tongue and sucked in his breath.

Then she went over by the bed and very quickly the bra and panties were gone. Dropped in a delicate heap beside the bed. She posed for an instant, and the terrible mixture of fear and lust brought perspiration to his body. He bent over to untie his shoelace.

"Honey," she said, "don't bother."

He knew then that she understood all about him. He felt foolish and embarrassed. She took his hand and pulled slightly.

It was over almost immediately, and he knew she understood even more about him now. He could not look at her. A sense of shame settled over him like a dark, ugly cloud.

She led him to the corner, to the pan of water, the soap, the small bottle of alcohol. And there she washed him as he stood shamefully before her. This done, she dressed quickly and pulled the robe around her. She opened a drawer, withdrew a dime love novel, lay on the bed and started reading as though he had already gone. Joel dressed. He wondered if he was supposed to compliment her, or say thanks, or laugh. He didn't know. He had seen whores all his life, but before it was different. Now he had known one.

Occasionally she glanced from the page and studied him impassively, as if surprised that he was still there. She did not look up when he left.

Joel had gone out into the street. The pimp was standing on the corner and he turned as Joel left the doorway. The pimp waved, winked and shifted the limp cigarette to the other side of his mouth with his tongue. Joel walked along the street. He sighed. The unrelieved tension caused a shudder in his chest. This was it. This was what they talked so much about. He felt dirty.

He climbed the stairway above the Green Parrot Bar and looked in his mother's room. She was sitting up now, a glass of bourbon in her hands, holding the glass tightly to keep from spilling the drink. Drawing it to her mouth, getting the amber liquid in her throat until the shaking gradually subsided. She glanced at him.

"Joey, baby," she said. "Mama's gonna be up after while. You go see your friends and be a good boy, Joey."

Joel found a towel and soap.

"What you doin', Joey?"

"I thought I'd take a bath," he said.

"Now?"

"Yes."

"Okay, Joey. You run take a bath and be a good boy."

Joel closed the door and went to the bathroom. He filled the tub and got in. Twice he drained the water and filled it again. He lathered his body several times and rinsed. When he finished, he got out of the tub and dried with the towel. Strangely, he still felt unclean.

As he dressed he studied his face in the mirror. They couldn't tell. It didn't change you in some secret way. Joel laughed, the fear subsiding. He'd lived on the street of whores all his life. Before they were just faces, laughing or crying or cursing into a bottle of beer. Now they were different. Now he really understood what they were like with a man, and it changed his entire outlook. For a reason he did not understand, he did not like them. He did not want to ever do that again.

He went to a movie that night. In the movie he saw a beautiful swimming star. It occurred to him that she smiled just like the girl in the hotel. A girl that pretty could be a movie star, too. She wouldn't need to do that at all. He tried to remember that the next time he saw her, he would tell her about it. No, he wouldn't tell her. She'd laugh in his face. He awoke as the usher shook his shoulder.

"Man . . . show's over."

"Oh . . . sure," Joel said. When he stood, his leg collapsed beneath him.

"You okay, man?" the usher asked.

"It went to sleep," Joel explained. He limped out of the theater, his foot feeling like a dead stump beneath him. In the lobby he noticed it was after twelve. He went back to Reno Street, to his room next to his mother's. But the nap in the theater had taken the drowsiness away. He lay for many minutes, watching the flashing neon lights reflecting on his wall. He counted them until he reached one hundred. Then he quit.

He did not remember when at last he fell asleep, but he remembered the dreams that followed were bad. He had them this way every night for a week. And every morning Joel examined himself in terror to see if he had caught the disease. He promised himself that he would never do that again. Until he knew at last that he did not catch it from her, and finally he forgot. Until the night that he went back to her. . . .

He pushed away from the curbing and crossed with the light. Joel wondered now what had happened to that girl. He passed a clothing store. In the window he glanced at a pair of worn paratrooper jump boots, khaki jackets, and a pair of fatigue pants that had been torn. They were repaired with red thread. He paused at the window. His mind drifted back again. He heard the deep-throated explosion of the grenade and saw a part of France briefly suspended in the air, showering over him, mixed with the jagged shrapnel from the grenade.

He felt it tear into his body and remembered the dull ache that followed, the blood soaking through the torn cloth. The almost pleasant relief as the sights and sounds faded into a great black silence, his face in the mud.

Later, the voice of a man at last probing through the silence, stirring him to response.

"That's the trouble with our army," the man had said lightly, "just a bunch of goldbricks. They'll do anything to get to sleep in a soft bed."

Joel opened his eyes to see clearly, though he had

imagined the man's face was dim and far away and the voice, a sound coming through an echo chamber. The man, he saw, wore fatigues and he needed a shave. He wore a fabulous red beard, and the face was a desperately tired face. But the voice was like a bassoon, deep and strong. A large hand rested on Joel's shoulder. He was aware of its warmth.

"Joel Brogan," the man said, "I'm the Chaplain. You're in the hospital."

"Hallelujah," Joel said acidly, though his voice cracked and turned to a whisper.

The Chaplain's red beard gave way to a grin.

"Would it help to know you aren't dying?"

Joel moved in the bed, then became aware of the sudden pain that must have showed on his face.

"Joel . . . do you want a cigarette?"

"Yes."

The big man took one, placed it in his own mouth. He flipped a lighter, then placed the cigarette between Joel's lips. It made him dizzy, and after a few drags, he declined the rest.

"How bad was it?" Joel asked.

"Not too bad. Your leg. It's all there, anyway most of it, enough to fill your pants."

Joel had the peculiar feeling that he actually had lost the leg. He started to examine himself, but became dizzy as he raised his head.

"It's there, son," the Chaplain said. "I wondered if maybe you wanted me to write a letter for you. It may be a few days before you feel like it."

The Chaplain opened a writing tablet. He pressed it against his knee.

"You ought to let them know at home so they won't worry."

"No," Joel said.

61

"Your wife? Are you married?"

"No."

"Your mother?"

Joel laughed. It was a sudden, instantaneous out-burst that bordered hysteria. He visualized his mother reading the letter. It would upset her. If she had been waiting an hour before she took a drink, she would decide not to wait. She'd pour one right then. She'd weep into her glass. But not because of him. Not really.

The Chaplain's face was frozen in an expression Joel could not exactly describe. It was the expression a man gets when he has given money to a beggar and, nearly out of earshot, he hears the beggar call him a bastard.

"Is your mother living?" the Chaplain asked.

"No," Joel lied.

But the Chaplain knew better. "A friend?" he suggested.

"No."

"Relative?"

"No."

The Chaplain folded down the cover of the writing tablet. "I'll see the men in your company. I'll tell them you made it."

"Don't bother," Joel said. Not bitterly. It simply didn't matter.

"A man alone. You are, aren't you, Brogan?"

To this he could have answered yes. But because of the fatigue, the weakness from loss of blood, perhaps because for the first time in his life he realized that he *was* alone, he did not answer. He closed his eyes, turning his head away from the Chaplain.

"You're wrong, Brogan. Somebody was very concerned about you."

62

The Captain? The Sergeant? Crazy Sam Warren from Walla Walla? Joel opened his eyes. Who had been asking about him? He had never been really close to any of them. He did what they said. That was all. Who cared?

"Your best friend, Brogan," the Chaplain assured him.

Joel's lips formed the question.

"God, Joel. He was very concerned."

Joel's head rolled on the pillow. "Oh, crap!" he said.

Then the torrent of uncontrollable, hysterical tears. The heavy sobs that brought pain to his leg. Until it was over and he had achieved a sense of relief, almost peace.

The Chaplain was smiling, a huge red-bearded monster with a gentle hand. A real man.

There were the days the Chaplain came to see him. Always the face was tired, as if the man never slept. The terrible moments when men died a few beds away, and the Chaplain knelt beside them.

And at last the day the Chaplain did not return. The day the doctor paused before Joel's bed, tapping an envelope. "How do you feel, Brogan?"

"All right."

"I've got some news. It's not good."

Joel had pressed his elbows into the mattress, raising his chest and head. Waiting.

"Chaplain Wallace. He's dead, Brogan."

His elbows slid down, his head dropped back.

"He was killed last night."

Somehow it did not seem quite right. Chaplains weren't supposed to get killed. They held services in the chapels and they sent letters to wives and punched TS cards and carried Bibles, but they weren't supposed to die. This huge man with freckles and red hair and a beard that was usually a week old because he didn't waste his time shaving. Who could have been a prize fighter, or a steeplejack. Who talked about God as though God wasn't on some distant planet listening in on the earth, pushing and pulling buttons that gave Sally a new mink coat, or saved a child from polio, or talked things over on a golden throne with Jesus. Chaplain Wallace's God was right there with him, sometimes seemingly almost visible, so that the Chaplain tilted his head up slightly and asked, "Father . . . what are we going to do with this Brogan?" Smiling as though he expected a voice to answer.

"Dead?" Joel said numbly.

"Yes. You were particularly close to him, I understand."

It had not occurred to Joel before. Until then he had not considered how often Chaplain Wallace had returned to his bedside, even after they said he was out of danger. But he had. He had probed gently about life on Reno Street. He had gathered a picture of Joel Brogan as he had once been. Chaplain Wallace was often so tired his massive head sagged occasionally. Talking about faith. Mercy. Forgiveness. And always about love.

"This letter was with his things. It's for you," the doctor said.

Joel took the envelope. The doctor paused. "I'll read it later," Joel said.

When the doctor was gone, he lay staring at the envelope. Calmly he opened it. It read:

Joel:
There was much I wanted to tell you, but I understand you will be leaving soon. The word I get is

64

that you'll be sent back to a hospital, maybe to England, maybe home. But before you go, I wanted to leave a final message. It's about the church. Joel, men make a lot of mistakes. The best men alive are still blind to what is really good. You always seem to see the nonsense in the church. You say if this is the way Christian people are, you don't want any. But that isn't the right approach. I've got a Chaplain friend. He's a Methodist. He told me that years ago the Methodist Church used to own slaves. Every Christmas Day the slaves were returned and sold again for another year. The money they made went into church funds.

Today we see how wrong this was. Someday the things we are doing now will appear as bad to another generation. I haven't been able to get close to you because you have too many of these objectionable things tucked away in your mind. Then, Brogan, for the time, don't be concerned with the church. The church changes. Concern yourself with God. Just Joel Brogan and God. Learn to love, Joel, and you will know God. Learn to forgive. As a favor to me, make a little effort. What have you got to lose?

It's late and I'm leaving in a few minutes to go back up front. Good by, Joel. I hope we meet again.

And the letter was signed: *Red*.

Joel had managed to locate a bottle. It was cheap French wine, but it did the job. Joel laughed drunkenly at the Chaplain. The stupid dead Chaplain who had no more sense than to get himself killed on a front where nobody expected him to go. But the memory of Chaplain Wallace existed after the wine was gone.

Joel had been returned to England. In the hospital,

he remembered the haunting voice of the red-haired Chaplain, and each time he rejected the appeal of the voice. But he could not bring himself to destroy the letter. Occasionally Joel read it. He did not want to bother with God. But Chaplain Wallace had died telling men about God, and Joel knew that the Chaplain had a very deep and real understanding. It was a thing Joel could not comprehend.

Once in the hospital, a clean-shaven young chaplain came to his bed. He had seen no battle. His voice was effeminate. He sickened Joel.

Joel said, "To hell with God."

Yet the great voice of Chaplain Wallace would not die. It was a desperately kind voice. "Brogan," it said, "there were things I wanted to say to you. But it boils down to this. . . . Don't fight it. It's there, boy. Take it. Use it as it uses you. I didn't come from a clean street either. Mine was in New York and it was dirty, too. I know Reno Street all right. Give God a chance for my sake."

And Joel replied, "The hell with God." Wearily.

Until he grew too tired. Until, after he had seen men die clutching the cloth that covered them, crying desperately. The puzzle of life and death gradually simplified.

Finally he called the Presbyterian chaplain. He said, "Tell me about God. Maybe just for laughs tell me about God."

This time he listened. He remembered Chaplain Wallace and he grew to cherish that letter. Very gradually he drifted into the church. He asked many questions, some of them astounding, but for each of them he expected an answer. *Why didn't Christ get down off the cross? Why didn't He take over right then and there?* He liked to be shown Scripture to prove

66

the answers, and this proof was not always available.

He was told that if a man had proof of all these things, he wouldn't need to bother with faith. Faith was the price man had to pay for Christian peace of mind. Joel's faith suffered many relapses. Yet his weakness became his strength. Joel Brogan was honest with himself. If he was a tough hood on a tough street, he did not pretend to be anything else. If he was going to believe in God, he was going to believe for all he was worth. Otherwise he would believe not at all.

He rebelled often, a rebellion growing out of an intense dissatisfaction with himself. But these were short escapes. He always came back to the hospital chapel asking why he had renounced God. He was told it was because he was afraid to love God with all his mind and body. But to do so, Joel reasoned, one became God's servant. He was told this was true. But that was the same as being a preacher, he suggested. Again, he was told this was true. The first time it entered his mind, Joel laughed, half surprised, embarrassed. Me? A preacher? Man, what would God do with me a preacher? And he was told to ask that question of God. Which he had done, long ago.

Joel left the window displaying the paratrooper boots. He crossed the street, pausing for a taxi that had sped through on the yellow light. The taxi stopped in front of him and the rear door opened. A young woman got out as the driver unloaded a suitcase. She paid the driver and stood looking at the large blinking neon sign of the Green Parrot Bar.

She seemed uncertain, perhaps afraid. She lifted the bag and pushed into the bar. Joel followed, holding the door for her. She turned to thank him.

She studied his face for an uncomfortable moment,

then as if jarred to reality, asked, "I'm looking for Charles Jackson. He owns this bar."

"Yes. I'll take you to him."

She leaned to place the bag against the wall. Joel took it from her. "I'll carry it for you. If you leave it here somebody will steal it."

He walked on, listening to her footsteps behind him.

5

"Whatcha say?" Uncle Charlie asked, lowering his paper, peering over his glasses.

"I said, I'm Lynn Halliday," she repeated. "They said you had rooms for rent."

Uncle Charlie blinked and glanced over the girl. She looked twenty-four, maybe a year or so more. She wore a brown tailored suit, plainly cut, but expensive looking. Her eyes were soft brown, alive with interest. The way she had said her name indicated that to some people it meant something. On Reno it meant nothing.

Here her sense of importance made her appear out of place, awkward. Her voice was registered low, yet slightly musical. Her mouth was full, her skin soft and smooth. Her hair had received expensive care. Joel knew that Uncle Charlie was thinking over the unwritten roll of underworld women, and he was finding no recollection of her name.

"Are you a hustler?" he asked.

"No." The answer came so quickly that without intention, she betrayed her discomfort.

"Sister . . . are we gonna play games?" Uncle Charlie asked.

"I'm sorry. They gave me your name at the Salvation Army. They said you had decent rooms to rent."

"You want a room?" Charlie mumbled uncertainly.

"Yes."

"Look, Miss . . . uh . . ."

"Halliday," Joel inserted.

"Yeah . . . Miss Halliday. I got some rooms, only I ain't in the hotel racket. I rent 'em along, see. Only if you can find some place else . . ."

"The rooms are decent. The place is clean?" She made it more of a statement.

"That's right," Charlie said. "And I don't allow no girls hustling up there. You tell me you don't hustle, and the next thing I know I walk by the door and it sounds like a bunch of chimpanzees playin' tag on the bed."

Lynn Halliday's face colored. "Mr. Jackson," she said, "I've been staying at the Mason Hotel the last two weeks. But a few people thought I was selling myself. That is not the case, Mr. Jackson. I'm looking for a decent room where I won't be bothered. I did not come here to hustle."

"Okay," Uncle Charlie admitted. "Good for you. What did you come for?"

"To write a book."

Uncle Charlie glanced at Joel uncertainly.

"Come off it, honey," Charlie said wearily.

"My last was *The Biography of a Schizophrenic*. It's about the problem of mental illness. I thought you might have read it."

"I didn't. You gonna write a book about crazy people on Reno Street?"

"No . . . it's a different type of thing."

Uncle Charlie turned to Joel. "What is this jazz?" he asked.

"She did write a book. She isn't a hustler."

"Okay . . . you can have a room."

"Thanks." With a faint flavor of sarcasm.

"Seven bucks a week. Sheets changed three times a week. You clean up," Uncle Charlie said.

The girl opened her purse, found a bill and put it on the bar. Uncle Charlie made change.

"Joey . . . put her in the room next to you."

Quite suddenly the girl turned and examined Joel again. She frowned. Uncle Charlie laughed.

"About him you don't have to worry. Ugly as he is, he's still a preacher boy."

The frown changed to curious disbelief. Charlie located a key on his ring, removed it. He handed it to her.

"I'll carry it for you," Joel said, gesturing to the bag.

"Thank you."

He led the way, out of the bar, into the doorway and up the flight of stairs. He held the bag as she turned the key in the door. Inside, he opened the window. The room was like his own, an iron post bed, a cardboard wardrobe, linoleum on the floor, a small bedside table and a chest of drawers. He put the bag on the bed.

"I didn't read your book, but I was sure you had written one. Was it successful?"

"It made a little money," she said. "Actually it was written just as a series for a newspaper in St. Louis. To get the genuine background, I go to the source. I spent a month in a mental hospital for the first. I expect to do the same here. My concern is the reality of my situation."

"And this is a book about life in the world of commercial vice!"

"Something like that," she said.

He smiled cynically.

"Mr. Jackson said you were a preacher."

"That's right. I was."

She was curious now, and quite charming. It was all too obvious, too phony, Joel thought.

"I'd like to know about you," she said seriously.

"About why a minister ends up on Reno Street?" His jaws were set and his eyes narrowed. He did not wait for her response. He disliked the way she put it. "Miss Halliday . . . I don't want to be a character in your book. I don't want to be immortalized in print. Thanks, anyway."

"I didn't mean to offend you. My work is an honest study."

He disliked her tone. She seemed altogether too stuffy. "I know. We've had writers here before. They turn over the rock and show the world what has crawled underneath. They've come from the magazines. I remember one title was "The Streets of Hell." It was an exposé type thing for one of the men's magazines. The same writer went to Chicago, New Orleans, San Antonio. Same old stuff. He could have written it in his own apartment. They were all alike. A guided tour of vice towns. He'd give a whore five bucks or a bottle of gin and she'd tell him a great story. The same whore could have told another writer an entirely different story a month later."

"That wasn't the sort of thing I wanted. I want to know why the girls do this. How it really is to live this way. That's why I came here. To understand."

Joel shrugged as if listening to an ambitious child, a precocious one. "Then you're wasting your time," he said impatiently.

"Oh . . . ?" Questioning his ability to judge.

"There's only one way to know how it is to live like a whore."

She waited. "How?" she asked.

"Be one. Then you'll know. They can't tell you."
He started to pull the door closed behind him.

"Thank you," she said icily.

Joel paused.

"For helping me with the bag," she said.

Joel shrugged again.

"You don't like me, do you?" she asked impulsively.

"First impressions aren't very reliable," he said, "but if you happen to be one of the bugs under the rock, you aren't supposed to like the guy that flips it over. I imagine you'll find that out."

"I see," she said. She turned her head at an angle. She was haughty, aloof. And self-important.

Joel closed the door. He was irritable now. He wished that Uncle Charlie had not rented her the room. Evita stepped to the door, jerking her head toward the new occupant.

"Who's the doll?"

"Lynn Halliday," Joel said.

Evita shrugged. "Nice. Does she work in a hotel or take calls?"

Joel laughed aloud. He wondered how many times the society of Reno Street would inquire about her. How many men would feast on her with their eyes, nudge her with their knees, pat her with their hands, unable to believe that she was anything but a high-class hustler. Why would anybody else come down to Reno and set up in a room? Crazy!

He imagined the men discussing her approvingly. *How much is that doll? Thirty bucks? Is it worth thirty bucks? I mean, hell, it's nice and all, but let's face it. It ain't no Sophy Loren. Buy 'er a beer and tell 'er you'll give twenty-five. That's a good price. She ain't no Loren. Got a nice wiggle though. Man!*

Joel frowned at his own thoughts.

"I asked you a question," Evita said, "and you made a face. What's with the girl?"

"She's writing a book," Joel said.

"Well, I'll be damned. What's the pitch?"

"It's a fact. She's a writer."

Evita studied this, which she now accepted as truth. "What's she write about?"

- "About people, what they do . . . you know."

"Is she a do-gooder?"

"I don't know."

Evita raised an eyebrow. "I don't know how she writes, but I bet I know a way she could make a lot more money."

Joel did not reply. He started down the stairs.

"We sure get the bubble brains in this place. Used-up preachers, screwball writers, drunken lawyers."

Joel glanced up the stairway. Evita had omitted herself. Joel waited as she searched for a way to describe herself.

"And the best ten-dollar whore in town," she said boldly.

Joel entered the Green Parrot. Uncle Charlie was seated on his stool behind the bar, his hand pressing against his side, his face pale, betraying the presence of pain. He removed his hand as Joel approached.

"You fix her up?" he asked.

"Yes."

"She like the room?"

"She didn't say. I suppose she did."

"A writer," Uncle Charlie said thoughtfully. "They must be a nutty bunch of people. I think it would be nice, though. I mean you got nobody tellin' you what to do. I used to dream up stories all the time."

"You did?" Joel was mildly surprised.

"Crazy stuff. Only I never put it down. You ever do like that?"

"Uh huh," Joel said absently.

Joel had been glancing lazily about the bar when he noticed the girl in the corner booth. She had a glass of beer before her on the table, but she had not touched it. She was perhaps twenty, but no more.

The girl turned toward Joel, as if drawn by the feeling that she was being watched. She was very young and fresh. Wonderfully alive. But unsure, timid.

Her eyes rested on Joel. They told all about her. She did not need to cross her legs carelessly as she did.

"Who is that girl?" Joel asked. "I haven't seen her before."

"New one. Her name's Rose Nickels," Uncle Charlie said.

"She's pretty."

"She gets twenty bucks," Charlie said, indicating that the price was perhaps the best judge of her beauty.

Joel shook his head. "Why?"

Uncle Charlie's face became a mask of wrinkles. "Now are *you* gonna write a book?"

"No," Joel said. "I was just wondering."

The girl realized that Joel was not going to join her at the table. She no longer invited him, but occasionally she glanced toward him quickly, then away.

A man came in, chewing an unlighted cigar. He headed directly to the table where Rose sat. He was Nick Martelli, but on the Street they called him Philosopher. He had a degree, or at least he had convinced everyone that he did, from Cornell. He also had a word of advice for everyone, which was usually good advice, but never taken, or meant to be taken.

The Philosopher was a pimp, and this girl was

apparently his newest. He kept a maximum of six, and when his crew fell below three, he would disappear for a few weeks, returning with fresh blood. Joel wondered where Nick had found this girl. What had he said to her?

They left the table and came toward the bar. The Philosopher was in a cynical mood.

"The good Reverend Brogan," he said, bobbing his head, his fingers tight around the girl's arm. "Rose tells me that she was involved in a light flirtation with you. She didn't know you represented the cloth."

Nick Martelli was perhaps an inch taller than Joel, but his shoulders had rounded and his spine curved so that he appeared shorter. Joel met his eyes steadily. He had the vague discomfort that he had always felt in the zoo snake house. He knew the slithering bodies could not reach him or touch him, but he still had a loathing of them.

Joel moved his eyes deliberately to the girl. She was embarrassed. Not because she was what she was. She had learned to accept that. But she was humiliated because her pimp was making a deliberate attempt to embarrass a preacher. She saw no use of it at all, no humor, or purpose.

"I didn't know," she said with a tone inflection that asked him to understand the rudeness of her manager.

The Philosopher was not receiving any attention. "In the case of ministers," he said, "we give the customary ten per cent discount."

Joel tried to disguise his disgust. If the man had been thoroughly vulgar about it, or profane, it would not have mattered. Joel kept his eyes on the girl whose discomfort grew more acute. "If he ever whips you, hits you, or abuses you in any way," Joel said, "you come to me. You don't need to be afraid of what he will do.

76

He's afraid of me." Joel trained his eyes on Nick Martelli. "He knows that if I broke his body into little pieces, nobody would care."

As he finished, Joel was short of breath. He drew air hungrily into his lungs, noticed the tense shudder in his chest. The Philosopher had been affected by the intensity of his anger. His reply came swiftly, in singsong fashion.

" 'But if ye forgive men not their trespasses, neither will your Father forgive your trespasses.' It would seem that the preacher boy's halo slipped." Martelli winked. "Ten per cent off. Any time, Brogan."

Then he was gone. Joel watched after him.

"What was that jazz he was sayin'? It's in the Bible, ain't it?"

"Yes," Joel said. His fingers trembled.

"You don't want to get wound up with an ape like that, Joey. He's strictly no good. He was settin' you up."

"I know."

"So be smart."

"All right. Does he whip them?"

"They all do," Uncle Charlie said.

"Takes their money."

"As much as he can get."

"And they let him. *Why?*"

Uncle Charlie's hand touched his shoulder. "Hell, Joey, even a whore's got to feel like she belongs some place."

"But the beatings."

"Beatin's now. Used to be spankin's when they was kids. If you ignore a kid long enough, he'll do somethin' bad so you'll spank him. It's a tough price to pay to know you belong. I read that once." The old man winked mischievously.

77

"Now you're the philosopher," Joel said.

"Yeah. When you get old enough that you got to get up during the night to go to the bathroom, you're a philosopher." Uncle Charlie lighted a cigarette. It made him cough which caused a pain in his abdomen. He dropped the cigarette in the tray and held his chest to stop the cough. When it had passed, there were tears in his eyes.

"Are you all right?" Joel asked.

Uncle Charlie grunted. "Sure." But he did not pick up the cigarette. He walked away, returning to his stool. When he sat down, his hand moved to his stomach and he pressed lightly.

Joel stayed with him until it was late. Then he climbed the stairway wearily. Evita's door was closed, the light inside turned on. Joel went to his room and sat down heavily on the bed.

It wasn't a very pretty world. Anywhere you looked, you saw people with rotten motives. And without meaning it, you probably had the same rotten motives toward other people. Maybe you found one person that you didn't hate just a little. Maybe if you were really lucky and not too greedy, you had six or seven people who cared a little about you. Uncle Charlie had a lot of people like that. Maybe because he was the Will Rogers of prostitute alley. Anyway they liked him. Trusted him. Nick Martelli probably didn't love anyone. Joel wondered if perhaps one day long ago Nick Martelli had been a brilliant young man. That he had fallen in love with a beautiful girl, and just when everything seemed perfect, somebody jerked the rug. When he got up, he got up hating. It might have been that way.

Or a man like Chaplain Wallace. People really loved him. Joel visualized the few people that he had known

78

in his life who had been genuinely loved. The kind of people who seemed to be surrounded by a warm glow. People who were at peace. Not necessarily Christians, or sometimes not even moralistic men. Joel did not know the qualities that made Uncle Charlie one of these gifted people. He could not lift a single characteristic out of the whole and examine it. Somehow it was not possible.

But these people left others with pleasure. Like, perhaps, a man was driving across the country on the way to commit murder or adultery or suicide. Anything, it didn't matter. But whatever it was, it was unpleasant, and the man was in despair. Then his car happened to come into the main street of a sleepy small town. Halfway through the town he smelled a bakery. He rolled down the window to enjoy that odor, and then too quickly he was at the edge of the town and it was gone. But for that one moment, the smell of bread baking had taken away the despair. Just a pleasant feeling. Like a man makes a feeling come into your life. Like Uncle Charlie or Chaplain Wallace. Like the old janitor at the church at Toyah, who brought coffee to his office every morning and sat there radiantly in his overalls.

Joel wondered whether, if a man looked for this kind of person often, really tried to search him out, maybe he'd be surprised to find that there were lots of men like that. That when he had found more and more he came to realize that the people who glowed so beautifully had been there all along. That it had been he who had been unable to sense the good feeling that radiated from them. That the only really evil person had been himself.

"Reverend Brogan."

Lynn Halliday was standing outside his doorway.

"What did you say?" he asked, shaken from his thoughts.

"Your name."

"That's not my name. Don't run around calling me that."

"I'm sorry. . . . I thought . . ."

"Reverend Brogan." Joel flipped his hand. "Here it isn't right. I don't have a church. It sounds phony. Did you need help?"

"I wanted to ask about laundry. Is there a place near by?"

"Yes. There's a little place around the corner. Come in."

She came inside, sat stiffly in a chair.

"How do you like the room?" he asked. He too was ill at ease.

"It's fine. I hope the typewriter doesn't bother anyone. You might think it a nuisance. In so many words you told me I was a corrupt, dishonest writer on a worthless project."

Joel detected a softening of attitude.

"I might not have been entirely fair. I don't know your work. I just know what other writers have done. They want to show these people in all this ugliness. But they don't propose anything to change them. I suppose you'd call it sensationalism. But maybe you won't write that way."

"I came with an open mind. In this business your success depends on finding a fresh angle. I don't know how I'll handle it. I did wonder about you, though. What was your church?"

"Presbyterian."

"You went to a seminary," she said.

"Yes. And a degree from the University."

80

. "I see." She studied his face intently.

"I know you're wondering. I was fired from two churches. When I was finished, I couldn't get another recommendation. You can't blame them."

"But there should be other church work," she suggested.

"I didn't inquire. I guess I was stunned. Actually it's not too unusual for a minister to fail. Some go into other work."

"Will you do that?"

"I don't know. I've been trying to understand myself."

"Perhaps a psychiatrist," she suggested.

"I won't say it wouldn't help. If you didn't sell two books, would you consult one?"

"That's different."

"Maybe not. I did my best, but it wasn't acceptable. I didn't have breakdowns. I didn't scream at the people. There was no unrest."

"That you could see," she added.

"Look . . . I'm not insane. I put it on the line. You go out and try to make people live their religion and you'll see. The deacon sleeps with his neighbor's wife, and then shows up on Sunday morning in church. You go try to straighten him out and see what happens."

"I can imagine. Did you do that?"

"I can't stand hypocrisy. It's hard for me to forgive and impossible for me to overlook."

"How about your own hypocrisy?" Her voice was a blunt instrument.

"Name it," he said angrily. "I wouldn't like it myself."

"Why aren't you working with these people? You don't like writers who call attention to their faults and

81

yet don't do anything to help them. Why don't you carry on your ministry here?"

"I could preach on a street corner?" he said acidly.

"Jesus did. I think too many of you theologians need a fifty-thousand-dollar building and a nice income before you become inspired."

Joel leaned over, resting his face in his hands tensely. "Nice shot," he said. "But they'd laugh me off the street. I couldn't get any place like that."

"Then you aren't serving your God," she persisted.

"I don't guess I am," he said. "Is that what you wanted to hear?"

"It's what you needed to hear perhaps."

"You're pretty frank, you know."

"You forget you've already told me my work was just so much corrupt sensationalism. I didn't thrill to that."

"So I did. But there wasn't a man in my seminary class that would stand on a corner and preach."

"Of course not. They expect the prestige of a church. But the Salvation Army does it."

"And they're laughed at."

"They help some. They couldn't go on if they didn't."

"True."

"But you don't want to take that abuse," she said.

"Will you play the drum?" he asked.

"I'm not the preacher. It's not my problem."

"Then don't solve it." By his tone he ended it.

They sat silently. He spoke finally.

"We got off to a bad start."

"I think we understand each other. Maybe it wasn't so bad."

Joel stood. "I've got a dime. You want a cup?"

"Yes, I do."

The top of her head came to his shoulder. She was

an attractive woman. Too obsessed with her career to let herself really be a woman. But still attractive.

When they reached the street, he walked along with his hands in his pockets, slowly, so that her short strides could keep pace.

6

Joel put the newspaper aside as soon as he had clipped the want-ad. As he shaved, he heard Uncle Charlie close his door and pad quietly along the hallway. Soon he heard a muffled alarm clock, clanging only briefly in Evita's room. She swore.

It was a sleepy morning. Evita's door opened. Joel heard her slippered feet scurry to the bathroom. Down the hallway, Judge Hanson's door opened. The old man coughed violently as he left the room. He pounded his cane along the hall, pausing as he reached the stairs. He hesitated, establishing his footing, then pounded his way down, until the cane struck against the last step and became muffled by the concrete sidewalk outside.

Through the wall Joel heard Lynn's typewriter carriage move haltingly, until the faint bell sound warned of the approaching margin. She shoved the carriage and began again.

Joel dressed in his brown suit and white shirt. He selected a conservative tie and flipped it around his neck. Of course, he could do the simple overhand, like the army ties, but he didn't like that style. He liked the neat triangle of the Windsor knot, but he had never mastered it. He tried twice, bending before the mirror. He gave up when the tie twisted and began to wrinkle. Joel threw open the door.

"Hey, sugar," Evita yelled, "you want a cup?"

"Yes," he answered, fumbling the tie in his hand.

"Well," she shouted, "come on in. We don't deliver."

Joel went to the door, still not looking in. "Are you decent?" he asked.

"Hah!" she laughed. He felt ridiculous when he realized the implication. "I'm dressed," she said. "That's the best I can do."

He went inside. Evita had her hair done back in a pony tail, a cigarette, as yet unlighted, hanging from her lips. She wore toreador pants and a loose fitting sport shirt. Evita was a short woman, very curvy. Her skin was tanned and her dark eyes betrayed a trace of Italian. She was, as they said on the Street, a box.

"Why so dolled up?" she asked.

"Oh," Joel said, "I was just going out."

Evita took two cups from a drawer and looked into the saucepan on the hotplate. "I don't have a pot. I just make it this way. You get a few grounds, but you can clean your teeth spitting them." She poured the coffee and handed him a cup. "Drink up," she said.

Joel sipped his coffee.

"What are you going to do, Joey?" Evita asked.

"I've been looking around."

"The coffee's rotten, isn't it?" she asked.

"No. It's fine."

Joel set his cup on the table.

"I'll run along. Thanks for the coffee."

Her voice caught him as he reached the door. He looked back.

"C'mon. I'll tie it."

He grinned.

"I've seen a lot of these things untied and tied back in my day," she said. She began looping the tie around his neck, looking up at him. "Okay," she said, "the ties I've seen tied weren't preachers'."

"Don't you ever wish you could get out of it?" He knew instantly that he should not have asked.

She smiled cynically. "Uh huh."

"Why don't you?"

"Sure, Joey," she said, a knife in her voice, but she was keeping it light. "I could quit and take my dough and go study to be a preacher. When I graduated . . . what would happen to me, Joey? God wouldn't have any use for me. Just like you. Because of that, I got no use for God."

"I don't feel that way," he said.

"You don't because you think the good fairy is going to knock on your door and give you a great big church someday. I don't. I've been on Reno long enough to know you don't get out."

"That's not true." His voice lacked conviction.

"What can I do? Can I be a secretary? I can't even write a letter. Can I be a salesgirl? Every time I made a sale I'd have to fight to keep from slipping the bills into my brassière out of habit. What the hell is left?"

"Maybe you could get married."

"Joey, you *are* stupid."

"There are lots of guys. You've got a little money . . . quit and move out and find some guy . . ."

"Can't you just see my wedding night, Joey?" Evita sassed. "Can't you see me flop in bed and say, 'Darling, I'm so nervous,' and then throw him the best . . ."

Joel put his hand on her lips.

She laughed. "You got to admit it would be funny." But her voice trailed away. "I'm not deceived by crap," she said.

Joel examined his tie in the mirror. It was perfect. "Thank you," he said. He went to Uncle Charlie's room and found the prescription box on the bedside

86

table. Joel opened it. It was empty. He slipped it into his pocket.

The morning sunshine was warm on his face. He walked up Broadway until he reached Main Street, the big street, the big glitter. He turned west at Main. Here was the orange-juice stand where they turned out real fresh juice, always kept a bowl of nuts to eat. The theater where two smartly dressed ushers stood at attention in the doorway. Joel knew a way to sneak into that place. He'd learned it when he was a kid.

Across the street were the big clothing stores, a shoe store. Veazey's Drugstore was near the corner. It hadn't changed since he was ten years old. He swiped a box of candy there once. Maybe Mr. Veazey wouldn't mind. It had been his mother's birthday.

Joel crossed the street. Over there was Brown's, the big department store, something like Macy's but on a smaller scale. He turned up Robinson and walked past the big bank building. He passed the newsstand. The white-haired, stooped owner appeared almost the same, a little older, but not much.

His hands were moist when he reached the office of the Dawson Church Supply Company. It was not a very impressive office. Emil Dawson's name was lettered unevenly on the door. Joel took the scrap of torn newspaper from his pocket and checked the ad. This was it. He went inside.

The man was chewing gum vigorously. He was a heavy-set creature, bearlike, with small pig eyes. His forehead wrinkled as he read a letter. His head was bald, perspiring slightly.

"Sit down, son," he said, not looking up.

Joel sat down. Still reading the letter, the man spoke. "Name's Emil Dawson. What do you want?"

"I read your ad in the paper, I'd like to discuss the job."

Emil Dawson made a clucking noise in his mouth and continued to chew his gum, at last putting the letter aside. "Stand up," he instructed gruffly.

Joel stood. Dawson examined him critically.

"What's your name, son?"

"Joel Brogan."

"What was your last job?"

This one Joel had thought over.

"I was in school. The jobs I had since then were just temporary."

"Ummmmm. You know anything about the Bible?"

"I've studied it."

"Think you can sell Bibles and church supplies?"

"I believe I can."

"Have you ever sold door-to-door?"

"No."

"We do that, too. It's not easy. Do you drink?"

"No."

"They all say that," Dawson said sourly. "I had a man out in the best part of town, anyway the best part to sell Bibles, and I got a call from the police. Damned fool had got drunk and decided he was a Romeo. Had some housewife backed right up to the bed. She was screaming like mad when the police came in. Terrible stink. Ruined that neighborhood for three or four weeks. I just can't use a man that drinks. Are you married?"

"No."

"That's bad. Young man like you gets out and some woman comes to the door in her undies and you drop the Bible and try to grab a handful. That's the trouble with young men. They jump four feet high when they see a woman."

88

"I'm not that kind," Joel said.

"I've heard that, too. Don't stand there, son, sit down."

Joel sat down.

"When I came here, I didn't have twenty dollars." Dawson stared at a fly on the ceiling. "Came right during the depression, and it was hell, I can tell you that. You're too young to remember, but I can tell you it was hell. Nobody had any money hardly. So I tried to figure out how to keep out of that damned Roosevelt's soup lines. I was lucky. You notice I didn't say I was smart. Not many smart men around. Mostly just lucky. Well, I was. I stumbled into this guy who had a whole crate of Bibles. He wanted to sell out, so I bought 'em. Got 'em for fifteen cents on the dollar. Then I went to the nearest church. I figured with everybody hungry, they wouldn't give a nickel for a new radio or an ice box.

"When a family gets in bad shape, they'll reach for a Bible. If they have plenty of money to spend, they buy beer, but when they are right down to the wire, it's a Bible they want. Now I said I wasn't smart. But I happened to know that much about people. God wouldn't have a single convert if He promised man that he'd live to be three hundred years old. Every bastard in the world would live to be two hundred and ninety-nine before he even thought about bein' saved. That much I know.

"But anyway, things was to the point where folks didn't see how they were goin' to live. That's when they turned to God. You'd just better believe it. So I went to this church and tried to sell the Bibles in a lot. The preacher didn't go for that. So I made him a deal. I got a list of the people on the church roll. I told the preacher I'd furnish the church with fans if

89

he'd give me the roll. Them days there wasn't any refrigeration. Church was hot as hell on Sunday. You can believe it. Are you an ex-convict?"

"No," Joel said, surprised.

"Good. I get a lot of cons. They figure they'll look good to the parole officers if they are out sellin' Bibles. Bastards'll steal you blind. Anyway, I didn't have the money to get the fans. I told the preacher I'd bring the fans later. So I started down the list. That's when I learned how to sell Bibles. I'd go in a house and I'd start off with a prayer. It lowers a housewife's sales resistance. Then I give a little talk. I'd tell how the preacher hoped the people can take Bibles, because the church got a benefit from it. Then I tell 'em that I only sold to the Baptists or whatever church it is. That I been goin' all over the country sellin' to the Baptists, because the Baptists are the only ones got the right idea. This makes 'em feel good.

"Then I'd get on this stuff about if more people really read the Bible and believed it, there wouldn't be no depression. Tell 'em that the preacher talked about how God punishes them that don't live by the word. And anytime the lady looked like she was about to say no dice, I'd jolt her. Like maybe a dirty little kid comes in the room. Always a bunch of kids around anyway. I been bit by more kids in my time than dogs.

"So I'd point to one of the dirtiest kids I could find and tell her that if he had this Bible as his own, to study and all, he'd probably grow up and really be a fine man. Then right quick I'd talk about all the terrible things kids do, like hatchet murders and all, and the idea is that if the kids had had a Bible when they were young, they wouldn't have done all that.

"By this time I had it pretty nearly done. I'd give her the Bible to look over. She'd thumb through it.

90

I'd tell her that I could tell people that really knew their Bibles by the way they looked through them. Let her know she was one of them that really had read her Bible by the way she handled it. Usually they'd put it down because, chances are, if you asked them where Micah was, they'd have gone to the door and looked down the street.

"Well . . . you know what happened. I sold all the Bibles at twice what they were worth. I practically stole a bunch of surplus fans from a funeral home and sent 'em to the preacher. Then I went to the Congregationalists. Only this time I told 'em I was from their church. I've even sold Bibles to folks that couldn't read."

Joel had taken the ad out of his pocket. He read it again.

WANTED. Salesman to introduce excellent quality Bibles and church supplies. Exclusive territories. Lists furnished. Only men of highest standards need apply. 412 Bancroft Building.

Joel folded the ad and glanced at Emil Dawson curiously.

"You won't start out with big sales at first. It takes time to get the pitch. This door-to-door racket is tough. We sell communion supplies, paintings of Christ, crosses, and all that. Once you get the hang of it . . ." Emil Dawson snapped his fingers, "you'll be on your way." The man pushed a Bible across his desk. "This is what you sell. This is a big item."

Joel examined the Bible. It was nicely bound.

"In the back it's got everything. Tells how to pray for the sick. How to pray for faith. Even interprets the scripture. It's a good gimmick. You tell 'em that this is the authentic interpretation by the Methodists, or the Baptists, any of them. Most of 'em don't know the difference. It's the King James version. Ain't many folks know the Anglican scholars did it."

"How much is it?" Joel asked.

"Here's the deal. I get three ninety-five for every Bible you take out of here. I give you the lists of the church rolls. We'll go out of town in a team. The real money is in the small towns. Usually we get five ninety-five. It's a fair price. Don't make the mistake of promising a lot of junk to go with the book because one guy is doing three years because he promised too much. An old geek made him put it on paper, and wham! My suggestion is to be perfectly honest. It always pays. Five ninety-five is a good price."

"How much are they in the stores?"

"About a buck less. But the people don't know that. How long has it been since you shopped for a Bible? You see? Then naturally we sell other stuff. Crosses that glow in the dark. They eat that up."

Joel nodded.

"What do you think, Brogan? I've got a place for you."

Joel put the Bible on Emil Dawson's desk. He was trying to think how he could get out of the office. The easiest, quickest possible way. He stood up.

"I'll let you know. I live with a friend. I told him I'd talk to you and let him know. I'll go send him to you."

Emil Dawson rubbed his chin thoughtfully. "Okay. Only I want strictly honest people. If he's a con or a drunk or got hot pants, I don't want him."

"I'll send him in a few minutes," Joel promised. He reached the door, waved and closed it behind him. Out in the hall he shook his head. *Man!*

He took the elevator and went into the coffee shop on the main floor of the building. He sipped the coffee slowly. *The Bible Belt.* That was what they called the midwest, particularly the southern part. Small churches all over the area probably had been visited at one time or another by these salesmen. The percentage they sold might not be high, but Joel remembered the people of Toyah and he knew that the sales pitch would have been effective there. Even in his church it would have been effective.

Today Emil Dawson was probably presenting a large cheap print of Christ in a frame to the ministers, in exchange for the membership rolls and some church business. Joel shuddered. He smiled to himself. *And the ad had sounded so promising.*

Maybe some other kind of job. Shoe salesman. Joel considered it. He simply didn't want to be a shoe salesman. It was nothing to him. Truck driver. A good job, but he didn't want it. But what? He had to do something.

What could be more useless than a preacher that nobody would hire? Preach on a street corner? That would be Lynn Halliday's solution. Except fortunately she was a writer. If a writer fails, he's quietly alone in a closed room. He can always try again. It just takes the effort to roll clean paper into the typewriter and he's back in business. It was easy for her to solve a problem she did not understand. Of course he wasn't serving God. That didn't mean he no longer loved the church, that he didn't believe.

Sure he had expected a church. He had studied nearly as long as a medical doctor. Was he wrong to expect a decent job after all that preparation?

Wait? How long could he wait? Sell Bibles for Emil Dawson? *Honestly,* like Dawson did? Surely God didn't intend that. Joel thought of the preachers he had known who had failed, and of some he had heard about, but had not known. One had become an alcoholic. One ran off with the organist's wife. One was shot in the head by the father of the soprano soloist. .

People didn't understand that preachers were ordinary, fallible human beings. Somehow people had created an image of a man who walked with God and talked with man. If a preacher slipped too far into the realm of ordinary men, he was criticized. Too human! If he firmly insisted on obedience to the teachings of Jesus Christ, he was a fanatic. The ideal situation was to remain in the God-man image, close enough to people to be helpful, but distant enough to be beyond reproach.

The problem was what to do next. He had failed. Obviously the church had not wanted him. He was not exactly certain why. He had most certainly expected too much of the congregation. He had tried to make them change, and he had not been very forgiving. He had battled church politics like a madman. All in all, he had not been a very smart young man. He had not said the things they wanted to hear. His suggestion to invite Negroes to the church had brought about a major crisis. But he did love God. And he wanted to preach. He could not preach while selling shoes or driving a truck. He couldn't actually preach on a street corner because that would be entirely too much like Christ, and they would probably put him in an insane asylum.

Joel finished his coffee. He was convinced that there was a purpose to his life. He could not believe that he had gone as far as he had without really belonging to God. God had something for him and in God's good time he'd find it. Until then, he had to do something.

Joel paid for his coffee and walked toward the Medical Arts Building. He entered the building, sniffing unpleasantly at the hospital odor.

He took the prescription box from his pocket and checked the doctor's name. Dr. Jay Sherman. He found the name on the large, black, glass-encased listing. Eighth floor.

He entered the office and sat down. The office was vacant. "It will be a few minutes," a woman's voice said.

Joel turned to see a small, attractive blonde in a white uniform.

"The doctor was in surgery this morning. But he will be back soon."

"Fine."

The nurse took pen and pad, then glanced at him quickly. "Your name?"

"Joel Brogan."

"What seems to be the trouble, Mr. Brogan?"

"It isn't about me. It's about my uncle. I wanted to talk to the doctor about him."

"I see," she said. "And his name?"

"Charles Jackson."

"Oh, yes . . . I remember Mr. Jackson. How is he doing?"

"Not very well. He ran out of these pills and he's been having a rough time of it. I thought I'd get the prescription refilled."

The waiting room began to fill up. There were overweight men who had difficulty getting their breath. There were very thin men who coughed into handkerchiefs. Mothers arrived with children, each hovering over her own, obviously fearful of the diseases possibly carried by the others.

Joel relinquished his chair when the room became

full. Finally the doctor came in, greeted the patients, and escaped into one of four doors marked private. Shortly the nurse gestured to Joel.

"Mr. Brogan," she said, "the doctor will see you now."

Joel followed her into one of the rooms. The doctor came in, a thin, angular man with a mustache and rimmed glasses. He smoked a pipe.

"You wanted to have a prescription refilled?"

"Yes. For Charles Jackson."

The doctor removed a pen from his white jacket and scribbled hurriedly, tearing the paper loose when he finished. "How is he?" he asked.

"Not well. He seems to be in pain all the time."

The doctor frowned, shook his head.

"Can you help him, Doctor?"

Dr. Sherman pondered this briefly. He sighed. "I don't think anyone can help him. I checked Mr. Jackson very thoroughly when he came to me a few months ago. I recognized the symptoms, made X-rays."

"What does he have?"

"He hasn't told you?"

"He avoids it. He passes it off lightly. But he can't seem to go on much longer. I wanted the truth."

"Inoperable cancer, spread to the internal organs. He came too late. Besides, he refused to consider an operation."

"How long . . ."

"I don't know. . . . I frankly didn't think he would live to exhaust the supply of narcotics I gave him. We can't predict how long it will take. He will become weaker until he is bedfast. It usually comes soon after that."

"Then he hasn't long."

96

"I'm sorry, Mr. Brogan. We didn't have a chance on him. See that he takes these capsules for pain."

"Yes."

"When he begins to fail, we can take him to the hospital. I don't advise taking him now, because we are desperate for beds. I don't mean to sound unsympathetic. He can see his friends more often in his home. If you could hire a special nurse, I think it will be the most satisfactory thing for him."

"Thank you, Doctor," Joel said. He reached the door.

"I'm sorry, Mr. Brogan."

Joel left the office and waited silently for the elevator, clutching the prescription. Then he was on the street, moving very rapidly toward the drugstore.

Joel went back to Reno Street. When he entered the Green Parrot Bar, he had made a decision.

"Hello, Uncle Charlie," he said, taking off his coat. He hung it on a peg, started away, then returned and took the coat down. Someone would steal it in two minutes and sell it at the nearest pawnshop. He folded it and placed it under the bar, took off his tie, unbuttoned his collar, and slapped his hands together. "Okay, old man," he said, "what do you want me to do?"

Uncle Charlie's mouth was ajar. "What do you think you're doin'?"

"I'm going to help," Joel said.

"You get the hell out from behind my bar," Charlie snapped.

"No," very softly.

Uncle Charlie got off the stool and moved closer. His face was drawn. He had changed considerably in three weeks. He was in pain. It showed in his eyes. "Am I gonna have to bounce you?" he asked.

Joel put his arm around his uncle's shoulder. "You kid everybody else, Charlie. Don't kid me. It's a little late for you and me to start that, isn't it?"

Uncle Charlie looked down. He was old and worn and tired and sick with pain. "It's a little late," he said.

"I'm going to help out."

"I don't want you mixed up in this racket," Charlie said.

"Would I be any worse? Will they change me, Charlie? Are you afraid of that?"

"No."

"Then I'll help you. I want to help you."

Uncle Charlie rubbed his hands over his thinning hair. "You mean that, kid?"

"Yes, I do. It won't hurt my chances for a church. So don't worry."

Uncle Charlie took a deep breath. "You can help me on my terms."

"Like?"

"You make change at the register. The girls serve the beer. I don't want you to do that. I just don't. You can sort of manage the place."

"All right."

Uncle Charlie gripped his arm, his head bending. He sighed deeply. "It was gettin' hard, Joey. It was gettin' so hard."

"Why don't you go upstairs and take a nap? It will be good for you. Here are your pills."

"I believe I will." Uncle Charlie started away, then turned. "I never thought I'd need anyone."

"We all need someone."

"Yeah. I guess we do. Well, I'll take a nap. Thanks, Joey. You know?"

"Yes."

Uncle Charlie went out of the bar slowly, his hand

against his side, not conspicuously, but pressed there just the same.

Old Viola came to the bar and leaned close to Joel, squinting her eyes in the dull light.

"I heard," she said.

"We can make it easier for him."

"You saw the doctor?"

"I saw him," Joel said wearily.

"What did he say?"

"He said Charlie is a sick man."

"He's gonna die."

Joel did not answer.

"He's a good man," she said. She left the bar, shuffling along until she reached a table. She sat down and lighted a cigarette. And watched it burn untouched in the tray.

7

Saturday was the big day. The oil field roustabouts, tool pushers, and drillers lathered up and shaved. They almost managed to rid the crude oil odor from their pores and most of the grime from beneath their finger-nails. This done, they piled into cars, heading for the city.

Some had wives and went home. Some had wives and didn't. Many of them turned up on Reno, dressed in plain, white, short-sleeved sport shirts and slacks. They mingled with men from the factories, the air base. The first project was to get the beer down. Leathery faces in contrast to the white beer foam. Hairy, muscled arms reaching for money, for glasses. *Get a load on, men. Get a few down.*

The freelance prostitutes liked the oil field jockeys. For one thing they didn't take much time, unless they were real drunk. After a week on the derricks, not many got that drunk.

Then the college boys. These were the most idiotic creatures on the Street. They wore fancy knit shirts, knife-edge pressed slacks, and smelled of cologne. They had crew cuts. Some sported fraternity pins. Most had read enough sex literature to think they understood women in general and prostitutes in particular.

These boys were apparently unaware that they were considered the biggest asses on the Street. But they

100

came, and drank, and fed their money to the vulture-like machine that sucked indiscriminately from one and all.

To the oil field worker or laborer, Saturday night on Reno Street was his weekly fling. He was not particularly ashamed of the women he met there. He took them out on a round of the bars. They were women available on quick notice, and for him that was enough. Besides, they were usually attractive, and if he spent his money freely, they were fair companions, in and out of bed. A man with twenty-four hours away from an oil camp learned not to be choosy.

But to the college boy it was entirely different. To him this was a night for slumming. He looked with contempt on the women he met there. If a whore appeared on the university campus and called his name (the fictitious one he had given) he would probably suffer palpitations. Yet he, more than the salesman, laborer, or serviceman, was most fascinated by the prostitutes.

The students gathered at tables in small groups, usually three or four, and tried to carry on conversations with the whores. Serious conversations about how she liked her work, how many men she had been with, how she got started, if she enjoyed men. Because of this sociological curiosity, the college boy was most despised by the girls.

The servicemen. The salesmen in the stores. The old men who were grateful for anything. The young men who wanted most to nurse. The degenerates who wanted to improvise. The sadists who wanted pain. For all of them an outlet on Reno. On Saturday night.

Joel knocked lightly on Lynn Halliday's door.

"Come in," she said loudly.

Joel entered to see her pulling brassières and panties from a cord stretched from the wardrobe to the window sill.

"You're going native," Joel said.

Lynn tossed the freshly washed things into a drawer. She wore jeans and a knit shirt. She even looked like a native. Had Uncle Charlie seen her like this the first day, he would not have believed she was an author. She smiled gaily.

"What's with you?" she asked. She was very much at ease today.

"I thought I'd tell you about Saturday. This is it down there. All the monkeys come out to play."

He glanced at the page in her typewriter and read a few lines unconsciously, then looked away.

"I'll have to take it in," she said.

"You'd be pawed to death today," he said. "The average idiot down there won't know that you aren't salable. But anyway you'll see the show, if that's what you came for."

"I'll see it," she said agreeably.

"Then don't get mad and slug somebody in the bar. Just raise your little hand and I'll come chase the bad men away. Down there, if you hit somebody, it's an unspoken signal for everybody to hit somebody else. When it's over, there has been a lot of damage."

"I'll keep an eye on you," she said. "And I'll lock on my chastity belt."

"How is your work going?" he asked.

"So so. I'm still not writing this book. I'm taking notes. When I get a bagful, I'll write. I'll be gone by then."

"I see."

"I have wondered about one thing. For skid row, I

102

don't see any drunks lying in the street, on the sidewalk. That sort of thing."

"You mean like Chicago or the Bowery in New York?"

"Yes."

"Doesn't happen here. Oh . . . to some extent it does. But not like those places. It's because Oklahoma was a dry state until recently. The real down and outers can't afford cheap vodka, which is what they drink mostly around here toward the last. Beer doesn't have enough kick and it costs too much. So when a man gets really down, when he starts drinking anything, Sneaky Pete stuff, he leaves. He travels to Chicago, or the West Coast, or New York. And the local police keep them moving."

"Why?"

"Because they won't work and they don't have any money. We keep the city clean on the surface."

"Then you wouldn't really call this skid row?"

"No, I wouldn't. These prostitutes make two hundred dollars a weekend. Some less, of course, and some more. I would say skid row is a place where the people have the same habits, but not the cash. This is the vice district. New Orleans has the French Quarter. Here it's Reno."

"New Orleans is tourist stuff."

Joel nodded. "Look around tonight. You'll see them. Once or twice a week they make it down here. Then they go back to other parts of the city. Or out of town. When they have a big convention, it's murder down here."

"Thanks, neighbor. I'll look for signs. It was nice of you to brief me."

She pulled the knit shirt down tightly, unaware that

103

the shirt molded closely against her breasts. Joel glanced away awkwardly. He was conscious of a sudden animal desire. "I'd better go," he said.

She had known at once and released her hold on the shirt.

Joel went to the door and started to close it after him.

"Leave it open," she called.

He noticed her thoughtful expression as he left. It had been unintentional, that gesture with the shirt. But it had called his attention to her. She was something other than a name on a book cover, an argumentative creature who seemed at times to heckle him. She was desirable, soft and warm. Touchable and exciting.

She, too, had noticed and had responded to his interest in that moment before he turned away, frightened.

Joel let his feet take the stairs two at a time, finding himself breathless at the bottom, standing stupidly in the morning sunlight.

He couldn't let himself become involved in something foolish. Yet he was conscious of his desire, his loneliness. That very loneliness stirred a need.

But this was impossible. He would forget it. She would be gone soon.

Uncle Charlie was cleaning glasses slowly. His weight was falling steadily. He showed little interest in food. Only his spirit remained. It was all that kept him going.

"How do you feel?" Joel asked.

"Like a million dollars," Uncle Charlie said with a scowl.

Joel raised an eyebrow.

"Well, a million after taxes, then," Uncle Charlie added, scratching his head foolishly.

He led Joel to the cash register.

"I ain't gonna push it today," Charlie said. "You sit here and rake in the money. I'll just horse around. I'm practically a retired man."

Joel sat on the stool. The place was clean, ready for the onslaught. The two regular waitresses were supplemented by an extra two. In addition, Viola kept things orderly among the girls. The two special girls were primping by the juke box. The two regulars, relaxing over cigarettes at the bar.

At exactly ten in the morning, Uncle Charlie spoke to Viola. "Okay, Vi, open the door and stand back."

And it was started.

The little man with red-rimmed eyes came in at five in the afternoon. He sat on a bar stool and glanced drunkenly around the room, until he spotted the three college boys. Then he smiled. Uncle Charlie nudged Joel.

"See that little old guy?" he asked.

"Uh huh."

"He's been here before. I know what he's gonna do, and I want you to watch this. Maybe I ought to stop the creep only it's so rare I don't think I will. Just keep an eye on him."

Joel re-examined the man. He wore a felt hat with a small red feather. That it was the middle of the summer did not seem to faze him. His suit coat was double-breasted, and, Joel imagined, unbearably hot. It had wide stripes, the sort popular ten or fifteen years ago. The pants were unpressed, a different material from the suit. To the shirt collar he had clipped a pale-green bow tie. He wore suède shoes. He reminded Joel of Harpo Marx.

The little man smiled at everybody, then got up and walked over in front of Joel and sat beside the

105

college boys, who turned and eyed him as if he were a leper. He chuckled to himself, his shoulders shaking mightily as though some private joke had just swept through his mind.

He pulled his billfold out of his back pocket. This he placed on the bar in front of him in plain view of the boys. The billfold was crammed with ten- and twenty-dollar bills, a thing Joel noticed, as did the college boys, almost immediately.

"Howdy," the little man said in a nasal drawl that Joel suspected came from the Ozarks.

The college boys mumbled arrogantly. An attractive prostitute named Sharon had noticed the billfold and had slipped onto the empty stool on the side opposite the college boys.

Joel glanced at Uncle Charlie who smiled patiently, almost cunningly.

"My name's Hank," the little man announced.

"My name is Benito," the nearest boy lied wisely, but glanced at the billfold, the fat, fat billfold.

Hank's soft, brown, cocker-spaniel eyes roamed the bar.

"Sure are lots of flies in here," Hank said.

The boy who had identified himself as Benito raised an eyebrow as if to ask from what hole this creature had crawled. Hank tipped his felt hat to Sharon and nasaled her a "Howdy" also. Sharon smiled back lustily, hungrily eyeing the billfold.

"I never seen the like of flies," Hank said. He waved them away as if he were being smothered. Two single flies buzzed along the entire length of the bar. Joel started to get the fly swatter, but noticed Uncle Charlie spread his hands in protest. Joel forgot the swatter, turned his attention back to Hank.

106

Hank looked directly at Joel. "Buddy," he said, "can I have a soda pop bottle full of water?"

Joel reached for a glass instinctively.

"A bottle," Hank insisted.

Joel found an empty Coke bottle and started to rinse it.

"No need to do that," Hank said. "Just fill it up."

Joel filled the bottle, leaving perhaps a half-inch air space at the top.

"No," Hank protested, "all the way up. Plumb full."

Joel put the bottle under the water until it ran over. Hank pointed to the bar in front of him and Joel put the bottle down.

At this Hank pulled a twenty-dollar bill from the billfold, which accidentally caused several other bills to slip partly out of the leather case. "Why don't you set me and the lady and Benito up for a beer," Hank said.

Benito said abruptly, "I'm with these people. . . ."

"Sure," Hank said. "Set all of us up with a beer. Live it up, I always say. Ain't that what you always say, honey?" Hank jabbed Sharon none too lightly in the ribs with his elbow.

Looking at the change from the twenty, Sharon painfully but pleasantly agreed.

Viola served the beers and the group thanked Hank, who was bobbing his head happily, drunkenly; and now singing a few lines from *Oklahoma!*

"A damn man has got to do something to forget. Ain't that right, Benito?"

"Sure," Benito replied, "if you say so."

"Damned right. The bastards got oil all over the fields and my cows can't find nothing to eat that don't taste like oil. And the smell. It's the worst, stinkingest,

awfulest smell I ever smelt. Son . . . you ever smelled
oil for a month at a time, day and night, every breath
you take?"

"No," Benito admitted, somewhat awed.

"It's horrible. And the noise. The damned things
out there all night long. Pump . . . pump . . . a man's
got to forget. Damn flies sure are thick in this place,
ain't they? You ready for a beer, Benito?"

Benito finished his beer quickly, though it nearly
choked him. "I guess so," he said indifferently.

"Set 'em all up again," Hank said.

Joel saw Hank's hand move in a single swift stab.

"I got one!" Hank shouted happily.

Sharon, Benito, the other college boys and several
people at the near-by tables looked up as Hank
shouted.

"What?" Sharon asked, alarmed.

"A fly. I caught one. That'll fix 'em," he said.

Benito winked over Hank's bobbing head toward
Sharon, who raised an eyebrow in return. Then both
glanced at Hank's bulging billfold.

"How long you think it takes to drown a fly?" Hank
asked.

Joel looked at Uncle Charlie, who smiled without
moving his mouth. Nobody answered.

"Three minutes?" Hank asked finally. "You reckon
it would take a fly three minutes to drown?"

"I have no idea," Benito said, drinking his beer.
He could not have cared less.

"I heard that flies is real tough to kill. I bet it takes
at least five minutes," Hank said thoughtfully.

At this Hank took the fly, which was still clutched
in his hand, and eased it into the Coke bottle of water
that Joel had given him. He pressed his thumb in the
bottle top and turned the bottle sideways. Inside, the

108

fly began to drown, fighting vigorously for a time, relaxing, floating motionless, then fighting again.

"Somebody look at the clock," Hank said, "and tell me when five minutes is up."

Joel glanced at the clock. "It's five twenty-five," he said.

"Good. When it's five-thirty, I'll bet I can take this here fly out and put it in a box and dry it off and in another five minutes it will just up and fly away."

"That is ridiculous," Benito replied.

"No," Hank insisted. "I heard that they was hard to kill."

Joel found himself watching the fly closely. Three minutes had passed and the fly was no longer struggling. Occasionally a single leg would move slightly. Joel kept track of the time and when the clock showed five-thirty, he called out. To his surprise, not only were the college boys and the prostitute bending close over the bottle, but a half dozen other people had gathered around. Joel examined the fly. It was obviously dead.

"I'll bet that if I leave him another five minutes, I can still make him fly away."

"That fly?" Benito asked incredulously.

Hank giggled foolishly. "I guess I'm crazy. But dammit, money ain't everything. Just think what them oil wells has already done to my cows. Ruined the whole pasture."

"How much," Benito asked cautiously, "would you bet?"

"Well . . . it's just for fun. Might as well bet a few dollars."

Benito reached for his billfold. "Now exactly what do you plan to do?" he asked suspiciously.

"Well . . . at the end of five minutes, I'll pour out the fly. Then we'll put him in a box."

"What box?" Benito asked sharply.

"The bartender has a match box. You do, don't you?"

Joel indicated that he had a box.

"Then I'll put this here fly in a box and cover it up with salt to dry it out. Then if the bartender will put the box under a light and shake it around, I say the fly will fly out of the box before five minutes is up."

"Let me see that bottle," Benito said. He studied the fly closely. "I'll bet you ten dollars that the fly won't fly away," he said.

Hank turned to Sharon quickly. "Honey, am I bein' an ol' fool?" Hank asked.

Sharon had reached inside her brassière and withdrawn a five-dollar bill. "No," she said, "but I want to play, too."

"Well, I guess you got a right to play, too." Hank gestured toward his billfold. "You take out the money and hold it for us. Will you do that?" Hank asked Joel.

Joel checked with Uncle Charlie who nodded agreeably.

"All right," Joel said.

The college boy beside Benito removed his billfold, but had not yet made a bet.

"Don't try to change flies," Benito warned.

"Now, son," Hank said somewhat pained, "I said it was just good clean fun. And it's only money. So why would I change flies?"

Benito accepted this, but kept a watch over the fly in the bottle.

Joel glanced toward the clock. Time was up.

"It's been ten minutes," he said.

Benito and Sharon practically pressed their noses

against the bottle. They smiled joyfully. The fly was quite dead. It had not moved for seven minutes.

Hank laughed wildly.

"I bet," he yelled, "I could give it another five minutes."

The onlookers went for billfolds at once, a sudden movement like a western gunfight showdown between the Clantons and the Earps.

Hands were pressing money into Hank's face.

"That wouldn't be fair to you, I reckon," he said to Benito. "Our bet was for five minutes. You might not want to wait any longer."

"No no." Benito choked. "Go ahead. I'll wait."

Sharon bounced on her stool. "I don't mind either. Go another five minutes," she said too eagerly.

"Take the bets then. After all, I did say it. I guess I just get too excited and . . . I'm just an ol' fool."

Sharon comforted Hank to a point bordering indecency. Joel took the bets, removing money from Hank's billfold while Hank held the bottle aloft. The bets finally came to forty-five dollars.

Benito and his college friends were in for a total of twenty-five. Sharon was in for five. And various others had made up the rest.

"One minute to go," Joel said.

"Now, son, you get me a penny match box and fill it half up with salt."

Joel emptied a box of matches and poured salt in the bottom.

"Good," Hank said. "I'll just give you the bottle and you ease the fly out. Then pick him up and put him in the box gently."

"Time's up," Joel said. At this Hank, under the watchful eye of a dozen people, handed Joel the bottle.

Carefully Joel poured out the water until the fly

flowed out. Using the edge of a piece of paper, he carefully lifted the soggy black mass that had once been a live fly up for all to see. He then put the fly in the match box.

"Now you just cover him all up with salt," Hank ordered.

Joel did this.

"Now hold the box under that light," Hank suggested. "It ought to be warm enough." Joel held the box under a small lamp at the end of the bar. "And shake it around, like you was about to roll dice."

Hank went about finishing his beer. He did not watch the progress of the insect in the box. It did not concern him any longer.

"A minute's up," he said, sipping his beer indifferently. "What's the fly doin'?"

"Nothing."

"Shake him some more."

Joel shook the box under the watchful eyes of the gamblers.

Suddenly Sharon screamed. "No!"

"What is it?" Benito asked.

"It moved. Oh hell, I swear it moved," she announced.

"Two minutes is up," Hank said, taking a cigar out of his coat pocket. He located a match and lighted the cigar with obvious pleasure.

"It can't be," one of the boys shouted.

"Did it shake the salt off yet?" Hank asked.

"It just did. It's standing up," the boy answered.

"Shake the box a little more," Hank suggested, breathing the smoke.

Joel shook the box. Quite suddenly the fly fluttered its wings, rubbed its legs about its head and, in one

112

surprising motion, flipped free of the match box and soared up toward the ceiling. Joel put the box on the counter and stopped in front of Hank. "Here's your money," Joel said.

Hank modestly accepted the money, did not bother to count it. "Set everybody up for a beer," he said, getting up. "I've got to be gettin' along."

Hank went to the end of the bar and paused.

"It was dead," Benito said sadly. "I saw it. How could it fly?"

Hank laughed softly, cocking his felt hat at a rakish angle. "The thing to know about a fly is this. It will live submerged in water for from forty-five minutes to an hour and a half. Just cover him with salt and get him warm and shake him around. Very sturdy little insects." Hank smiled roguishly and left the Green Parrot Bar.

Sharon sat glumly staring at her beer. Benito and his companions began to argue until Uncle Charlie lifted a hand and said, "Easy, men." They settled down.

"You knew what he was going to do?" Joel asked.

"Yeah. The guy came in a couple of years ago. He never misses. Everybody looks at that billfold of his and they get greedy, real greedy. Besides he acts like a simple fink, you know? He just lets them force the money on him. Lives that way all year. Drives a four-door Cadillac. A pretty dumb guy."

Joel scratched his head. "But who would believe the fly was still alive?"

"Nobody," Uncle Charlie said. "It cost me ten bucks last time he came. I couldn't believe it either. And that pitch about the oil wells. That's the best of all. He's got something better than oil wells. They go dry.

113

But he'll never run out of suckers." Uncle Charlie shook his head and went over to his chair behind the bar.

Rose came in and sat at the bar. "Hello," she said.

"How are you, Rose?"

"Okay."

"Did you want a beer?"

"I guess."

Joel motioned to one of the waitresses, who brought a glass of beer. Rose opened a small purse and paid for the drink. She took several swallows before she looked up.

"I'm sorry about what Nick said the other day. I didn't know you were a preacher. He made me feel awful."

"He did?"

"That about ten per cent off. He didn't have to say that."

Joel sighed. "The Philosopher," he said thoughtfully. "He had to show a little contempt toward God. He didn't care about me."

"You know . . . really . . . I think that's right," Rose said.

"He hates too much. It'll make him sick."

"Yeah."

"Has he ever hit you?"

Rose sipped her beer.

"Why do you let him?" Joel pressed.

The conversation was making her nervous. "I don't guess that's my business," Joel said.

She looked at him curiously. She seemed so innocent. So clean. "I don't mind," she said. "Maybe we could be friends. Not real friends like, you know. But just friends, if it doesn't make any difference about what I do."

"We're friends, Rose," he said, "and if you ever need help, you let me know. You remember that."

"Okay."

A sailor leaned against the bar. He appraised Rose hungrily. Occasionally she glanced toward him. She smiled shyly. "Baby," he said at last, "I'd like to get to know you."

She blinked innocently.

"Twenty dollars," she said, drinking her beer.

The sailor appeared surprised at first, then recovered quickly. "I'll buy that," he said at last.

Rose finished her beer and slid off the stool. The sailor took her hand. " 'By," she said to Joel. She smiled shyly again. "And thanks."

So they came and went. Lynn Halliday came down when it was getting dark and sat on a stool near Joel. "How do I get protection?" she asked. "Scream?"

"No . . . I'll keep an eye on you."

The room was crowded. Shrill laughter occasionally screeched over the mumbled conversations. The juke box played almost continuously. Couples danced. Some just leaned against one another. Others stood against the wall talking intimately.

The three teen-aged boys came in about seven-thirty. One of them, Joel remembered, had been with the group that had tormented Pencils in the alley. He had very blond hair, combed to a duck's tail in the back. His eyes were pale blue, like the flame of an acetylene torch. He wore a loud sport shirt, the collar turned up in the back. Without a word he leaned over the bar as a waitress passed, and moved his hand quickly. A match in his hand burst into flame and he lighted his cigarette. The waitress stopped, put her tray on the counter and moved toward him.

"Now don't get excited, baby," he said, blowing

smoke across the bar. "I just needed to strike a match."

"Well, buster, you picked the wrong place to strike it," she said, rubbing herself.

Uncle Charlie eased from his stool before the waitress could reach the kid. Joel left the register and followed. "Hold it," Uncle Charlie said. "What's the trouble?"

"This jerk struck a match on my . . . dress," she said. A very thin dark line of evidence showed on the tight-fitting skirt.

The kid looked blankly innocent. "I didn't think. I just reached out to strike a match and her . . . she just happened to be there," he said arrogantly.

"Whitey," Uncle Charlie said, "that'll cost you two bucks."

The boy acted as though he was going to make a big thing of it, but he found a superior smile in time. "What's two bucks?" he said. He reached into his pocket and peeled off two dollar bills.

"Don't get loud, Whitey," Uncle Charlie said. "If you do, you go, but fast."

"I am an angel," Whitey said, balling his eyes, turning his hands palms up.

Uncle Charlie returned to the stool. The waitress took the money and marched away victoriously, but still not exactly certain how this came to be a victory.

Joel followed Charlie to his stool. "Who is that boy?" he asked.

"Name's Homer McMillin, but on the Street he goes by Whitey. That's all you ever hear. The others is his stooges. He usually has a couple around."

"How old are those kids?"

"Sixteen. Maybe seventeen."

"Why do you serve them?"

116

"Joey, I ask them kids for identification. You got to be twenty-one. They smile like cherubs and open up a billfold. In the billfold, which they have copped, is this driver's license and social-security card and it says they are twenty-one. If you still refuse to serve them, they give you the bird. What am I supposed to do, make 'em bring their birth certificates? These kids, is wide awake."

Whitey grabbed an empty beer bottle, intent on becoming the main attraction, raised it near his mouth and shouted.

"Ladies and gentlemen. This is Bill Stern speaking to you from South Bend, Indiana. Hey, baby, bring me a Bud. Get that? A Bud. What's for you guys? They want Buds too. That makes three. One, two, three, testing. One two three. This is Bill Stern at South Bend. Ladies and gentlemen, there are thousands of fans gripping the edge of their seats. Notre Dame has the ball. They are down on the Oklahoma seven-yard line. It is fourth down and goal to go. Only two minutes remain on the clock.

"Ladies and gentlemen, this is the last chance for Notre Dame today. They have won one thousand and fifty-three games in a row, and they are trailing by six points. Quarterback Leshitsky . . ." Whitey paused for a laugh from his friends and a couple of drunks who were leaning close to the group. "Leshitsky is going into the huddle. This is the last play for Notre Dame. If they don't score, they will lose the game. Ladies and gentlemen, do you hear that roar?" Whitey paused to make a sound very faintly suggesting a lion. The crowd became larger. Two or three prostitutes were taking it in and a half dozen people holding bottles of beer stood about. Somebody turned down the juke box.

117

This apparently pleased Whitey, because now he didn't have to compete. It was his show. Big and important. He was somebody. It showed on his face. They were listening.

Clutching the empty bottle for a microphone, Whitey went on. "Ladies and gentlemen, the coach is pacing the sidelines madly. He'd like to send in a play, but there isn't time. The quarterback looks over the defense. This is it, ladies and gentlemen. This is the critical moment. Is Quarterback Leshitsky going to call a pass? Is he going to run it? What would you do? Ladies and gentlemen, I'm asking you, *what would you do if you was in his place?*"

A waitress paused in front of Whitey. "Three Buds, sister. If we don't get three Buds, this game ain't ever gonna get over with. Okay, okay. The quarterback is scratching his head. He don't even know what to do. Nobody knows what to do. Wait! Wait! They're taking time out. And, folks," Whitey said softly, abandoning the feverish pitch of the game, "if you don't know what to do, let me tell you. Go out to the telephone and call up the nearest beer joint and say, 'Bring me over a dozen cases of that famous beer. You'll like the tangy taste. It is smooth like hydrochloric acid.' " Whitey paused for the laughter from his audience. For some reason, this was thought to be very amusing. "Always keep eight or ten cases in your refrigerator. Drink it. . . . You'll like it! And now back to the game."

Whitey changed back to the feverish pitch. "The official blows his whistle. Ladies and gentlemen, this is Bill Stern." Whitey apparently threw that in for the late-comers, as a large crowd was growing about him. "What would you do? The quarterback comes out of

118

the huddle. He bends over the center. He barks the signals."

Whitey stopped to bark like a dog. This was greeted with applause. "One, two, three. Three! Three beers! Baby, if you don't bring me them beers, I'll scream." About this time the beer was placed before Whitey and his friends. Whitey took the empty from his mouth and began to fumble for his money.

"Here," some fellow in the middle of the crowd said, "I'll pay for the beer. You go on. Man, you're the greatest."

Whitey could have died happy at that moment. Joel had him figured now. Whitey plunged back into his work.

"The center snaps the ball. The quarterback fades back. He's back to the twenty. He's looking for a receiver. There ain't none. He fades back. He's being rushed. What is he going to do? Hell, who knows what he's going to do. He don't even know himself. He's at the fifty. They are swarming him. No, wait. He breaks in the clear. He's in the open. *Ladies and gentlemen, he's in the open streaking down the sidelines toward the goal. He gets by one tackler. Two. Three. He's going all the way. He's at the twenty. The fifteen. No one in sight. He's at the five. They're only five seconds left. He is going . . . Wait!*" Whitey stopped, calmly picked up his bottle of beer and drank while the crowd tensely awaited the outcome.

"*Ladies and gentlemen. He fell on his butt on the three-yard line. And there goes the gun. The game is over. Oklahoma wins 20 to 14.*" Whitey accepted the applause modestly.

"You're great," a drunk said. "I mean, you're the greatest."

"Yeah," Whitey said, pursing his lips. "I'm the greatest. We got to face it."

The crowd began to dissipate. Joel turned to Uncle Charlie. "Did you hear that?" Joel asked.

"Joey," Charlie said, "that was heard three blocks from here."

"That kid's good. He clowned it, but he does things to people."

"He sure does," Charlie said.

"What do you mean?"

"I mean he could con you out of your last cigarette and then make you feel like an idiot if you don't light it for him."

"What does he do?"

"Like I said, he cons."

"What?"

"Anything. He'll roll a whore, a drunk. He'll steal a car for a ride with the boys. He ain't immune to nothing."

"Is he in school?"

"He just got out. A year in Stringtown for takin' a car for a joy ride. I think he got a good education."

"Charlie," Joel asked, "why do you serve him?"

Uncle Charlie let his hand rest on his stomach, pressing against it. His face was very weary. "There's a bootlegger around the corner that'll sell 'em 100-proof. He can get that in five minutes. He can get a joy stick if he wants it at the poolroom. But right now he's satisfied with a couple of beers. He's got a phony ID card. I figure if he stays on a few beers, he might be all right. If I run him out, he'll really get into it. It ain't easy, Joey."

"Isn't there any hope?"

The old man smiled. "There's always hope, ain't there?" A pain contorted his face. He couldn't make it.

120

"Why don't you go upstairs? Do you want me to call a doctor?"

"No. I still got some pills."

"Have you been taking them?"

"No."

"Why don't you go upstairs and have one?"

"I might."

"What did the doctor say about when it hurt like this?"

Uncle Charlie slipped from the stool. "He said not to play too much tennis."

Whitey watched Uncle Charlie leave. To Whitey, this seemed to mean something. It showed all over his face. Whitey's eyes shifted to Joel where he sat by the cash register. Joel thought it would be best if he got things straight at the beginning.

"Charlie's gone upstairs to rest, Whitey," Joel said. "But his rules still go. I'll crack your head."

Whitey lifted the bottle of beer. "Sure. Sure. Hey, preacher," he said smiling crookedly, "you want a beer tonight?"

The kid didn't miss anything. "Be careful, Whitey," Joel said.

"Sure. I'm always careful. You preaching tomorrow? Huh?"

Joel's jaws tightened. *That's what he wants. That's how he knows he has you, when you react. Keep yourself under control.*

"I don't have a church any more."

"No kiddin'? What happened?"

"I got fired. I got fired twice. Everybody knows that around the Street, kid. Don't you get around?" Joel smiled evenly.

It killed Whitey. The kid hadn't expected Joel to admit the truth and it put him at a disadvantage. He

121

didn't like that business about not getting around either. He fought back.

"Yeah. I get around. I heard a long time ago about you. You and your big buddy Jesus. What a laugh."

Joel smiled. "You're really afraid of Him, aren't you?"

"I'm not afraid of nobody, mister. Don't you ever forget that."

"Then why does He bother you?"

"Who?"

"Jesus."

Whitey laughed. "Are you gonna preach?"

"No."

"Good. I don't pay my money to listen to you."

"No, Whitey," Joel said softly, "you pay money to listen to yourself."

It took a moment for that to register properly. The effect was devastating. "Look, buster. You want my business?"

He had a point, Joel admitted silently. When you ran a bar, you had to take the gaff that went along with it. You couldn't get too choosy about your customers. Not on this street anyway. "Yes," Joel said. "But be a good boy."

Whitey finished the bottle of beer and shoved it toward Joel. "Gimme another one of those," he said.

Joel turned his back and walked away. He called the waitress. "Send that boy a beer." Joel looked back. Whitey was frowning. He'd found a man who didn't con very easy . . . who didn't con at all. "On the house," Joel said. "Then don't serve him any more. He's had enough."

Joel leaned against the cash register. Whitey reached for his money. The waitress told him it was on the house. Whitey raised the bottle in thanks. But

122   •

he was not sure about things. Joel could feel it. That was all right. Joel figured that the skirmish had been a draw. Whitey finished his beer, nudged his companions and left the Green Parrot. Joel was glad to see him leave.

Judge Hanson plodded his way to a table. He drank alone, sipping his beer. He did not remove his coat or his muffler. But he did lay the worn Homburg on the table. The juke box throbbed to the savage beat of the jump music. As the evening wore on, the beer flowed more slowly. A few people became completely drunk. Joel called cabs for some of them, asked others to go home. If they had a home. It was pathetic to see them when they reached the stage of helplessness. A few real drunks were mixing vanilla extract with beer. One by one the freelance prostitutes found company and left.

At eleven forty-five the bar was nearly deserted. The smell of spilled beer was everywhere. Joel went to the stool and sat down. He noticed that Lynn Halliday had left, but couldn't remember seeing her go. Old Viola was sitting in a chair smoking a cigarette, her eyes closed. The other waitresses were lingering with the few drifters who remained at the bar. Engagements were being made for the remainder of the evening. The girls seldom went home alone.

Countless staggering characters paraded before Joel like a monstrous dream. They were all running from something. From themselves, from love, from responsibility, police, job, fatherhood, respectability. Every one of them had a monster they tried to escape. But the monster they created was more terrible than the one they ran from. These were no longer once-a-week drinkers. These were the ones who didn't worry about breakfast in the morning. They thought about whether or not they had saved one drink to get up with. They were in various stages of alcoholism. Even Whitey, he was going to make it too, between prison terms.

Joel studied the hulking form of Judge Hanson at the table. His head sagged and bobbed. But there was half a glass of beer left. He would discipline himself to finish it. Even if it made him sick.

"I want a beer," someone said.

Evita slid on a bar stool. She studied him carefully.

"Say," she said, "you look beat."

"I am. You want a beer, you say?"

"Yes. I'm through for the night. I'm loaded. Now I want to get drunk," she said.

"I guess it follows," he said.

She began to laugh. "Like hot dogs at a ball game."

A waitress came to the bar, opened the case, and slid a can of beer before Evita. She flipped Joel a half dollar.

"Keep the change," she said. "I'll have another."

"That's something you could do," Joel said.

"What's that?"

"Work in a bar."

"Isn't that compromising with sin, Mr. Preacher?"

"I'm not the one to say. But you'll have to admit it's a step in the right direction."

"Joey," she said, her voice quite sharp, "are you going to give me hell tonight?"

He turned away. "No, Evita."

Her voice softened. "I won't try to make a prostitute out of you if you won't try to make a Christian out of me. Okay?"

"All right," Joel said.

"Come off it, Joey," she said angrily. "This ain't a church."

124

He frowned.

"I'm sorry," she said. "Just get off my back." She drank from the can as though she were starved for a drink. She put down the empty can and walked around the bar and opened another. "What you need is a good woman," she said. Joel looked intently into her face. "Not me," she said. "Don't be stupid. I mean a *good* woman. You and me wouldn't work. I don't want your kind of life. I wouldn't want it even if I wasn't what I am."

She drank deeply from the can.

"I love you, Joey. I love you more than I love anybody in the world, but I don't love you like that. It could never be like that. I love you because you tried to get out, and I wanted you to make it, and even if you didn't, I still love you for trying. You did what none of us had the guts to do. Do you understand that kind of love? Or is that love?"

"Yes."

"Are you afraid of it? You think I'm kidding myself?"

"You never did kid yourself," he said.

"Good. So now when I make a crack, don't look like you think I'm trying to trip you into a bed. Sometimes I've got to joke about it. Sometimes . . ." She moved the can away angrily. "Now you've ruined me. I don't even want to get drunk any more."

The juke box played a slow sad ballad.

"You know what we talked about before?" Evita asked.

"Yes."

"And I made fun of me getting married, about the first night and all . . ."

"Yes."

"I've thought about it." She reached for the beer and sipped it. "Do you really think that somebody would have me?"

"Sure." He knew she wanted to believe it. Now especially after the parade of men had used her body and left. She was a product, not an individual, and she fought against it. She would not change, but she clung to the idea that change was remotely possible, even as she ridiculed his words.

"Who?" Evita asked.

"I don't know who. But there are lonely people . . . it's the world's greatest disease."

"I know. I made a hundred bucks off them tonight. But that isn't my idea of not being lonely.".

"No."

"If I meet a guy in my line of business, you know what *he* wants. If that's what he wants, I don't want him. And that's the only kind of guy I know. And these bastards have wives at home. I'd kill a man that did that to me. How could you ever trust one?"

"I can't answer that. I can . . . but it'd be breaking our agreement."

"You mean take it to the Lord in prayer?" She took a drink of the beer.

"I made you a promise. I'll stick to it."

"No, dammit. Forget the promise. Dammit, let's hear your angle about prayer."

"Evita, do you want to know?"

"No. Dammit, I don't." She finished the beer and sat angrily looking about the room. The music was haunting. Her face betrayed frustration. "Yeah . . . how do you do it?"

"Remember when your dad used to hold you on his knee?"

"Boy, is that ever going back to the middle ages."

126

"Didn't he ever do that?"

"When he was drunk, he did."

"But you liked it."

Evita thought about that for a moment. "He meant well."

"Did you ever tell him you loved him?"

She nodded. "Yeah . . . the slob."

"And that you wanted to be a good little girl?"

"Yeah."

"That's how you pray, Evita."

Old Viola peered through squinted eyes from the table. She raised the cigarette to her mouth, took a final puff, and dropped it to the floor. She sat very still.

"That's how you pray?" Evita asked.

"Yes."

"What's that got to do with me finding somebody good. I thought you had to ask Him and all that and say *Thou* and *Thine* and get on your crummy knees and . . ."

"Just the part I told you. You don't have to ask Him for anything. He knows."

"I thought you had to be tuned in like a radio or something and that . . ."

"Just like when you were a little girl," Joel persisted.

"That's all?"

"Yes."

Evita sat and sipped the beer quietly. "And He'll help?"

"Yes."

"Joey . . . I can't believe that crap. Only an idiot would."

"I know you can't. But it's that way."

"You know why I can't?"

"No."

"Partly because of you."

"Is that why?"

"That's why a lot of things on this street. You got burned and I figure Jesus done it. If He's such a great guy, why did He jab you?"

"Evita, you've got more sense than that!"

"I'm just telling you," she shrugged.

"You expected *He* should have given me the world on a string?"

"I expected you'd get a better pitch than you got. I'll say that."

"My chance will come. If it's preaching or driving a truck or . . . it doesn't matter. He'll take care of me."

"Like a little kid?"

"Yes."

"Boy, that's hard to swallow." She tasted a fresh beer.

A tall man, dressed in a neat sport coat, strode to the bar and slid in alongside Evita. "Hello, baby."

"Haul it," she said not looking up.

"I've got the money," he said. "Let's go."

"I'm through for the night."

"Come on, sister," he said. "I feel like it and I got the cash. Let's go." He took hold of her arm and she came up off the stool slowly.

Her voice was death. "Take your hand off me."

He laughed, leaning back, roaring, but the laughter was cut short as the blade of the knife snapped open and locked into place. His eyes bugged, the knife resting against his belt, cutting edge up. He released Evita's arm, his face pale.

"Don't ever try that again," she said. "Now get lost."

He backed away, backed until he bumped a table, then turned and made his way to the door. Evita hid the knife as quickly as she had taken it from her purse.

She watched the empty doorway, listening to the few

passing cars. "Don't preach to me any more. I don't want to hear it. If I do, I'll tell you."

"Evita, you said . . ."

"I know. I asked you. But I don't want any more."

"All right."

She left.

Old Viola came to the bar. She was smiling. "Just like a little kid," she said. "Joey, what chance has she got?" Then she held up her hand. "I know. Charlie always says there's hope. But I'd like to hear that sister pray."

Joel agreed. "So would I."

They closed the Green Parrot at two in the morning. Three of the waitresses left with customers. Viola waited as Joel locked the door. "You'll see about Charlie?" she asked.

"Yes."

"How long has he got?"

"I don't know."

Viola shook her head and walked down the darkened street. Joel went up the stairs. He was tired. He stopped at Uncle Charlie's room and opened the door a few inches. From the light of the flashing neon sign, he could see his uncle lying on the bed, his chest moving rhythmically. His face was softened in sleep. Joel closed the door.

He fell on the bed without undressing. What a day! He thought about Lynn Halliday, remembering her that morning, the feeling of that one moment. He forced his mind away from thoughts of her.

Instead, he thought of Uncle Charlie in a drugged sleep down the hall . . . Judge Hanson making the effort to drink the last of the beer in the glass, trudging along, pounding his cane, pretending to be eternally busy . . . and about Whitey and the kind of life he had chosen. It might end on a misty street at the end of a drag race in a stolen automobile. It might end as he ran down the darkened alley ignoring the policeman's warning, falling, bleeding, and dying a hoodlum, abandoned even by his friends. Or it might end in Mc-Alester in the electric chair.

Evita . . . struggling for escape, feeling used and cheated, bitter and vengeful. At times gentle and honest, fighting and surrendering to life, running like the rest, away from a monster, into the waiting arms of a greater one. Would she learn to pray after she was old and diseased, when she had nothing to give God in return? Or would it come at all?

Joel thought of dozens of them, and as he thought of each one, he said a prayer for them. These are the forgotten ones, by man, by decency, by honor, forgotten by all but God. And they resisted Him like death.

. When Joel finished, he heard the low, deep voice calling back to him. The voice of the girl in the room down the hall. He saw her standing in the doorway. "Thanks, neighbor," she had said. "Leave the door open." Joel turned restlessly in the bed.

It was unbearably hot. He got up and opened the door. He saw the glow of a cigarette.

"Can't sleep?" Lynn asked. He went out into the hall. She leaned against the wall, looking up at him. "Do you want a smoke?" she asked. He did not, but said he did.

He saw her flip the end of the cigarette around in her fingers. She put the filter tip to his lips. He inhaled and saw her in the dim glow. When she removed the cigarette he tasted the lipstick.

Joel exhaled and reached until his hands were on her waist. She came to him hurriedly, breathlessly.

130

8

"Hey, Brogan," the voice warned, "grab for cover, here I come."

Joel was on his stomach, a pillow over his head shielding the morning sunlight. He heard the door open, was aware of her quiet presence in the room.

"Lazy."

He smiled, unseen by her.

She sat on the edge of the bed beside him. He stiffened as she ran a fingernail along his spine. There was no more awkwardness between them. The night had taken it away.

"Hey," she said softly. "Hey, Brogan. Tomorrow is here."

"Good," he said sourly into the pillow.

She took the pillow from his head. He squinted into the bright light. "Turn over," she said.

He rolled over. Her eyes were laughing.

"How do you feel?" she asked.

He thought for a moment. "Loose," he said.

"You didn't get the lipstick off."

She examined the part of his chest that showed above the sheet.

"Hairs. Ghastly hairs. Men are so nasty," she said.

With the speed of a cat she struck. Pinching a half dozen hairs between her fingers, she jerked, and he roared.

"Happy Sunday," she said, examining the hairs distastefully. "I have a present for you."

131

Joel studied her. He had a most unholy desire to draw her under the sheet with him. Not easily, he resisted the thought.

"Thanks," he said.

"You get up and I'll give it to you." Joel's trousers were hanging over the chair by the window. She followed his eyes to them. "You suit up while I go after it."

"Okay."

"Hurry," she said, running from the room.

Joel whipped out of the bed and grabbed his slacks. He had them zipped and was reaching for a shirt when she returned, carrying a long square box, with two smaller boxes stacked on top of that.

"Lynn . . . what have you done?"

"It's a surprise. Open."

She put the packages on the edge of the bed. Joel opened a drawer, located a pair of socks and slipped into them. He stepped into his shoes, then sat on the bed and snapped the bow from the first package.

"Shake it," she said.

He shook it and it made no sound. She laughed at him.

Inside he found a three-quart saucepan. In the second package was an aluminum six-cup coffeepot. In the largest was a two-burner electric hotplate.

"Well?" she asked.

"How come all this?" He was overwhelmed.

"It was because of yesterday in the bar."

"So?"

"You did something nice. I saw it. It was very good, so I ran out to buy you a present. Besides you protected me from bad men."

"You must be nuts."

132

"Uh huh. Anyway I like surprises."

"And what about that business in the hall last night?" he asked.

"Oh that," she said. "Very interesting."

"What does that mean?"

"The pan is for hot water," she said, ignoring him. "So you can shave with hot water. Do you like that?"

"You bet!"

"And the coffeepot is for me, too. So I can come in and make a pot when I'm working. Would you mind?"

"No."

"I might just knock a hole in the wall between the rooms."

"That I wouldn't do," he said.

"I guess not. You're an animal, too."

"If we had some coffee we could make a pot," he said.

"Evita has some," Lynn suggested.

"Sure," Joel said.

"Ask her over."

"Okay."

"Brogan . . . would you ask her if she'd let me interview her?"

Joel paused at the door. He glanced at the shiny coffeepot and pan. Her face sobered quickly.

"Never mind," she said coolly, her eyes bearing a subtle hurt.

"I'd have asked her to talk to you. If these things were to soften me up . . ."

"No . . . forget it. I can ask her. Do you *always* search for evil motives?"

It was a terrible situation. Joel leaned against the door. "Lynn, it just came too quickly after the gifts. I still don't understand about the gifts. It isn't done around here much, you know."

"Brogan . . . do you know why you got fired at those churches?"

Joel's fingers tightened on the door knob. "No."

"I can tell you."

"Be my guest," he said, sharing the hurt now.

"Because you're too rigid, too inflexible. You wouldn't let people just be people. You had to constantly hold them up to Jesus Christ. Just so they'd know they weren't really good. And I'm wondering if you did it because you honestly wanted them to be good. I'm wondering if maybe it was because you wanted them to be bad so that you could be holier than thou, so you could escape the stigma of Reno Street. You're awfully ashamed of your background. Awfully aware of it, aren't you?" She spat the words, cutting them sharply. Her mouth pinched in anger.

Joel sighed. "Then why would I come back to it? Have you figured that, too?"

Lynn's mouth softened. "Because maybe you are happy here."

"Happy? You are crazy!"

"I wonder. Here you don't have to try to impress people. You can be yourself. These people appreciate you, in their own way, they do. Joel Brogan is accepted, even admired. Probably you love them, too. You don't condemn Evita . . . or those others. Oh, sure, your faith outlaws their sins, but that same faith makes it easy for you to forgive them as individuals. You can understand why some of them are this way. That part of you I like. That's why I got these things. Why did you have to suspect me? If Evita had given them to you, it wouldn't have occurred to you."

To himself Joel admitted it was true.

"I'm sorry, Lynn. I'll get Evita."

"Not now. Maybe later."

"Are you sulking?"

"Nope."

"I'll be right back then."

Joel left, hurried down the stairs, jay-walked across the empty street and reached the Poor Guy Café. He went inside.

"Hi, Joey," the waitress said.

"You have some coffee I could buy?"

"Are you nuts? I got ten gallons of it made."

"No. I want the grounds . . . you know."

The waitress reached under the counter and came up with an envelope. "This is restaurant coffee. It's a quarter pound."

"How much?"

"Two bits, I guess."

"Fair enough," he said.

Joel pocketed the coffee, dropped another twenty cents on top of a stack of newspapers and took one. Then he hurried back across the street, up the stairs. Lynn was plugging the hotplate cord into the socket when he came in.

"Coffee we got," he said.

Lynn smiled.

"And Sunday papers we got," he said.

"Aren't we family-like?" she said.

"Yeah. How much coffee do you put in?"

"Where is your spoon?"

"Haven't got one," Joel shrugged.

"We'll guess," Lynn said.

"Here's a spoon," Evita said from the doorway.

Joel and Lynn turned as Evita came into the room. She had a spoon, a can of coffee and several cups.

"I heard you discussing it," she said.

Joel glanced at Lynn quickly.

"Relax. I'm not the sensitive type. Besides for ex-

135

clusive information about the happy world of the prostitute, I claim the right to use this pot when I damn
well please."

"Granted," Joel said.

Evita put the spoon and cups on the table.

"Nice hotplate. Very nice gift," Evita said.

"Have you been listening in?" Joel asked.

"Hell, I'm not deaf," Evita said.

"We'll have to talk softer," Lynn said.

Evita glanced toward the bed. "You two been playin'
house?"

Lynn blushed.

"It looks like it," Joel said, remembering the lipstick. "Did you hear that part about knocking a hole
in the wall?"

"No . . . you gonna do that?"

"Well . . . we talked about it," Joel said.

Lynn was measuring the coffee.

"What about whores?" Evita asked abruptly.

"Why are they?" Lynn asked, still busy with the
coffeepot.

"I'm not sure any more. At first it was for the money.
Make a big killing and get out. It was always tough
when I was a kid. I'd slept with boys since I was fifteen.
I was a real woman at fifteen. The older boys didn't
waste much time showing me. But I liked it. Anyway,
I did then."

"But how did you start professionally?" Lynn asked.

"I was hanging around the bars. I was eighteen then
and knew the score, or thought I did. I'd let a guy
buy me drinks and if I liked him, I'd go home with
him. If I didn't, I'd go home alone. Usually I found
one I liked. Then, it happened gradual like. The guys
started leaving five or ten bucks on the table in the

136

morning. After a while I expected it. Finally my old man found out what I was doing. The reason it took him so long was that he had been sleeping with some old bitch and seldom made it home at night. He blew his stack, but he didn't really care. Anyway he did throw me out. That's when I got down to business."

"What did you do?"

"I went right to a call house. And applied for a job."

"Then?"

"The guy that ran it said he'd try out the merchandise. He wasn't too dumb. He put me on the list."

"Was it hard for you to take?"

"Yeah. Every time is hard to take. It's not fun, if that's what you think. You feel dirty. You hate the bastards that come to you. A lot of them are married. You wonder if there's a decent man in the world. They're all johns. Just johns. With hot pants and empty heads."

"Why do you do it?"

"Mainly the money. If a girl really wanted to, she could quit. Not many do. She'd probably have to leave town. And she'd keep bumping into the johns and they'd be trying to trip her into a bed all the time. Usually by the time you want to get out, it's nearly impossible. Like me . . . what could I do?"

Lynn did not offer a suggestion. Joel watched the coffeepot as it began to perk.

"Joey says I could get a job. He's after me to play on God's side."

Her voice was acid and Joel studied her curiously.

"I'm all for you," Evita said to Joel, "but I don't see much in this God racket. I believe there is one. I guess I do. If there ain't, a lot of people sure are fooled, and I'm not the one to say they're nuts. But I

137

don't bother God and He don't bother me. We don't see much of each other. Besides, half the johns that sleep with me on Saturday night are in church on Sunday.

"If there is one thing a whore is, it's honest. A naked whore can't kid even herself. I don't think I'm one thing on Sunday and something else on working days. I'm a whore. I've got a few years left before I begin to sag and wrinkle. It's tough then, but that's a few years away. There ought to be a whores' retirement fund. Honestly, I think most whores would pay for it. You think I'm kidding. I'm not. That's what we fear worst. Knowing that someday they won't buy us. When that's gone, we got nothing. Besides we aren't much anyway. You can't be proud, or clean or happy when some fat ugly old slob puts his money on the table and grabs you. Some girls go crazy, or turn into drunks. Stuff like that. I worked into the racket easier. It wasn't so much a shock to me, maybe that's why I've never tried suicide. But once in a while in a bar a little snotty girl comes up and asks me who to see to get set up. It always makes me want to vomit. How's the coffee?"

Joel glanced at the pot. It was perking, the coffee odor escaping with the steam.

"I'll pour," Joel said.

"What else?" Evita asked indifferently.

"Do you ever enjoy it?" Lynn asked.

"You're kidding," Evita snapped.

"What do you feel?"

"Disgust, mostly. But I act like it's great. That's what they pay for. A joy ride. I give it to them. But I hate it. Sometimes I get more than I can take. I cry. They like that the best. They think you're enjoying it. Can you beat that? A woman lying on her back with

138

tears running down her face, sobbing so much she can't stop, and some hungry bastard thinking she's enjoying it."

Joel put Evita's coffee on the bedside table. She did not seem to notice.

"And some johns always want to think you like them especially. They know you'll take anything that can manage to get into bed, so why do the bubble brains think they're special? Usually the young ones think like that. The older ones are more businesslike. I've got several of those steady. One even offered to set me up in an apartment. But I figured I could make more my way."

"What do you do with the money?" Lynn asked.

"A lot for clothes. Sometimes a guy wants to take me some place, specially the convention johns. So I have to dress. Anyway, a well-dressed woman is sexier. Even a homely woman that dresses well attracts men. And for drinks. I save some of mine along, but most girls don't. Sometimes I save two hundred a month. But most girls don't save a dime. They think they can last forever, I guess."

"Don't you have enough money to quit?"

"No. I'm still good for a while. When my body gives out, I'll have enough saved to see me through."

Joel put his cup away.

"Evita . . . you'll be sick then. You won't enjoy the money. You'll just be used up."

"Like some preachers I know," Evita answered quickly.

Joel's jaw sagged from the impact of her voice.

"I didn't mean it that way," she said.

"It's all right."

"No . . . when I'm down, I'll have it coming. I

whored a long time and I guess I deserve it. But you didn't earn the treatment you got. You tried to be good. I shouldn't have said that."

The sting of it had gone. "Have some more coffee," Joel said.

"No . . . I don't want any. Sometimes I just try to hurt everybody for no reason."

"I know that."

"Is that all you need to know? The story of my life. Hah!"

"Thank you," Lynn said.

"You gonna put me in the book?"

"Yes."

"My name?"

"I'll change that."

"I wouldn't care. I'm honest about it. But tell one thing. They call us dirty names and the vice squad rides us hard and the do-gooders talk about how sinful we are . . . and they forget just one crummy thing. They forget that it takes two. If all the johns that were married stayed at home nights, and all the momma's boys in college stayed in at night and studied, and all the others that are so innocent stayed home, there wouldn't be many whores. Every time the vice squad boys pinch us, they tell the man to go on home. He never pays a fine. He's never fingered. He's never shamed. His money doesn't make him innocent by a damn sight. He's as dirty as we are. Only he leaves Reno Street and acts like he's a real good Christian. That makes him worse than us. He's not only dirty . . . he's a liar."

"I'd never thought of that," Lynn said.

"You write it in for me."

"I will."

Evita went to the door and opened it. "I know a

couple girls you should talk to. One is a drunk. The other's been in the nut house. They could tell you a few things."

"Thanks," Lynn said.

Evita closed the door. Joel and Lynn looked at each other solemnly.

"Whew," Joel said softly.

They heard Evita's radio playing. Evita turned it up. She knew they wanted to talk.

"Pretty rough," Lynn said.

"Yes."

"I talked to some psychiatrists before I came down here. They don't see it quite her way."

"What would they know?" Joel asked.

"They've analyzed a few," Lynn said.

"That's it. A few. How many prostitutes go to a psychiatrist? I'll bet not one in a thousand. And those not the lower paid ones."

"That figures," Lynn agreed.

"What did they say?" Joel asked.

"Well . . . most of them are resentful, like Evita, plagued with guilt feelings, which I guess is typical. Evita exhibited that."

"So?"

"So the doctor worked with one girl. He helped her get rid of her guilt problem. Finally he had the girl pretty well adjusted. She was still working in a hotel, but she didn't resent it like she had before."

"A prostitute who enjoyed her work," Joel said thoughtfully.

"That's how it read."

"What happened?"

"The girl quit going. She told the doctor if she kept seeing him, she'd end up giving it away."

"Do you believe that?" Joel asked.

"Not exactly. But I think analysis could help the girls if they were trying to quit. This one wasn't."

"But when he starts talking morals, he brings back guilt feelings."

"Maybe. Maybe that should be the preacher's job. Teach her morals without the guilt association toward her past. Emphasize Christian forgiveness of past sins. Why wouldn't that work?"

"It might," he admitted.

"We're real smart, aren't we? We've solved a problem that's been going on forever. In fact, we must be brilliant," she said sarcastically.

"Have another cup of coffee and we'll solve the problem of world peace."

"And farm surplus," she added.

Joel poured coffee until she raised her hand. He filled his cup and sat down.

"Thanks for the rig. It was very thoughtful," he said.

"I surprised you," she said.

"You did."

"You thought I was a stuffy career girl who looked at life through a microscope."

"Let's face it. I was wrong," he said.

"After we eat, let's go for a walk," Lynn said.

"All right."

"To that little park by the auditorium. We could sit on the grass."

"And get chiggers," Joel added.

"Yes. That's all you'll get," Lynn said suggestively. "Do you like me?"

"Are you writing a book?" he asked clumsily. It was an idiotic thing to say.

"No. I'm serious. Do you like me?"

"Yes."

142

"But you won't fall in love with me. Not the kind that tears your heart out."

"Why?"

"Because one of these days I'll leave. I don't want it to kill us."

"All right."

"We'll turn it off. Won't we, Joel?"

"I've never been in love, Lynn."

She nodded. "I know. I won't let you get in too deep."

"You'll turn it off?" he asked curiously.

"Yes."

"You're sure you know what you're doing?"

"I think so."

"Okay." He didn't want to talk about it, or do anything to ruin it. Already it had became important.

She slipped her arms around his neck. "We make sparks," she said. "Did you know that?"

He did not reply. He could feel her heart beating against him.

"Hold me, Brogan." She closed her eyes and her voice was a whisper. "Make sparks," she said.

9

It was during the lonely, pensive hours that he rediscovered himself. Things he had known and believed, but had forgotten somehow, became clear once again. The concept of God had not changed. Only he had changed.

His fervor, his love for God and man became dulled by both his hatred and sympathy for himself. These things he had first learned so long ago, and had so recently forgotten.

But Joel could not exist in this withdrawn state. He wanted again the peace that came in the lonely hours. The quiet giving of himself for others. The outward worship of God, praising Him, asking only for guidance. Needing only that part of the prayer which stressed God's will be done on this earth.

So it was now that he had rediscovered the sweet calm of prayer. The magnificent sense of relief that came when he turned over his life and cares and troubles and joys to the hands of a God whom he had once again learned to trust.

It came slowly, this rebirth. It began when Lynn Halliday asked him a meaningless question across the bar.

"Joel," she said.

"Yes."

"Why don't you ever laugh?"

Joel had been indifferent at the time. But later in his room he began to examine himself. Why *didn't* he laugh? He became aware that if he lived or died, or succeeded or failed, it would all be over in a, fantastically brief instant in the immeasurable expanse of time. That his troubles would be gone only too soon. Why did he not love and laugh and deliver himself over to God in unreserved surrender. . . .

Why not?

Joel Brogan . . . a man given but a little talent. He could not orate. His voice was not magnetic. He could not sing a hymn and make them cling to each sound. Not a brilliant man, wise in advanced theology. Not a gifted church organizer able to transform chaos into order.

Joel Brogan . . . an ordinary man. But not a waste. He was not that. He had small talent perhaps, but he could be a turtle of Christianity. He could plod. He could bend his neck and move slowly ahead, turning himself outward, living the teachings of Christ. He could help someone, sometime, somehow. The opportunity would come. He didn't need a pulpit. If he was inadequate for a fifteen-thousand-dollar-a-year church salary, he could still carry those teachings of the Christ in his heart. Joel Brogan's mark might not be large. But though it be small, he would make it.

This was hard to face. For many years there had been the Joel Brogan that he had wanted to be, that he had imagined himself. This man was clothed richly. He stood in the shadow of wealth. His great church towered high in the city. Those who came to hear him went away inspired. He blew the breath of God across crowded church pews and he was loved greatly. He was a giant.

But he was not. He was none of these things. Probably he would never be. And his voice was not the breath of God. It was soft. It was weak. There was no great wealth. He was not clothed richly. Joel Brogan was a reality . . . a small man with a small talent. But he was still Joel Brogan and he had been given life and that life he surrendered. He would be himself.

Following this understanding, he walked along the hall in the evenings to Uncle Charlie's room. Under his arm he carried the Bible. He sat beside the bed and read slowly, explaining as he went, adding information and background. When he finished reading, he discussed and answered questions. He experienced peculiar joy the evening Uncle Charlie told him he wanted to be a real Christian. By this act of ministry, Joel Brogan became an implement of God.

Joel located the prescription box on Uncle Charlie's table. It was empty.

"How do you feel?" Joel asked.

"Don't schedule me no fights for a day or two," Charlie said.

"Do you feel like getting up?"

"No," Charlie grunted. He glanced at Joel apologetically. "I'm weak, kid."

"Do you hurt?"

"Not yet. Maybe when the last of that dope wears off."

"I'll get you some pills."

"Okay."

"Anything else you need?"

"Yeah . . . my tennis racket is busted. Get it fixed."

Joel grinned. "You take it easy. I'll go get you some dream powder."

When he reached Lynn's room she was standing at the door. "How is he?"

146

Joel shook his head.

"How long?"

"I don't know."

"Should he go to the hospital?"

"Yes, but he won't. He says he can see his friends here. Besides he hates hospitals."

"I don't blame him really," she said.

"I'm going to the drugstore. Want to go?"

Lynn glanced at her typewriter, made a face. "No. I've got to work. I'll go with you to visit Charlie tonight."

"Okay."

Joel walked down the hallway. Evita's door was open.

"How's Charlie?" she asked.

"No better."

"Dammit! What can I do for him?" She was impatient.

"Nothing. Just a visit. Let him know you care."

"He knows that."

"Remind him."

"He don't want flowers. He can't eat. Maybe I could buy him a radio."

"He wouldn't listen to it," Joel said.

"Yeah . . . it's a tough way to go."

"He has a chance to see his friends. I think he prefers it this way."

"I hope a building falls on me when it's my time," she said.

"Well, I've got to go after some pills. Want to come?"

"No . . . I'll look in on him in a minute."

Joel went down the stairway.

The street was already crowded. Joel passed the pawnshops where the owners waved, whistled, called, anything to get you inside. *Inside* if you had the

147

money. If you didn't have money, they watched you as they would a scorpion. Somehow they seemed to know. They couldn't get rid of you quick enough if you were broke or had nothing to sell. Usually for good reason. They almost had to nail the merchandise to the counters.

In the windows they displayed diamond rings, watches, guitars, trumpets. Joel knew of a trumpet that had been in one of the windows even before he went to the army.

He reached Saul Bernstein's Honest Loans and Saul shifted the short, unlighted cigar in his mouth.

"Hi, Joey. How's Charlie? He okay now?"

Joel paused. "He's not doing so good."

"What you want me to do?" Saul offered.

Joel rested his hand on his shoulder. "Nothing. Go see him maybe."

"The shop. All the time the shop. Maybe I'll go when I close."

"He'd like that," Joel said.

The little man's face was sad. Joel had not helped his morning at all. Long ago Joel had learned that the Jews on South Broadway start the day with a mood and they do not often change in midday. But thinking about Charlie had changed Saul's mood and he would not be happy all day.

"Hello, Joey."

Joel glanced around. The voice had come from a darkened staircase leading to a two-story hotel. One of the prostitutes who came into the Green Parrot was sitting on the steps in the morning sun. She was part Indian, very dark, very sensual. Her name was Tana.

"Good morning," Joel said.

"How's Charlie?"

Joel shook his head. They had noticed when Charlie

148

stopped staying downstairs all the time, when he began to lean against the bar for support, when he left holding his side. The word had spread quickly along the streets.

"Not so good," Joel said, pausing at the entrance. The girl was young, but most of them were. The market demanded youth. Joel sat down on the step beside her.

"You can't stay long," she said.

He started to leave, but her hand on his shoulder restrained him.

"Not yet. In a few minutes maybe. Today's payday."

"Payday?"

"The vice squad boys collect this morning."

Joel understood. Tana was paying her bribe so that she could go on hustling unmolested.

"Sure," he said.

"About Charlie . . . he's pretty sick, huh?"

Joel nodded.

"Charlie's a nice guy. He was good to me once.

"He's that kind."

"You know what he did?"

"No."

"One night in the Green Parrot, I was sick. I had a virus or something and I was broke and I needed to turn a couple of tricks, but I felt awful. So Charlie came over and pressed twenty bucks in my hand and told me to go see a doctor. He said to get some pills so I'd feel better. That was nice, wasn't it? I mean, it was damned nice."

"That's Charlie's way," Joel said.

"And you know what? When I got okay, I made some dough and took it to him. You know what he asked me to do?"

Joel indicated that he didn't know.

149

"He said to keep the money and buy a bus ticket and get a job some place . . . you know, a job like working in a store or something."

Joel turned to her. "Why didn't you?"

The girl shook her head. "I don't know. I had it all figured then. I was going to make a lot of money and quit."

The old, old story.

"Did you make it?" he asked.

"No . . . I blew it on stuff. Who can save money?"

"You're a pretty girl. You should . . ."

"Thanks," she interrupted. "From a preacher boy that's something."

A tall heavy-gutted man in a dark-brown suit appeared, moving along the sidewalk toward them.

"You better go, Joey."

Joel got up and started away. He memorized the face of the payoff man. This one he wanted to remember.

"You tell Charlie I hope he feels better," Tana said.

"Sure."

In the reflection of the pawnshop window he watched the man pause at the entrance of the small hotel. Tana went up the stairway. The vice squad officer followed.

Joel reached Main Street, went into the drugstore where he had the prescription filled. He bought two magazines that he hoped Uncle Charlie might enjoy and went back to Reno Street. Evita was standing at the top of the stairs.

"Did you get the pills?"

"Yes."

"Hurry up. I been with him and he's hurtin' bad."

Joel went to Charlie's room. Uncle Charlie was sitting up in bed smoking frantically. He could not disguise the pain. Joel took a capsule from the box and poured a glass of water. "Here you go," he said.

Uncle Charlie took the pill and settled back.

"I was ready for that one," he said.

Joel waited until the pill had taken effect. Charlie's hands began to relax.

"That's better," Charlie said. "Who's keepin' the store?"

"Viola opened up. I'm going down in a few minutes."

"Okay." Charlie shifted in the bed. He was pale. Very thin. "This girl, Joey . . . this Lynn. You like her?"

"Sure. She's fine."

"I mean at first you didn't. I could tell. You two didn't mesh at all."

"Well . . . sometimes we still don't."

"But you like her."

"You're trying to say something."

"Why don't you marry her?"

"You're kidding," Joel said.

"No . . . I saw you playin' kiss on the mouth. It looked good. So why not get married?"

"No. That won't get it."

"Why not?"

"She's just here to get background for her book. She'd never fit here. Or with me. She couldn't take Reno for long."

"It used to be all people had to do was be in love. What the devil happened?"

Joel shook his head.

"She's smart. She'd make you a good match."

"You look silly playing Cupid, Charlie."

"You'll get a church. What's Reno anyway? It's a dot on the map. You can get a church some place and

151

get together. Have babies and things. She can write books, too. You can write books any place."

Joel did not reply.

"I guess," Charlie said thoughtfully, "I'm tryin' to get everything all arranged so's I can go ahead and die. You're a big boy, Joey. I guess you know what you're doin'."

"She's coming tonight."

"Good." Charlie seemed pleased.

"I'd better get downstairs," Joel said.

"Yeah . . ."

He went to the door.

"You know what, Joey. I wish I could live long enough to see you marry that girl. Or some girl. Have babies. I'd like to take your kids down to the ice cream store and to the park." Charlie closed his eyes. As he stopped speaking, his head sagged against the pillow.

The drug had taken hold.

Joel closed the door. Evita was waiting down the hall. "Is he feelin' better?"

"Yes. He's asleep."

"I'll go sit with him in case he wakes up and wants something. I can hear the phone from there."

"Thanks," Joel said.

He went downstairs and entered the bar. Inside he saw the man from the vice squad sitting at the bar sipping a beer. His face was puffy, his body heavy and soft. But the eyes were cruel, shrewd.

"You come from up there?" the man asked Joel.

"Yes."

"That girl up there now?"

"What girl?"

"You know what girl."

"Yes."

The man finished his beer and flipped a coin on the

152

bar. He turned the corner and climbed the stairway.

"He comes once a month," Viola said bitterly. "Then once a month they pick her up and book her. That's it. If she don't pay, she stays in jail so much she can't make a dime. They pay. They always do."

"Yes, I suppose they do," Joel said.

Joel watched the flashing neon sign, shouting in blue light the brand of top beer. The smell of the bar was nauseating. The bubbling juke box was silent. Joel felt a sickness, a regret. Old Viola sat at a table, puffing a cigarette, her eyes closed again, a sadness in her worn face.

"Viola," Joel said.

She turned speculatively.

"Why don't you go get some soup and maybe a loaf of bread and take it upstairs for Charlie?"

Viola pushed away the chair and shuffled toward the door.

Joel remembered what Uncle Charlie had said in the Poor Guy Café that morning about old Viola taking nickles for quarters. But he had said it without malice. He had never seemed to notice how slow she was, how she could not see, how she sat down so often to rest when the bar was filled. It would be hard on Viola when Charlie was gone.

"You asleep?" Evita asked.

She was dressed for the street.

"No . . . how's Charlie?"

She swore softly. "He didn't eat hardly anything."

"Is he asleep?"

"No . . . we been talking."

"Oh . . ."

"I got a call. I didn't want to go, but I got a call."

"Sure."

Evita avoided his eyes. "I want a beer first."

Joel hesitated.

"A beer, Joey. The guy ain't gonna kiss me," Evita said irritably.

He opened the can and Evita dropped the change on the bar.

She drank quickly, as though she were in a hurry to get the drink inside, to cloud thoughts she was unwilling to face. She finished her beer and slid from the stool.

"You look nice," Joel said.

"Good. Maybe today I'll raise the price."

Joel looked away.

Evita rounded the bar. "You better check on him. He's pretty weak, and when he needs them pills . . ."

"All right."

Evita left the bar.

Joel went to the juke box and dropped a quarter in the slot. He searched the list of old favorites for a song. There were so many, but he found one he remembered. "All the Things You Are." He punched the song five times.

The music began, a chorus singing *You are the angel's glow that lights the stars. . . .* Joel listened thoughtfully. *Someday my happy arms will hold you. . .*

He walked the length of the room toward the bar. A drunk had passed out in a booth. Joel went outside, hailed a cab, then half-carried the drunk to the cab and paid the driver. When he went back inside, the song was playing a second time.

Joel sat alone. *When all the things you are are mine.*

"Hello, Joey."

Joel turned. Lynn slipped onto a bar stool and smiled. Joel touched her hand lightly. "Listen to the music," he said.

154

"I like it," she said.

"Shall we dance?"

Joel took her in his arms. It had been a long time since he had danced.

"Rusty," he confessed.

They whirled around the room. When the music ended, they were both breathless. Joel laughed and led her toward the bar. He saw the boy standing soberly in the doorway. He was about twelve, with black hair and black eyes. He held a note in his hands.

"Are you Brogan?" he asked. His voice was already crisp with the wisdom of the Street.

"Yes."

The boy handed him the note. Joel read it. Three words. They were scrawled on the bottom of a piece of newspaper. The letters were wildly distorted, as though written by a hand crippled with palsy. *Help me. Rose.* That was all.

"Who gave you this?" Joel asked.

"The girl. She's sick."

"Where is she?" Joel asked.

"I'll show you."

Joel turned to Lynn. "Would you ask Viola to come down? Something's wrong."

Lynn left hurriedly.

"You say she's sick?"

The boy agreed.

"There's blood all over the bed," he said.

Viola entered the bar.

"I'll be back," he explained. "Come on, boy. You show me where to go."

"For a quarter." The boy's lip twisted cynically. Joel handed him a quarter. Victoriously the boy led him along Reno Street, flipping the quarter in the air.

10

The boy stopped in front of a doorway. "I don't wanna go up. She might make me sick, too."

"Where is she?" Joel asked.

"In that room up on the left. You'll smell it."

The boy flipped the quarter, walking away indifferently.

Joel paused at the door on the left. He knocked softly. There was no answer.

He turned the handle and opened the door a crack. The odor of heavy air, of stale urine, was so strong he cut his breath short. Joel pushed the door open farther, and saw her on the bed. She was nude. She had taken the sheet from the bed, wadded it up, and pressed it between her legs. The sheet was stained with blood. Joel went inside and touched her forehead. She was hot with fever, her face almost scarlet. Her breath was shallow and fast.

"Rose," Joel called. She did not respond. Aside from the bed there was nothing in the room except an empty hot tamale can. This was what Rose had used for the waste of her body. In her delirium she had knocked it over. The urine had soaked into the rough wooden floor.

Joel ran out of the room, breathing the clean air. He stumbled hurriedly down the stairway and burst into a bar three doors away. "Where's the phone?" he asked.

A peroxide blonde with brown teeth jerked her head toward the booth. Joel located a dime and placed a call for an ambulance. Then he left, hurrying back to the room.

"Rose . . . Rose . . ."

The girl stirred, opened her eyes slightly. She stared through him.

"It's Joel," he said. "I'm here, Rose."

She seemed to understand. She tried to speak, but could not find her voice. Her lips were dried and cracked. He took her hand and, with a strength that surprised him, she drew him close. Struggling for breath, she whispered, *"Zeuses."*

"It's all right, Rose. You're going to be all right."

She shook her head. Then she tried again. This time her lips cracked to shape the word. A thin line of blood burst through the swollen mass and stained her teeth. "Jesus," she whispered. "Jesus."

Joel's stomach vibrated violently. He knelt beside her. The prayer unfolded, violently, desperately. *God in heaven, this is Your child. This broken one. God, have mercy. Mercy . . ."*

The siren sang in the street, as the men came up the stairs. The examination was brief.

"How long has she been here?" the intern asked.

Joel shook his head.

"Get the stretcher." Then to Joel. "Who are you?"

"A minister," Joel said. "She sent for me."

"I think she needs one," the intern agreed.

They loaded her onto the stretcher carefully. Joel followed down the stairs, through the collecting crowd that waited curiously by the ambulance.

"You'll come along?" the intern asked.

"Yes."

The attendant closed the rear door of the ambulance and hurried to the front. "Roll it," the intern shouted to the driver.

In a burst of sound and fury, the ambulance moved out, passing the cars, being waved ahead by policemen who directed traffic at the busy intersections. Ignoring red lights.

Backing into the ramp. Wheeling her into the emergency room.

"Sit down," the intern said, gesturing to a bench outside the emergency room. Joel sat down. He had been seated only a few minutes when a doctor came out of the room. His eyes were hard, angry.

"The attendant said you were a minister."

"Brogan," Joel said. "Joel Brogan. She sent for me."

"We report these things. An investigator will be coming over from the attorney's office. Will you wait?"

"Yes. The girl?"

The doctor lighted a cigarette, exhaled the smoke through his nostrils.

"It may be too late. She's a sick girl. It's a bad job."

"What did they do?"

"Took the easiest way. Whoever it was wouldn't even pay for an abortionist. They used a glass tube, inserted it and broke it off. Then they packed a rag to stop drainage. They probably told her to call you when the blood and infection came through the rag. It's an old trick. It would have been three or four days. Apparently she waited. I can't imagine why."

"I think I know," Joel said.

"Well . . . they took care of the pregnancy. They may have taken care of her, too. It's the worst I've ever seen."

"When can I see her?"

The doctor waved his hand futilely. "If she comes

around. Infection . . . It depends. I'll be working on her today. If you'll make arrangements at the desk . . ." he said, dropping the cigarette in the sandbox. "I'll go in. They should be about ready."

Joel left the bench, rode the elevator up one flight, then went to the business desk. He gave his name, address and information about Rose. "Do you need a deposit?" he asked.

The Catholic Sister glanced up from the paper. "No," she said. "The doctor mentioned that you were a Protestant minister."

"Yes. Presbyterian."

"If the patient asks for you, what is your church address?"

"I can be located at the Green Parrot Bar," Joel said.

Her eyes bounced from the page.

"I don't have a church. As a matter of fact, Sister, I was fired."

"Oh." Kindly.

"You people don't have that sort of thing."

The Sister laughed, a joyous cackle.

"Now that isn't quite true. We had a boy named Luther once. He got the boot. But we don't like to talk about it much at all."

Joel found himself relaxing.

"We have a blank for the patient's occupation," the Sister said.

"She was a prostitute," Joel said.

The Sister filled in the blank. "How is she?"

"Very bad," Joel said.

"We don't have a private room. There just aren't any available."

"I understand," Joel said. "You take care of that. I'll go back downstairs."

Joel took the elevator down. Two men were standing outside the emergency room, waiting.

"Are you Reverend Brogan?" a lean light-haired man with a tenor voice asked.

"That's right."

"Jack Walters," the man said, explaining that he represented the county attorney's office. They shook hands. Walters introduced the other man as his partner, Otto Marshall. Walters opened a notebook.

He asked Rose's name, her address. With the minor details out of the way, the investigator sighed. "Who did it, Brogan?" he asked.

"I don't know," Joel said.

"You suspect somebody?"

"She had a pimp. His name is Nick Martelli. I imagine he'll have a better alibi than you boys."

"We'll see," Walters said.

"It makes a difference if she dies," the other remarked.

"If she dies," Joel said wearily, "it makes no difference at all."

"I didn't mean . . ."

"Sure. I know that. I was thinking of something she said when I found her."

"Did she mention someone?" Walters asked eagerly.

"Yes," Joel said in a voice not steady, "Jesus."

"Oh . . ." The investigator considered it insignificant.

"We'll run along," Marshall said. "We'll check out this pimp. If you hear any more, you'll let us know?"

Joel agreed, and leaned back against the bench. He waited for a long time. He found he could not think of Nick Martelli without anger. But he did not think of the Philosopher often. His thoughts were with Rose, and the battle she now waged against the advanced infection in her body. The beat of her heart, pulsating

160

unclean blood through her body. A heart trembling with fever. But still beating.

The flow of antibiotics, meeting infection, waging cellular war. Her conscious mind sealed off, uninvolved in this survival struggle. The body delivered unto the power of a God to whom she had called when the end was near. A God to whom Joel Brogan had knelt in the stench-filled room. Had prayed to for mercy. Had begged.

The rubber glove snapped as it pulled free of the fingers. The doctor popped the second glove from his hand, reached for a cigarette and lighted it with a hand that trembled slightly.

"It's up to her now," the doctor said, drawing deeply on the cigarette. He sat down beside Joel.

"When can I see her?" Joel asked.

"Not today. She's out. If she dies, she won't flutter an eyelash. We'll just try to kill the infection and wait. I think she wanted to die. She went right down to the wire before she sent for you. There was no purpose in that. The baby was out of the question long before then. Did the investigators show up?"

"I saw them."

"They won't do much, I'm afraid. Unless the girl tells about it. That's if she lives. I doubt if she'll talk. They are usually afraid. I'd like to see them get this character."

"Rose won't tell. I don't believe she would."

"They could prosecute her. They won't, of course, but they might frighten her into some conversation."

"She doesn't frighten easily."

"That's probably true."

"When will you be able to tell about her?" Joel said.

"The longer she lives, the better the chance. Tomorrow morning maybe. She's taken a terrific jolt. If her body can last it, she's got a good chance. But she may die while we're talking." The doctor smiled. "Now I've got you running scared."

Joel studied the doctor for a long moment. He was about to speak when the doors opened and masked nurses pushed the cart into the hallway. Joel stood.

Her color was improved, Joel thought. Her mouth had been cleaned and her hair pulled back off her face. But her eyes were closed and he could not see her breathing. They pushed the cart into the elevator.

"Pretty girl," the doctor said. "Why do they get into jams like that?"

"Are you asking my opinion?" Joel asked.

"No. I think they're just after an easy dollar."

Joel watched as the doctor lighted another cigarette. "It's not an easy dollar, Doctor. You said I could see her in the morning."

"I didn't say that, but I imagine you can."

"Thank you, Doctor."

Joel left the doctor who was looking strangely superior, blowing smoke fiercely, tapping his fingers nervously, waiting for another broken body to reach the factory. Joel found a cab and went back to Reno Street.

It was late in the evening when he called the hospital to ask about Rose. He was able to pry but little information from the nurse. Rose was still alive. They said she was doing as well as could be expected. Which was to say nothing.

Joel climbed the stairway and Lynn came to her door.

"I heard about it. Was it bad?"

"Yes."

"Will she be all right?"

162

"I don't know. I really don't know."

"I saw Uncle Charlie. I didn't tell him."

"Good."

"He mentioned that we were coming tonight."

Joel remembered. He was not anxious to go. He was sick inside and tired all over. But he had to go.

"I had forgotten with all the worry about Rose."

"I thought you had."

"I'll get my Bible. Does he want me to read?"

"Yes . . . I'll read if you like."

"No, I don't mind. I like it. It's just that the whole mess was so rough. She couldn't make sense, but she kept trying to say 'Jesus.' All she could do was whisper.

"I suppose that was enough," Lynn said.

"I imagine it was," Joel said.

Joel took the Bible from his table. Lynn was waiting when he came out.

"You look exhausted," she said. She held his hand as they walked along the hall. He tapped on Uncle Charlie's door.

"Come on in!" Charlie yelled, a cheerful but weak greeting.

"How do you feel?" Joel asked.

"Lousy."

"Last night it was like hell. I guess this is an improvement."

"Yeah . . . How's Rose?"

Joel glanced at Lynn.

"Joey, I been on this Street a long time. I hear an ambulance and I know somebody ran out of luck. It figures I can find out who it is. How is she?"

"Better . . . I think she'll make it," Joel said.

"Evita said she asked for you. Is that the story?"

"Ummmmmm."

"You got one. That's good."

Uncle Charlie craned his neck and saw the Bible in Joel's hand.

"You gonna read tonight?" he asked.

"Yes . . . if you like."

"Good."

Lynn tightened the sheets on the bed.

"You know," Charlie said, "a long time ago I used to be crazy about Lou Gehrig. You remember what he said when he was gonna die, that day out there in Yankee Stadium?"

"Uncle Charlie . . ."

Charlie waved a weary hand. "I know I'm gonna die. But I ain't afraid. You know it, too. Like you said, it's a little late for us to start kiddin' each other."

Joel did not answer.

"But Lou . . . he came out there in front of all those people and he said he was the luckiest guy in the world. I used to think about that. I used to think Lou was crazy as a loon. Now I think I know how he felt. It ain't dyin'. What's that? Nothin'. But it's knowin' all the friends you got. It's knowin' that . . . Look at this room. Flowers . . . all that stuff they brought. Yeah . . . I think I know what old Lou meant. I'm a lucky old man. I seen 'em die down here in them flophouses with nobody to even take the body. They was buried by the county. Read it to me, Joey."

Joel opened the Bible and began to read. When he reached a familiar passage, he looked up at Uncle Charlie who listened through a drugged mind, with only the faint bite of pain to keep him awake. Joel read, not hearing his own voice, not conscious of the chapters. Lynn sat at the edge of the bed, watching him.

" 'I will have mercy,' " Joel read, " 'for I am not

164

come to call the righteous, but sinners to repentance. Then came to him the Disciples of John saying . . .' "

"Wait, Joey. Read that again," Charlie said suddenly.

"What?" Joel asked softly.

Uncle Charlie raised his head from the pillows. "Where He says what He came for."

Joel looked above and repeated, " 'For I am not come to call the righteous, but sinners to repentance.' Is that it?"

"Yeah. I know what that means. Don't read any more. I want to think about that."

Joel closed the book.

"Jesus . . . He meant that He loved the sinners. Isn't that it?" Charlie asked.

"Yes."

"I mean . . . one time you read about that blind guy and there was a lot of big shots around Jesus, see? And this old blind guy was on the side of the road and he asked Jesus to stop and those big shots told him not to bother Jesus. But Jesus stopped and He made the man see again. That was the kind of guy He was."

"Yes."

"And if He was here . . . He'd help these people down here on the Street. He'd stop for a drunk, and He'd stop for a whore, and it wouldn't matter that they was dirty and had done bad things, He'd help them. Right down here on Reno Street. Jesus would come right down here, wouldn't He?"

"He would. Yes."

"Read that one part again."

Joel repeated the passage, and when he finished, Uncle Charlie was smiling. "Gimme a pill," he said. "That's great."

Joel located the medicine. Lynn filled a glass with

water. Uncle Charlie took the capsule, tossed it into his mouth like a grain of popcorn. He drank a swallow of water.

"Nothin' to it," he said, wiping his lips with his sleeve. "Only when I was a kid I liked to have never got pills down. My old man beat me nearly half to death once to make me take a pill. Finally I just chewed the thing up and ate it. Boy, it was nasty, I can tell you. Anyway, I like that thing about the sinners. You take the people down here . . . you can figure they're sinners, but even if they wanted to go to a church, there ain't one to go to. Sure, they can go up the hill, but I tried that. People up there wasn't rude. I don't mean that. Only they just don't let you fit in. And I guess maybe you don't fit in. So the thing is, what are all the Christians doin' to help the sinners down here?"

"They aren't doing much, Uncle Charlie," Lynn said.

"That's no joke. Around the corner we got a couple of missions. I mean, the scum comes in and they get doughnuts and watered coffee, and for that they got to listen to some blabbermouth. He's strictly a hallelujah boy. He's strictly a big noise. And they never let the drunk quite forget that some big, rich church give 'em the money to buy the coffee. You know what I mean? You find these guys makin' fun of the missions. All down the street if a guy goes, he's an oddball. That ain't right."

"It's natural for them to resist God, Uncle Charlie. It's their frame of mind. It's not the missions."

"Maybe . . . only why didn't Rose call for the hallelujah boys? No. She calls for you. Because you understand. This street needs a preacher like you, Joey."

166

"Maybe I'd better read before I turn into an angel," Joel said.

"Don't be funny," Uncle Charlie said. "The thing is that these people don't need to be shook up about hell fire and all that. They been shook up already. They need to hear this stuff about Jesus and how He forgives. And love. They need to know about that."

"We all need that," Lynn said.

"So would a guy be able to walk these streets down here and teach about Jesus, or is this Christian stuff a bunch of crap the rich people talk about? A place they go to wear their fancy hats? Well . . . is anybody gonna answer me?"

"It works," Joel said.

"It worked with Rose. She turned to you." Charlie snapped.

Joel remembered her agonized whisper. "To God," Joel corrected.

"Okay. That's what I mean. I sure like that deal about Jesus coming to save sinners. He wouldn't be ashamed of people like me."

"He spoke wherever he went," Lynn said, flashing a meaningful glance at Joel.

"Right. I like that. It makes me feel good inside, and I ain't felt good in there for a long time. You know what I mean. Joey . . . I got this idea."

Joel had been staring into the gold letters on the Bible. He turned to face Uncle Charlie. The old man's face was so thin the flesh was stretched tightly over his cheeks. But from the face radiated a warmth, a faith.

"When I die . . ."

"Uncle Charlie . . ."

"Come on . . . when I die, I'd like to leave something to help these people on the Street. I mean I can't leave

167

you no bar, Joey. What would that be? A preacher inherits a bar. That's crazy, you know? But I got some money saved, and some insurance, and that's yours. You know that. Then the building, that'll be yours. Which is altogether not peanuts. No real big thing, I know, but it's all I could get together, and that's for you."

Joel could not raise his eyes. He listened, aware that both Lynn and Uncle Charlie were watching him.

"I would like . . . Joey, you listen, please, I may only say this once . . . I would like to give you all this. And I'd like for you to tear down the fixtures in the bar. Get rid of all that. And I'd like for you to put in a bunch of seats and a pulpit and a cross . . . whatever it takes to make a nice, real decent little church, and call it the Reno Street Church . . . and you be the preacher. Then I'd feel like some good came of the fact that once an old guy named Charles Jackson used to live down here. Course, I know you can't just up and clap your hands and decide, or nuthin' like that. You got to pray about it and feel that God wants you to do this. So you do all that. Then when I'm dead, if you get that feelin' that it's right, you can do it. I'm only tellin' you that I'd like it. I think my street needs a real church. I think my street needs you."

Joel raised his head. Lynn's eyes rested on him heavily. *What could he say?* He had to respond.

"I don't know. We'll pray, Charlie. Both of us."

Uncle Charlie smiled and blinked wearily.

"It's a beautiful thought, Charlie. It stopped me cold," Joel said.

"I been thinkin' about it. Before you go, you read me that verse again."

168 ·

Joel did not open the Bible. He spoke the words, watching the peaceful expression on his uncle's face.

When he finished, he left the room. He heard Lynn following behind him. Joel went into his room and sat down, exhausted.

"What time is it?" he asked softly when she came into the room.

"After midnight," Lynn said.

Joel asked for a cigarette. Lynn lighted it for him, then slipped it between his fingers.

"This is it for you. Right?" she asked.

"Yeah . . ."

"You've got a decision to make. It's been dumped right in your lap."

"Right."

"And you aren't ready to make it. Maybe you won't ever really be ready."

"You haven't missed yet," he said.

"But if you make it wrong, you're dead."

"I suppose that's true."

"You can't be entirely convinced that you could do it. You might not want to be laughed at by the hoods. Spat on by the whores. Or even sure that you could help them."

"Go on," he said, drawing on the cigarette.

"One question," she said.

"All right."

"Are you really convinced that Christianity could stand the test of Reno Street?"

"That I believe. But am I the guy to do it? That's it. Being nice and reading the Bible once in a while is one thing. Making a live-or-die project out of it is something else. I am not sure I want to try it. But most of all, could I do it?"

"Who else, Brogan," she asked, "if not you?"

She took the cigarette from his lips and inhaled, then gave it back.

"I'll leave so you can get some sleep."

"What do you think?" Joel asked.

"I don't know. I'm neutral, so I can see it from both sides. He's dying. His life is slipping away and he wants to leave something good behind. In doing it, he thinks he's giving you a job, and I guess he would be. I'd like to see it work for his sake. On the other hand, I've been here long enough to know that it would be a battle all the way. Churches around the city aren't rushing to set up down here. No priest walks this street. No Episcopalians or Methodists or Presbyterians . . . none of them. This is no man's land. They stay out because they don't know how to work with these people. It would take a man who has really grown to understand them. He'd have to know them. Love them enough to forgive the insults he'd reap. Brogan, I don't know whether you are that man or not. I'm the kind that would like to believe it could happen. It may be a fairy tale."

Lynn went to the door.

"It's a tough one. Good night, Brogan."

She closed the door. Joel fell back across the bed. He inhaled from the cigarette. Joel knew that Uncle Charlie had been thinking about it for a long time. He'd waited until Joel finally came to a significant verse of scripture. Using it as a weapon, he had presented the plan to make a church on Reno. The old man was not stupid. He had figured every angle. Even had taken into consideration Joel's final decision after his death. It was a trap. Joel could not drift any longer. He had to get in the boat or stay home. He began to figure an escape from the trap.

170

11

Joel sat in the coffee shop across the street from the hospital. The place had only four booths, a half dozen stools at a counter. It was occupied mostly by nurses and hospital attendants. A juke box was playing as Joel looked out the window at the neatly starched uniforms moving like ghosts across the green lawn between the nurses' home and the hospital. A clarinet was playing, a good clarinet which Joel soon recognized as Benny Goodman. He found he was tapping his foot to the music.

"That guy in the wreck? The one with the head?" a voice inquired.

"Yeah . . . he died. Anybody for a bet on the ball game?"

"Who's playin'?"

"Red Sox and . . . hell, I can't remember."

"You know Doc Harbison folded at the table? Had a guy's intestines spread around like spilled spaghetti and out he went."

"What was it?"

"Heart, I guess. He's had trouble before."

"Who finished?"

"Doc Jacobs. He was assisting. Probably could have done a better job anyway."

"How's Doc Harbison?"

"Complaining. Worse than any patient I've ever seen. And smoking. These jokers really take their own advice."

"Yeah."

Joel finished his coffee. It was nearly ten. Visiting hours were about to begin. He paid for his drink and walked up the concrete path. It was a cool morning for a change. Very pleasant. But the mornings would not be too hot from now on. Summer was practically over. Joel hadn't been aware of the passing days.

He looked up at the old, ivy-covered building. He counted six windows west of the corner of the third floor. Rose's room. A pot of flowers in the window.

She had made it now. The first day had been touch and go. The doctor had asked him to stay only a few minutes. In that time she did not speak to him, but he talked to her softly. He thought she knew he was there, but he could not be sure. Occasionally she would open her eyes and then, as if the effort had been too great, the lids would fall.

The second day she was better. He knew then that she would make it, though the doctor was cautious in predicting recovery. Rose seemed confused that she was alive. Apparently she had made the decision to die, then in her delirium, had revived with clear enough mind to scribble the note to Joel. Perhaps she did not remember that he came, or even that she had asked for him.

Joel had not stayed long that second morning. He showed her the flowers. They were from Uncle Charlie's room, but Uncle Charlie had insisted. Joel did not tell her that no one from the Street had sent her a gift. But perhaps she knew.

Now she was sitting up. Recovery presented problems. Joel brought his Bible into the room. She greeted him pleasantly, but she did not smile.

"How do you feel?"

"Stronger. I can tell." Her hair had been combed, and Lynn had sent a frilly gown. She wore it now.

For several minutes Joel chatted about people who had asked about her on the Street. This done, a difficult silence followed. Joel did not know if it was time yet to plunge into reality. She relieved his apprehension. She touched a flower blossom with her fingers. She examined it sadly.

"I guess I'll be back soon," she said.

"What do you mean, Rose?"

"I'll be getting out of here."

"But you don't really mean back. Is that what you want?"

"I just know how to do one thing."

"You aren't still afraid of Nick? Are you?"

Her mouth hardened. Tears formed in her eyes. "No."

"Do you *want* to go back to prostitution?"

She did not reply. Her fingers caressed the flower.

"Did you enjoy it?" he asked.

She shook her head that she did not.

"But you're afraid you'll end up in it again."

To this she did not reply either. But she looked from the flower to Joel, and back again.

"Rose . . . you owe me nothing. I was on that street before you were born. I'm not asking you to hand out literature or sing hymns or play a flute. So don't play me for a sucker. Let's find out what you want and I'll help you. I'm one guy that isn't trying to get in bed with you. It's time you got over that. Do you want to go home, wherever that is?"

"No!"

"Is it a mess?"

"Yeah . . . it sure is."

"Then that's settled. How far did you go in school?"

"High school."

"Graduate?"

"Yes."

"That's good. Can you type?"

"No."

"Have you ever worked?"

"Baby sitter. Ended up in bed with the father."

Her eyes clouded. She turned her head away. She had not forgotten the baby. Joel waited.

"What would you like to do?"

"I don't know." Her voice was hard.

"Now, Rose . . . the world doesn't owe you a living. If you start feeling sorry for yourself, you'll be back where you were. Maybe you enjoyed that."

"Cut that out," she said.

"Fine. With a high school education, you could be a sales girl. Or a telephone operator. I think you could get a job here in town. I'll help you. Maybe at one of the department stores. Then you could enroll in night school. They've got a school for secretaries over on Broadway. You study typing . . . shorthand . . . that sort of thing. Then you could get a job that really pays money."

"I'm too dumb."

"You aren't that dumb."

She smiled for the first time. Joel lighted a cigarette, very relieved.

"Maybe I should leave town," she said.

"No. Until you get set up, we can't do that. If you got to brooding, you might fall back. You'll have to be independent first."

"I was independent before, and look what I got."

"Like I say, Rose . . . I was on the Street before you

174

were born. I don't want to keep telling you that, but let's face it. You weren't too smart, and so far you haven't done much with your life."

"You seem to be taking over," she said quickly.

"That's right. Just for a while. Until you get set up. Unless you want to go the other way. Maybe you'd better make a decision. You sent for me, you remember."

"I'll go along. I owe you anyway," she said.

"Come off that," Joel said. "If you pay back the money, that's fine. I'd appreciate it. Right now it makes no difference. I'm not buying you."

"So I'm sorry."

"This school idea. Do you like it?"

"I guess. If I can learn." She was taking it lightly, not entirely believing.

"You can learn," he assured. "You'll need help. You can live in one of the rooms over the bar."

"Down there?"

"Right. Are you afraid of it?"

No answer.

"The only way you'll ever regain your confidence is to look the problem right in the face. Soon you'll feel big inside. You won't have any doubts. If you run from anything, it grows. Besides, the room is free."

"Why do you do this?"

"One reason. I told you I'd help you that day in the bar. I've told a lot of people that. But you called me. So I'd like to see you through. If you make it, and, Rose, you will, it will be easier for the next girl."

"That sounds like AA."

"In a way. When you move away, you can send us money for the help. Maybe we can start another girl with it."

"What about God? Do I have to buy that, too?"

Joel drew on the cigarette and thought his words through before speaking.

"That's your business. If I can help, I will. You ask for help. Just like you did when you were sick. If you ask, I'll be there."

"Suppose I don't?"

Joel looked at the flower. It was pink. He knew nothing at all about flowers, did not even know its name. But the petals were beautiful in the soft morning sunshine.

"About this whole thing," he said, ignoring her question. "It's a deal?"

"Yes."

"Then it's settled. Let's don't worry about it. What did you tell the investigators?"

"Nothing."

"Why?"

"I just wouldn't."

"Protecting him?"

"No . . . I just won't tell them. It happened to me. I let him do it to me. I told him I was pregnant in the first place, knowing he'd have it knocked. Besides I just won't tell."

Rose looked out the window.

"There's that lady that writes," she said.

"What?"

"The one that lives up there by you. She's coming up the walk."

By the time Joel reached the window, Lynn had gone inside the hospital doorway.

"She's probably coming to see you," Joel said, very pleased. He was sure that this business with Rose would turn out all right.

"I asked the doctor," Joel said. "In case you want to

know, you aren't ruined. You can still have a baby."

Her face became soft, not at all happy, but soft. He detected a touch of tragedy in the eyes, but not despair. Rose had hope, a feeble, uncertain hope, for the future. It would grow to confidence, but that would take time.

He heard the knock at the door, got up and gestured to Rose. "She did come to see you," he beamed.

Joel opened the door. "Good morning," he said too loudly. He was glad that Lynn had come. It would be a lift for Rose. Lynn could convince Rose.

"Brogan . . . can you come outside," Lynn said softly. She glanced at Rose, then back to Joel quickly.

Somehow he missed it. "Come on in. I've been telling Rose . . ."

"Joel . . ."

"Just a minute, Rose," he said finally.

Out in the corridor he turned, questioning.

"Joel . . . your Uncle Charlie died a half hour ago. I'm terribly sorry."

Nurses passed along the hallway carrying bedpans and water pitchers. A Sister walked along talking to a doctor. Joel was numb. He nodded and kept nodding as though unable to stop, and yet unaware that he was nodding at all.

"Joel . . ."

He looked down at her. She had tears. She bit down on her lip. "Were you there?" he asked. His voice was a whisper.

"No . . . I found him."

"I see."

"I thought I'd better come. I didn't want to tell you on the phone."

"He was good. When I was hurt, he was always

177

around," Joel said blankly. "I should have been with him."

"Do you want to leave now?"

"Yes," he said.

But he did not move. He remained immobile.

In a moment he remembered Rose. He opened the door. "Rose, I've got to go. I'll get my Bible."

"Something's wrong," Rose said.

"Not exactly wrong, Rose. Uncle Charlie is dead. He's in good hands."

"I'm sorry," she said.

Joel took his Bible. "I won't come tomorrow. . . ." He left the room. Lynn slipped her arm around his. They walked along not speaking until they were out in the sunshine. Joel looked up into the cloud-dotted sky.

"Are you all right?" Lynn asked.

"Yes. Suddenly lonely. I suppose you always are. But not crushed. I've a feeling about death."

She did not prompt him. He walked a few yards.

"If you really love right, you give yourself. And when someone dies, you still give. You still love. The people who are crushed the most when death touches them are the people who love possessively. They don't give. They take. When someone dies, it means they can't take any more. The supply is cut off. I don't love that way. Not any more. A chaplain taught me that."

They reached the corner.

"A cab will be along soon," Lynn said.

Joel laughed to himself, a laugh choked with emotion. He was limp, weak. A cab wheeled around the corner. He raised his hand and it stopped. When they were on the way, he asked about the others.

"Viola?"

"She's in the bar. She's torn up. She won't leave."

"Judge Hanson?"

"I couldn't find him."

"Evita?"

"She's in her room."

"What did she say?"

"She's sitting there getting drunk."

Joel rubbed his eyes.

"Joel?"

"I'm all right. Just overcome. I wasn't ready."

He dropped his hand in his lap and watched out the cab window. As they neared Reno Street, the cab driver half turned his head and shouted over the motor, "If you two are gonna have a good time, I know where you can get a real good bottle. Cheaper than the liquor store, too."

Lynn's face flushed with anger. Joel touched her hand softly.

"No, thanks," he said gently. The cab stopped in front of the Green Parrot Bar.

12

Joel noticed that the typewriter noise had stopped. He lay on the bed, his head turned toward the window. All he saw was the shaft of light, the darting flash of the neon signs on the barren bricks of the building next door.

He had not been listening to the typewriter, but he noticed when the sound no longer came. He heard her footsteps in the hall. She tapped his door lightly.

"Come in," he said.

She opened the door, poked her head in first.

"I thought you might be sleeping," she said.

"No." He turned on the lamp.

"You look tired."

"I knew you were going to say that."

"Are you?"

"Drained is more like it. Out of gas."

"I could sneak down," she whispered, "and buy a half dozen beers. Real cold. Would you like that?"

Joel laughed. "No . . . but you make it sound delightful."

"Well, if you won't get soaked, how about some coffee?"

"I'd like that." He started to get up.

"Stay put," she said. "Let me wait on you."

He sat up anyway, slipping his feet into his shoes.

"I'm out of smokes," he said.

She took one of hers, struck a match and lighted it for him. "There."

"Thanks," he said. "I'd better go check on Rose."

"She's asleep. I noticed as I came down the hall."

"Good."

Joel played with the cigarette. He did not really want it.

"You look back on it, it's an ordeal. I'm not going to have a funeral," he said.

Lynn paused as she turned water into the coffeepot. She filled it and put it on the hotplate.

"I'm serious," he said. "The people are already in grief. Lots of them have had about all they can stand anyway. So they've got to parade it in front of everybody. For what? Charlie didn't enjoy it."

"Brogan . . ."

"I'm not upset. I mean it. I think it's a racket. We're all too afraid of what people think to break it off. Except me. I prohibit a funeral. I want a wooden box with little holes so that the water can get in and get it over with." Joel sighed. "Now I'm sick."

"Then for heavens sake, shut up."

"Okay."

"What are you going to do?"

"I knew you'd been hashing that around. Well, I've decided. I've been thinking about it. I figured it out very reasonably. I even made a list. I put down all the things against the Reno Street Church. Then I put all the things for it. And I had a clear view of the entire problem. A practical view, you see?"

"How did it come out?"

"Nothing at all reasonable about a church down here, Lynn. Honestly. For me or anybody to start. The odds are terrible. The punishment . . . it's ridiculous."

181

"I don't blame you. It really isn't practical," she said, her voice edgy. "You've got to think of your future."

"What the devil are you saying?" he asked.

"You decided against it."

"I didn't say that. I said it was unreasonable. Not impossible. I admitted that to Uncle Charlie. And to you."

"You're going to do it?" she asked cautiously.

"It was never really a contest. I'm going to start tomorrow. Frankly, I'm scared. This could be murder."

"I think I'll cry," she said softly. She was obviously affected greatly.

"Are you crazy?"

"I was positive you would rationalize your way out of it. All week I wanted to ask you. I can't believe it."

"You really care," he said, somewhat surprised.

She sat beside him, turned his face with her hands and kissed him. She did not laugh. She warned, "I should never kiss a man on a bed."

Joel fell back laughing, more elated by her real interest in his decision than by her remark. When he sat up, she had poured the coffee. Her face was bright with excitement.

"It will be a terrific job. But I think you can do it."

"The money is the only worry," he said.

"Why?"

"I can last a year or so . . . well, maybe two . . . without any church income, but by then it's got to work."

He sipped the coffee. It was very strong.

"Wow!"

"It walks," she admitted. "But I was nervous."

"One thing, Lynn, they can't fire me. Man, I've really got that beat this time."

182

"Maybe you won't be such an idiot either," she added.

"This stuff I can't drink. I ought to get some doughnuts from the Poor Guy. Would you like that?"

"Yes!"

"I'll run over there." Joel located his billfold on the table and descended the stairs. He was gone for only a few minutes. When he returned, he found Lynn standing very quietly, her finger over her lips.

"Shut the door," she said.

"Okay. What's the mystery?"

"Rose's boy friend came to see her. He asked me if he could."

"Her what?" Joe's shoulder muscles crawled.

"He's down there. I was being quiet so we wouldn't disturb . . ."

Joel jerked the door open. His feet moved swiftly along the hallway. He reached Rose's door, blasted it open with his fist. Nick Martelli was bending over Rose, talking softly. Nick jerked upright immediately.

Joel's mouth tightened across his teeth.

"What do you want, Nick?"

The Philosopher shrugged, and made an ugly U shape of his lips. "Just came to visit the little girl."

Joel eased across the room, his feet flat on the floor. He balled his fists tightly.

"Get out," he said.

"Now, preacher boy . . . you don't want to . . ."

"Shut up, Nick. You nearly killed this girl."

"Oh, no . . . No, sweetheart. You got it all wrong. I was out of town when angel face got it."

"I warn you, Nick . . ."

Joel pressed closer.

"What did he say, Rose?" he asked.

The girl did not answer. She was terrified. Joel kept

183

his eyes on the Philosopher. He asked her again.

"Rose . . . answer me." His voice was only slightly under control.

"I was just seein' how the kid was." Nick was surly.

"Rose . . ." Joel prompted.

"He said he'd make me go back. He said he'd get me in trouble with the cops."

Joel smiled. The smile cut tightly across his teeth and his eyes grew narrow.

"Nick, if you ever open your slimy mouth to this girl as long as you live, I'll beat your head until your brains spill on the floor."

Joel's smile widened. His body trembled visibly, but his voice was soft, almost inaudibly gentle.

Nick shrugged angrily. "Don't play Jesus with me."

Joel's fist smashed with a hideous impact against Nick's face.

Nick fell back, bending forward. He coughed violently from deep in his throat until a tooth dropped on the wooden floor. He got up suddenly, drinking in air through his bloody mouth. An empty spot revealed a fountain of blood where the tooth had been. The click of the knife alerted Joel, and he stared at the blade. He still smiled. His chest heaved as he breathed, but his expression was frozen on his face. A cheerful hate.

"There's your little man, Rose. Look at him."

"I'll call the police," Lynn screamed from the hall.

"No!" Joel shouted.

Satisfied that she had not moved, he fixed his eyes on the weaving pimp.

"No . . . we're going to give the little man a chance to go to the electric chair." Joel took a step forward.

"You hit me. I can defend myself," Nick assured.

184

"Sure, Nick. The jury hears Lynn tell exactly what you said, they'll love you. They'll remember that I hit you then."

Joel took another step, ignoring the knife.

"Cut me, Pimp. You don't need to reach out for it. I'll push it in your dirty face. You just stick it in me and turn it around and around and you'll be there when they pull the switch on you in the chair."

"I don't want trouble," Nick said.

Joel walked into him. He felt the knife blade against his chest. He reached and took the knife out of Nick's hand. He dropped it to the floor.

"Don't hit me."

Joel shoved him against the wall, pressing his hand around Nick's throat. Nick's face began to turn red, then faintly blue.

"You get off this street. You get off before morning. Do you hear me? You be off tonight. Because . . ." Joel tightened his hand until Nick's face became a ghostly white-blue. As Nick sucked for breath, Joel tightened his grip. "If I see you again, I'll see that you end up with the rap for that job on Rose. She'll talk this time. Now you get out. Fast!"

Joel removed his hand suddenly and the Philosopher dropped heavily to the floor. He clutched his throat and struggled desperately for air. Joel stood over him silently. At last the man was able to roll over on his stomach. He tried to vomit, but his convulsive motions soon stopped. He lay for several minutes. At last he drew his knees under him, as the color returned to his face. He pulled himself to his feet and glanced at Joel fearfully.

"Get out," Joel said evenly.

Nick, holding his throat, went through the door,

185

his footsteps fading as he left the building. Joel turned to Rose. "He won't ever bother you again," he said.

"I thought you'd killed him," she said.

"No . . . I was letting a little blood through . . . a little air. I could feel his knees give."

"You have the most terrible smile I've ever seen," she said.

"You go to sleep, Rose," Joel said. "You didn't know the big man could be afraid, did you?"

"No . . ."

"He only knows how to fight women. He may even give that up. But I'll bet he isn't in this town tomorrow. You're safe now. Good night."

He left the room. Lynn was waiting in the hallway. She followed him silently to his room. There she spoke softly.

"You'd better wash your hand. He cut it with his tooth."

Joel held his hand under the tap while she soaped it. It burned.

"You must be crazy. He could have killed you."

"No . . . he's not a knife man. He's never used one."

"There's always a first time."

"He held it blade down. If a man cuts you, he's got the cutting edge up. All he could do was thrust. I was ready for that."

"Did you see his face? I'm like Rose. I thought he was dead."

"You've never been on an advance night patrol."

"Have you killed men like that, Brogan?"

Joel sighed regretfully. "I shouldn't have made a remark like that." He was immediately ashamed.

"Here, I'll dry you off." She rubbed his hand gently with the towel. "You were furious."

186

"I was," Joel admitted.

"Very suddenly."

"He tripped it. I gave him every chance. He knew what he was doing."

"He just thought he did," Lynn said.

"Were you afraid?" Joel asked.

"I've still got a scream that didn't come out."

He laughed. His shoulders began to loosen. He let his arms hang limply, but he could still feel his heart throbbing in his chest. He could feel it in his ears. Joel swallowed and the pressure eased noticeably.

"I got the doughnuts."

"I can't eat them," she said.

"Neither can I."

"How about a cigarette?"

"I'll buy that."

She took two, lighted the first and gave it to him. The second she lighted and puffed vigorously. Joel sighed deeply, then inhaled.

"Will you be a two-fisted preacher?" she asked.

"Oh, no!" he said quickly. "I don't get mad like that. I'll have to take a lot of gaff down here. And I can't hit every meathead that insults Christ, or myself. Still ... I knew Nick. He'd have stayed after Rose. It wasn't her. It was just that she'd kicked him. His other girls would be getting ideas. The only way was to get him out for good."

"And I thought you had," she said. "I didn't know you were so strong."

Joel howled. But he was man enough to enjoy it.

They heard footsteps on the stairs.

"Maybe he went to the police," Lynn said.

"Him?" Joel scoffed.

He went to the door. Evita topped the stairway. She had been drinking. She was not happy.

"You got coffee?" she asked.

"Yes," Joel said. "Come in."

Evita came into the room and sat down heavily. Her hair was out of place and her eyes streaked. She gulped the coffee.

"God!" she said when she tasted its strength.

"It'll be good for you," Joel said.

"How's our wounded butterfly?" Evita asked, gesturing toward Rose's room.

"You'd better talk softly," Lynn warned. "The big man here might get rough."

"What's this?" Evita asked.

"Drink your coffee," Joel said.

"That man that used to own Rose came up and Joel caught him trying to get her back."

"Well, goody," Evita said drunkenly. "What did he do?"

"Brogan nearly killed him. Knocked a tooth out and choked him until he was green. That man has left town!"

"Joey . . . I'm proud of you," Evita mouthed.

"Drink your coffee," Joel said.

"It's crazy. Man spent ten dollars to get me drunk. So I'm drunk and got to ruin it. Ten bucks." She drank from the cup.

"Do you want to tell her the news?" Lynn said.

"Not now," Joel said, holding the coffeepot in readiness.

"What news?" Evita asked too brightly.

"Brogan's going to make a church out of the bar downstairs."

Evita put the cup down and her face sobered considerably. "Don't do it, Joey. They'll beat you to death. Take everything you got and get out."

"No," Joel said.

"That figures. I feel for you. You poor stupid bastard. You want me to move?"

"Why should I want that?"

"You want a whore sleepin' over the church?"

Joel grinned. "I'd much rather have her sleeping over it than in it."

"Oh . . . I ain't goin' to it," she said.

"That's up to you."

"Who do you think is gonna go?"

"I don't know."

"Let me tell you about it. Ain't nobody gonna go. Just a bunch of horses' asses down here. I wouldn't have 'em in my church," she said righteously.

"More coffee?" Joel asked.

"No . . . I'm for bed before I get sober."

She left. Joel turned to Lynn.

"And she may be right," he said.

"You don't believe that," Lynn said.

"No . . . I don't want to."

"I'd better go to bed. Good night, slugger," she said.

She paused at the door and leaned against the wall.

"Kiss me?" she asked.

Joel drew her close. Her body molded against his. Passion mushroomed within him. She leaned her head against his chest.

"I must be in heat," she said.

"You can knock a hole in the wall between the rooms while I work downstairs tomorrow," he said, still stimulated by the excitement of the fight.

"I may do that."

He watched her until she disappeared into her room. She closed the door and Joel went back to the bed and

189

sat down. His hand was growing sore. He examined it, saw the marks the teeth had left. He could not get mad. He'd have to remember.

Joel got up and threw his slacks over the chair. He turned out the lamp and slipped between the sheets. His hand throbbed in the darkness. He thought about Uncle Charlie for a while. The Reno Street Church. When he had become humble enough, he closed his eyes. And prayed.

13

It did not take many tools for the job, and the work progressed much faster than Joel had imagined. A hammer. A square. A screwdriver. The booths were set in place with large screws that had apparently been put in to stay.

Because it was warm, he left the door of the bar open. He still thought of it as a bar. Only when the open-mouthed Green Parrot had been removed, replaced by the sign of the church, would the building become a sacred place.

During the frequent resting periods, Joel was visited by the curious, most of whom had been customers of the bar before Charlie's death. Jelly McSpadden, bottle bulging his hip pocket, paused along his way, noticed the booths being made loose from the wall.

Jelly rubbed his eyes as if unable to believe.

"Joey . . . for Chrissakes, what you doin', Joey? You ruinin' the place? It don't look right."

"No . . . I'm changin' it," Joel answered, breathing heavily from the physical exertion.

Rubbing a four-day-old beard, Jelly walked about the room. "Joey . . . I ain't tryin' to tell ya how to run a bar. Only for Chrissakes, they's nobody that's comin' in here to sit down in a mess like this to drink beer. You ruint the booths already."

"I'm going to make a church out of the Green Parrot," Joel said.

191

The drunk stared at him a moment, letting this information find its rightful place in his muddled brain. "Joey . . . I got only one thing to say. And that is to say you are crazy."

He left, weaving his way to the door, out into the street, wailing that Reno Street was being ruined.

Joel began to work again. Each time exhaustion came to his arms sooner than before.

That morning the salesman from the fixture company made a bid on the bar, booths, chairs and refrigerated cases. They reached a two-thousand-dollar compromise on nearly five thousand dollars' worth of fixtures.

This done, Joel returned to work only to smash his thumb with the hammer. The pain knifed to his shoulder. At this he stopped and walked to the drugstore for an adhesive bandage.

On the way back he stopped to visit with Saul Bernstein.

"How's the arm, Joey?" Saul asked. The little man laughed and hit Joel's arm a sharp blow with his fist.

"It's sore," Joel said. "Take it easy."

Saul laughed. Today he felt good.

Joel turned back onto the sidewalk, bumping suddenly into an unyieldling chest. He backed away, looking into Whitey's eyes.

"What say, preacher?" Whitey said through a cigarette that drooped from his lips. "You 'n' Jesus gettin' us some place to pray?"

Joel's lips became taut. He was in no mood to be pushed. "Yes," he said simply, controlled anger in his voice.

"Good . . . real good." Whitey turned to the boy standing beside him. "Jimmy, you ain't seen the

192

preacher before. He's come down to Reno to save us all from hell." Whitey laughed.

"You boys," Saul said, "leave Joey alone. I call the cops if you don't beat it now."

"Shut up you fat Jew bastard," Whitey said.

Saul's face paled. He went inside and stood with one hand on the phone, wagging his head sadly.

"Whitey," Joel said, "let me tell you something man to man."

"See, Jimmy?" Whitey said to the boy.

Only then did Joel notice the long knife scar on Jimmy's face, the ugly scar tissue that was a badge of honor in the eyes of Whitey and his friends.

"The preacher's gonna give us some Bible study. Tell us about old buddy Jesus."

The tension mounted. "It's this way, Whitey. I've been every place you've ever been and back a dozen times. I've done everything you've ever done except maybe I did it better. I've got a couple of buddies that I used to run with that are down in the State Pen now. Only I quit all that. A man can't live like that. Not for long. He murders himself inside. But I haven't tried to make a Christian out of you. I haven't asked you to hear about my buddy Jesus, as you put it. If you want to hear me, you come to the church. Right now you're wasting my time."

Whitey's face tightened slightly. Then he relaxed, spitting the cigarette from his lips.

"Hear that, Jimmy?" he said. "This guy's a real cat. He's been down here on Reno for a long time. But he's quit all this sinful stuff. And he's got him a real nice girl. You ought to see her, Jimmy. She's a real classy roll in the hay. Is that pretty good stuff, preacher?"

Joel narrowed his eyes. He put down, after considerable effort, the fury that sent stinging nerve impulses through his body. He did not answer Whitey, nor his scar-faced friend whose lips were curled in evil humor.

"You know where the church is," he said. "You'll be welcome." He walked around the unbudging Whitey and his friend. He trudged back to the bar and went inside. He was very depressed, possibly because Whitey was so much like he had been once. Joel knew that in those days, no man could reason with him. He had known all the answers, just as Whitey knew them now. A boy eighteen years old is the wisest creature on earth. Joel smashed his hands together fiercely, painfully remembering the ache in his thumb.

Joel found Angel Demarcus in a bar. Fortunately Angel was relatively sober. Angel leaned against the bar, singing happily along with the music from the juke box. There was little doubt that Angel was trying to figure how to make a couple of bucks. His face was unbelievably distorted from its original cast. His ears were stretched and flattened from too many falls on the canvas, too many punches. The nose was a mass of seemingly boneless flesh, flat and soft.

The facial structure was puffy, scars accenting his eyebrows where gloves had opened gashes. Angel was forty, perhaps forty-five, years old, but there were still many who remembered his fighting days. After he retired from the ring, he had made a living down on Reno Street as a bouncer in bars. He had been fired several times for threatening customers because they refused to buy him a beer. Now he drifted.

Joel had searched him out, not for his pugilistic ability, past or present, but for another talent. The Angel, as Angel Demarcus was more often called on Reno, spent his spare time painting chalk portraits, or

194

sketching caricatures for a beer or two in the bars. He was a copyist, could reproduce anything he saw.

"Hello, Angel," Joel said, resting his hand on Angel's shoulder.

"Wa' you say, Padre? How's it?" Angel replied, returning to his off-key imitation of Perry Como, who was now singing on the juke.

"I need a job done. You want to work a little?" Joel asked.

Angel sang on . . . at last interrupting himself. "Padre," he said in an effort to force his tongue to respond to the nerve impulses from his battered brain. "Padre, I can' work. Ya know. Ussa be able 'a go, ya know. Bu' I ain' go' i' no more."

"I want you to paint."

"Ohhhhhh. Well, Jees . . . I mean . . . labor like lif'in', I can' lif' no more. Go' a hyena." The Angel patted his lower abdomen, indicating the point of injury.

"But you'd paint a window for me?"

"Oooooooh ya . . . sure I pain' a winnow."

Joel took the Angel's arm and led him out of the bar.

"Padre, why ya wan' a pain' a winnow? Winnows is 'a see from."

"I want you to paint a picture of Christ," Joel said.

"Man . . . Chris'? I oney pain' dollies in bars. How'm I gonna pain' Chris'?"

"I've got a picture. All you have to do is copy the picture. But I want a good job. A really good job."

They walked along discussing the painting of Christ. Occasionally the Angel went off on his imitation of Perry Como.

Joel opened the Bible to the illustration of Christ

195

standing with his arms outstretched. Joel let the Angel study the painting.

"Can you do it?"

The Angel nodded. "Ya . . . I can do i'. Jees . . . tha's real good, ain' i'?"

Joel located the ladder he had borrowed from the Majestic Hotel. The hotel used the ladder to replace the 25-watt bulbs in the rooms when they burned out, which was often, because the guests frequently fell asleep with the lights burning.

Joel placed the ladder in front of the clear window. It had taken him the better part of two days to scrape the old green parrot from the glass. He had used Windex repeatedly until now there was no trace of the large parrot that had for so many years been a landmark on Reno Street.

"What I want, Angel," Joel explained, "is the figure of Christ, and all around his body I want the window covered with black. Then on the black part, I have some things to be lettered in white. But the main thing is to get the outline of Christ first. Angel, do you think you can do it?"

"I don' know, Joey . . . I' sure is a nice pain'in'."

"Why don't you sketch the outline first? Then we can tell."

The Angel climbed up the ladder, nearly losing his balance, and began to sketch the outline of the Savior in black paint. Joel had placed all of the colors he would need on a small table beside the ladder.

Joel sat down and watched. The Angel's hands were trembling violently. But when he placed the brush against the glass, by some mysterious inner control, the hand steadied, the brush moving gracefully, artistically, across the glass.

"Padre," the Angel said, "I know ya wanna see, on'y i' makes me shook. Ya know?"

Joel understood. He retreated to the far end of the room, and busied himself with the arrangement of the altar, glancing often at the entrance.

When the outline was finished, the Angel climbed down from the ladder and stood away, studying his work. Joel praised it. It was too early to tell, but the outline seemed to follow the painting.

"Padre," the Angel said, "I ain' had no dinner."

"Sure," Joel said, "go ahead."

The Angel did not move. His distorted features remained impishly immobile.

"What's the matter?" Joel asked.

"Well . . . Joey . . . I go' no cash. I tho' maybe you could advance me some dough."

"For lunch, sure. I'll take you to lunch."

The face of the Angel again became frozen. The eyes expressed intense boredom. "No, ya see, I ea' this same place always. On'y I owe some back. Maybe you can advance me so I pay wha' I owe 'em."

"How much?" Joel asked.

"Five," the Angel said impassively.

"If I give you the five," Joel said knowingly, "I want you to know you don't get the rest until the job is finished. Angel, this is Christ you are painting. You wouldn't pull a fast one under these circumstances. You wouldn't, would you?"

"No . . . Joey . . . No. I on'y owe five an' I can' ea' unless I pay 'em."

Joel handed the muscular giant the five-dollar bill.

"I see ya," the Angel said jubilantly, "an' don' worry none."

Joel watched him leave. Joel was certain that the

197

Angel could do the job because he had seen examples of his work before. And Joel wanted the work to be done by someone who lived on the Street.

Joel closed the door and skirted to the Poor Guy Café for a hot lunch special. Sixty cents.

When he finished, he returned to the project only to find the Angel leaning idly against the building watching a flight of pigeons circling a half block away. Joel had not taken over twenty minutes himself and he could not understand how the Angel had finished so soon. He opened the door and they went inside.

"Did you pay your bill?"

The Angel jerked his head crookedly, as if ducking some stiff right hand of many years ago. "I paid 'em. Boy . . . was they ever glad. Din' believe I'd pay. Ya know."

The Angel sang with great cheer as he climbed the ladder. He still had only learned the first line of Perry Como's record. In all probability he would never learn another word of it.

Joel retired to the pulpit, giving the Angel all the room he needed, occupying himself with odd jobs he had overlooked before, keeping an eye on the painting. For two hours he kept watching. The longer the Angel painted, the better he became, and the louder he sang.

Joel was relieved, because at this point he could tell that the painting was going to be satisfactory.

Joel first began to suspect something was wrong when the Angel switched keys in the middle of one line, jumping it several notes higher, out of reasonable range for his gravel-like voice.

Joel approached slowly. The Angel waved the paint brush vigorously, took a step down the ladder, laughed foolishly, missed the step, grasped for a hold on the ladder, missed the hold and crashed through the partially painted plate-glass window with a terrible shattering of glass. Joel jumped through the opening and reached the stunned Angel, who still held firmly to the brush. Then he caught a brief whiff of the Angel's breath.

Joel examined him carefully. He had a few minor lacerations on the face and lower arms, but that was apparently the extent of his personal damage. Joel helped the Angel to his feet.

"I . . . uh . . . boy, I really come down, din' I?"

"You bought whisky with that money, Angel," Joel said solemnly, as though he were speaking to a naughty child.

A fearful expression swept the Angel's face. His hand whipped into his bulging pocket. He withdrew the hand, almost smiling.

Joel quickly pressed his hand against the bulge and felt the contour of an unbroken pint bottle. Joel turned away and went inside the building, leaving the Angel out on the sidewalk.

Joel sat down, buried his face in his hands in frustration. He heard the crowd of curious, asking what had happened.

A huge hand dropped on his shoulder.

"Padre . . ." the Angel said, "here . . . I done wrong."

Joel looked up to see the Angel surrendering the nearly finished pint bottle. Joel took it and looked away.

"Joey . . . you gonna have a new winnow. Maybe I could pain' a new one."

Joel laughed. He did not want to laugh, and the expense of a new glass was not exactly amusing. But the apelike creature hovering over him with bleeding arms, asking if he couldn't try again, bordered on the ridiculous.

The Angel smiled in response to his laughter, as though he knew that he had done something amusing, and was in his own way proud of his accomplishment, even if it did involve falling through a plate-glass window. Joel overcame his brief flare of humor and set down the terms.

"You owe me, Angel."

"I know . . . I owe ya, Joey. I really do."

"You'll paint another Christ and you won't touch a drop."

"Okay . . . okay."

"It will be the finest painting you have ever done. It will be the most beautiful Christ in Oklahoma City."

"Okay . . ." The Angel was still agreeing, though not as certain that his work could be quite so professional.

"All right. Now get out of my sight. Don't come back until you're sober, which had better be in the morning early. I'll pour this whisky," Joel added, referring to the surrendered pint, "out in the street."

The Angel frowned, but did not speak. Joel knew that he was thinking that pouring whisky in the street was a terrible waste, a really terrible waste . . . but under the circumstances, the Angel did not protest. Again dodging a long-forgotten punch, he staggered to the door. Why he bothered to use the door when the window was knocked out, Joel could not understand.

When the Angel was gone, Joel located a broom and went out on the sidewalk to sweep up the broken glass. He swept the glass into a box, then turned away wearily. He had to order another window. Tomorrow the Angel would be back at his work if he was sober. Joel thought that he would be. He also had to shop for a small organ. He couldn't forget that. That would leave him only three days to visit all the flophouses,

200

hotels, bars and apartment buildings to invite people to attend the opening ceremony on Sunday.

Joel took a notebook from his pocket and jotted these things down. He also wanted a large portrait of Christ for the wall. And a pulpit Bible. Candles. Communion equipment. There were many things to do.

14

The Reno Street Church was in letters three inches tall, white on black. The outstretched arms of Christ, His face serene in this jungle of sin, the pulsating sights and sounds of Reno. His robe was white, unstained, pure. His hands gracefully reaching out. Silently calling the diseased, the broken and torn, the demented, the soul-sick masses stumbling through life day after day, growing weary, struggling blindly. It was completed.

Joel contemplated the church and silently dedicated it to those he hoped to serve. At times his lips moved, but no sound came from them. It was for him a solemn moment.

This church is yours, he silently said to the Street. It is no mission. The rich churches have not given pennies to offer you a prayer and a doughnut, a cup of watered coffee, only to send you on your aimless way. We offer you no uniforms. No bells to ring. No literature to sell. By you it will struggle and grow, or wither and die an infant.

We will ask no charity. But know this. If these doors close forever, it will be because you alone have rejected the higher community of man, the body of Christ.

For you it shall be a place for rest, an ever-burning light to guide your steps. Pause along the troubled way and enter. These doors will be open. Locks will

202

not be installed to safeguard your church from thieves, because all who enter are considered thieves in the society of man.

In this city there are great churches that men bless with the wealth they have won, and with their personal service. There are churches of poverty, where there is no wealth except the wealth that is the love of God.

But this church is neither one of wealth nor one of poverty. This is a church whose members live in the world of professional sin. Yet free perhaps of much crippling hypocrisy. Which one of you could turn to your neighbor and think that he has sinned more than you?

The whore, the alcoholic, the thief, the bastard who lives to hate a man whose name he never knew, the deserter, the opiate peddler . . . down here on these streets a breath away from hell, not one of you enters to condemn another, because you know . . . *you know.*

There are churches whose membership rolls are filled with names of men who have served half a century, and in that service there is quiet pride. But the Reno Street Church will never have such honored names on its rolls. Because when you learn . . . you will leave. You will abandon your illicit trade and move on, shedding the evil of the past for a new self-respect, for abundant life, for daily communion with the God who has given you escape from shame.

And the prostitute. When you have seen Him and felt His love, you will leave your shabby bed and escape these streets. You will look with compassion at those women who are less fortunate than you. Your body will again become a sacred temple, not to be violated by strange men. Our love will go with you.

And you, whose body is a living sacrifice to opiate,

203

or drink, you, too, will leave when He touches you. When His mercy and love give you the strength to win, as He has given strength to others before you. As you leave our street, a great love follows you. As we have prayed, you will emerge into a world where no guilt need weigh upon your heart.

But there will be others. Your younger sisters, your sons will be here. We cannot destroy sin. We can only win out, overcoming it, step by step. Uncertain, afraid, falling and standing once again, until at last you walk with solid footing. This is our church. We take them as they come. Our hands always outstretched, as His hands are outstretched, painted on a glass window, lighted by the neon flashes from the bars and the hotels where the contracts with sin are being made each moment of the day.

Here stands a living fountain of love for those who know no love. The door is open, this Christ waiting silently for these people, His children.

As he finished these thoughts, his dark and broken face was stained. Joel tucked the Bible under his arm. It was time to begin the walk from door to door to issue the invitation. These things that he had been thinking, he had to get across to them. They had to understand what this church really was, and the job would not be easy.

The painting of Christ was artistically good. The Angel had kept his word, his hands were steady. The inside was finished, the altar, pulpit, the second-hand pews. A small organ was placed at the side, below the pulpit, keys polished like freshly brushed teeth.

Perhaps the organ would herald an occasional wedding. It would say farewell to some who fell a final time on the street. On Sunday its voice would fill the room, like the sound of near-by thunder, giving the congregation support, enabling them to follow the notes of the used hymn books Joel had brought. He was pleased with the organ.

On one wall the painting of the Last Supper. Behind the pulpit Joel had hung dark drapes. High on the wall a white cross and beneath the cross a portrait of Christ.

This was the Reno Street Church. In a few days the opening service would begin, promptly at eleven. The building was no longer a bar, not even simply a vacated building. It was a church. And on the window, lettered in very small letters, was his name. *Joel Brogan, Minister.*

Joel glanced a final time at the front of the church. Then he climbed the stairs. When he reached the top, he knocked on Evita's door.

"Who's it?" she yelled.

"Joel."

"Give me a minute. I'm a mess," she said.

"I'll be back," he answered.

Joel walked down the dark hallway, toward the room where Uncle Charlie had given birth to this fantastic idea of a church where once a bar had flourished. To the end of the hall where he knocked lightly.

"Yes," the voice answered gruffly.

"Judge Hanson," Joel said, "this is Joel Brogan."

He heard the springs of the bed, heard the soft steps inside. Then the rattling of papers. "Come in, my boy," Judge Hanson said.

Joel opened the door. The Judge was seated at his desk, his eyes puffy from too much drink, small red and purplish lines beneath the skin of his cheeks.

"Judge," Joel said, "I've finished with the church. Our first service will be Sunday morning. I'd like it very much if you could be there."

"Yes, boy . . . yes . . . I've been busy. Very busy lately."

Joel watched the old man's hands. They trembled badly. He needed help.

"I don't guess you've seen the inside. When you go downstairs, maybe you can take a look. We have an organ," Joel said proudly.

"Son . . . God and I haven't been on very good terms."

"Well . . . maybe it's time to get acquainted again. I'm sure He's willing."

"I'm not interested in God. I owe God nothing. Render unto Caesar that which is Caesar's and unto God that which is God's . . . however it goes. I'm not interested. No, boy. God didn't do anything for me. If taking my family in the fire was God's idea, then I'd as soon be in hell. At least they tell you what you're going to get. I have no use for your idiotic God."

"You really don't mean that, Judge. You're a brilliant man and . . ."

"Take your God and go, Reverend Brogan."

Joel opened the door. "When did you eat last?" he asked.

"Get out!" The old man's body was trembling. Joel reached into his pocket. "I don't want your charity. Take your God and leave."

Joel sighed. "Good-by, Judge. I'll be down the hall if you need me."

He closed the door, prayed silently. He heard the old man shuffle to the bed. Joel returned along the hallway thoughtfully. There would be many like this. The majority would not come. Many would resent him, would be openly antagonistic. But there would be some at the crossroads who would listen. He had to see them all.

206

"Evita?"

"Come in now, Joey," she said.

Joel opened the door. "I came to invite you to church Sunday. We have an organ."

"Yeah, I saw . . . only who's gonna play it?"

Joel laughed. "I don't know. But there's always somebody around a church that can play hymns."

"Maybe not this church."

"You've got a point there. Anyway I'd like for you to come."

"Sorry, Joey . . . I don't want any."

"This is not my day. Judge Hanson won't come either."

"You associate with the wrong people," Evita laughed, lighting a cigarette. "I warned you. They'll murder you out there."

"Maybe . . . but I had to ask you. You do understand?"

"Good luck, Joey."

"Thanks."

Joel went down the stairs and strolled along the street. He went into the Blackout Bar where Luke Jensen was polishing glasses with a rag. The bar was empty.

"How's business?" Joel asked.

"Not so good," Luke said, rubbing his eyes. Luke had a habit of rubbing his eyes. He kept them inflamed most of the time because of it. "What's with you, Joey?"

"Not much . . . Say, Luke . . . you know when you've got no business at all, sometimes you get that sick feeling, like you couldn't make a dime in the Government mint?"

"You ain't kiddin'. I know that feelin'."

"That's good. I'm having my first service Sunday.

And I don't want to be up there without any business.
So maybe you'll come."

"Me, Joey . . . me?"

"I've got seats to fill," Joel said.

"Joey, I ain't been to church since . . ."

"I'm not asking you to sing a solo. I'm just asking
you to come."

"I'll think about it." Luke started to rub his eyes,
then refrained.

"You've got a boy . . . don't I remember you've got
a boy?" Joel asked.

"Yeah . . . kid looks like me. Too bad for him."

"Why don't you bring your wife and son? You can
have a pew all together."

"The old lady would like that. She spends enough
time raisin' hell with me. Joey . . . you want a beer?
On the house?"

"I'll take a rain check. I've got to see a lot of
people. Some of them would swear I was drunk."

A small, well-built, red-headed woman came into the
bar and sat down. She lighted a cigarette.

"What's her name?" Joel whispered.

"They call her Dolly. She's in here all the time."
Joel approached the girl. "Dolly . . ."

"You buyin' or bummin'?" she asked abruptly.

"Neither."

"Then beat it. Hey, Luke, bring me a beer."

"I'm Reverend Joel Brogan," he said. "We have a
new church on Reno. The first service is Sunday morning."

"Bully for you," Dolly said. "Now go die some place
where you won't smell."

Luke was about to place the beer in front of the
girl when she made the remark. He withdrew the glass.

"This credit?" he asked.

208

"Put it down! I'm dry. I'll pay. I always do."

"It just so happens I don't like your attitude. You're suckin' credit out of my place and you act like a rat to the preacher."

Dolly sighed. "Sorry, preacher. Now gimme the drink."

"No," Luke said.

"What I gotta do, kiss him?"

"He asked you to go to church Sunday. At least you can give him a decent answer."

"Why, you house ape. You tellin' me if I don't go to church on Sunday I don't get credit?"

"I ain't tellin' you that. I just ain't givin' no beer on account of the way you act."

The girl turned on Joey. "What'd you do anyway? Hypnotize him?"

Joel laughed. "I'd like for you to come, Dolly. That's all. He'll give you the beer."

"Do you want whores in your church?"

"I don't classify sinners."

"So maybe. Now beat it, preacher boy."

"You could pass the word for me."

"No . . . I ain't no radio station."

"Just tell the girls that work in the same hotel."

"They wouldn't come."

"Good-by, Dolly," Joel said.

"Okay, big boy," Dolly said, "gimme the beer."

Luke put the beer down and blinked, then began to rub his eyes. Joel went on down the street.

He saw Saul Bernstein standing in front of his pawnshop, chewing happily on an unlighted cigar.

"Joey . . ." he shouted, "come in and let me sell you something."

"What did you have in mind?" Joel asked, pausing leisurely in front of the pawnshop.

Saul took his arm and led him inside. "Now I got a croquet set here. I had this croquet set for five years. Why did I buy it? You tell me. Why did I buy a croquet set down where there is no blade of grass and no place to put it down? How much you give me for it?"

"I don't want it," Joel said.

"Joey . . . you always think wrong. If you see a bargain, you buy. Someday later you may want it. So it's a bargain. You better grab it now."

"That's what you did," Joel said, "and you can't get rid of it."

"So now I'm a business failure? How's the church?"

"Finished. First service Sunday morning."

"Fine . . . I saw the window. It's a good window."

"Thank you."

Saul dug into his pocket and came up with a roll of bills. "Joey . . . that's not my faith, but I put a donation in the plate for Sunday. I give my temple a little less. Okay?"

"I don't ask you to give to a strange faith."

"Joey . . . you are *not* a smart boy. For years I think that you are smart, but no. Joey, when you are a preacher or a rabbi or what have you, and somebody makes a donation to the church, you take it fast before they can change their minds. Now take this donation."

Joel opened his hand. It was, startlingly enough, a twenty-dollar bill. Joel looked down on the little man gratefully.

"Now . . . you wanta buy a croquet set?"

"How much?" Joel asked.

"Two bucks. A steal. It kills me. Two bucks."

Joel laughed. "I'll give you a dollar."

Saul's eyes darted at him appraisingly. "No . . . two

210

bucks. Look at the balls. Not a dent in the balls. It's got a case, handle and all."

"A dollar. That's all."

"Get out of my store," Saul said.

"A dollar and a quarter."

"Look at the handles. This is a new set. I should get ten dollars for it. I must be crazy."

"One dollar and twenty-five. That's all. I'm leaving." Joel reached the door.

"Hey."

He turned.

"Dollar and a half," Saul taunted.

Joel started out the door.

"Hey . . ."

He turned.

"One dollar and a quarter. Pay me!"

Joel reached into his pocket and handed over the twenty-dollar bill which he had just donated. Saul frowned. This was painful.

"Is that all the money you got?"

Joel went deeper into the pocket. He found a dollar bill and two dimes and five pennies. He gave it to Saul, who was beaming.

"Good. Now get that croquet set out of here. I am sick of it."

Joel took the utterly worthless croquet set in his hand and started for the door.

"If you can conveniently tell the Gentiles that we've got a service Sunday morning, I'd appreciate it."

"Sure. I'll put a little sign in the window. I'll put it by the pistols. Good-by, Joey. And I would have taken fifty cents for that croquet set. You aren't gettin' any smarter."

Joel laughed and started down the street with his

211

Bible under one arm and a croquet set in the other hand. It caused a great deal of speculation, he noticed.

From hotel to hotel he went. From bar to bar. He found Viola working in a bar on California Street. Uncle Charlie had also left her some money, and he was surprised to see her working.

"I thought you had retired," he said.

"I'd go nuts. I had to work."

"This place all right?"

"Sure . . . I don't make much, but I didn't figure to. What you up to? Slummin'?"

"No . . . The church opens next Sunday. I'm trying to visit everybody I can before."

"How does it look . . . I mean, the old place?"

"Different . . . but in a way the same. It's how you feel, I guess. Are you coming Sunday?"

"No, Joey . . . I . . ."

"This was Charlie's last wish."

"I'd like to come. But, Joey . . . I don't think I'd join."

"Did you think I would insist on that?"

"I didn't want to disappoint you."

"You won't. Just come Sunday. And any Sunday. If you ever want to join, just step up and join. Nobody's after you."

"Okay . . . I guess I'll show."

"Is there anything you need?"

"No . . . I'm fine."

"Would you like to move up above the church? There's a room vacant."

"Charlie's?"

"If you want it."

"No . . . I couldn't."

"Sure you could."

Viola considered. "How much is the rent?"

212

Joel appraised the situation. Viola knew that old Judge Hanson had not paid anything but token rent for years to Uncle Charlie. But Joel knew Viola would not accept charity. "Twenty a month," he said.

"That ain't bad. I'm payin' nearly thirty where I am."

"I'll get the place cleaned up for you."

"Okay . . . but, Joey . . . don't be after me to join the church."

"That isn't part of the deal. That's between you and God," he said.

"I'll send my stuff over."

"Good . . . So long, Viola. Church starts at eleven."

Back out on the street, Joel sighed. Uncle Charlie would be happy if he knew that Viola was safe and warm and had someone to see about her.

During the afternoon he had a tough time. A drunk standing on the street spat at the Bible in his hand and cursed him. He was miserable. He had known it would not be easy. But he had not bargained for this.

There were many more to see. This was only the beginning. He could not falter now. If he touched only one in twenty, he would feel that it was worthwhile. On this street one in twenty made terrific odds.

15

He awoke early, tried to fall asleep again, but was unsuccessful. He gave it up and got out of bed. This was the day.

He took his dark-blue suit out of the wardrobe and brushed it carefully although it did not need attention. He had done it the night before.

Once again he checked his shoes. They were shined to perfection. He inserted a fresh blade in the razor, then checked the coffeepot. As he spooned the coffee, his hands trembled uncontrollably.

Downstairs everything was ready. He had gone over the church with a dust rag carefully, appreciating the work that church janitors had always done for him before.

When the shaving water was hot, he poured it into the sink, added cool water until he had the right temperature. He would be especially careful not to nick his chin this morning. As he was shaving, he heard the knock at the door.

"Come in," he shouted nervously.

Looking into the mirror, he saw Evita open the door.

"I smelled coffee," she said.

"It's about ready. Help yourself."

Evita pulled the knot of her robe tighter. She poured a cup of coffee.

"You want one now?" she asked.

214

"Not yet. I'll get one later."

"All set for today?"

"Yes." He had difficulty with his voice.

He scraped too closely to his chin and the blade tried to dig in. Joel rubbed his chin, but no blood appeared.

Evita sat on the bed beside his suit, and watched him quietly.

"You want to practice your sermon on me?"

"No . . ."

"Where is it? I'll read it."

"I didn't write it. Maybe I'll do better this way. I just made a few notes."

"I'd forget what I was goin' to say."

"I may do that myself," he said.

"I ain't goin'," she said, almost apologetically.

"I know that, Evita."

"I'm leavin' until it's over. All that singin' an' stuff . . ." She made a face.

Joel finished shaving, rinsed his face in the water, then dried it carefully with a towel.

"I looked in last night. Place looks like a church all right."

Joel took his white shirt out of the wardrobe.

"You better drink your coffee first," she said.

"I guess so."

"Are you nervous?"

"Yes."

"I'd be nervous, too. That bunch may be half drunk."

Joel sat in a chair and drank part of his coffee. Lynn appeared in the doorway in a dress he had not seen before. She looked edible. Seeing her gave him a lift. She poured herself a cup of coffee, then sat beside Evita.

"You look nice," he said.

"Well . . . it's a big occasion. Are you ready?"

"Yes."

"You seem nervous," Lynn said.

"He is," Evita answered. "Nervous as a whore in church. And if you've ever wondered how nervous that really is, maybe there'll be one down there today!"

"Are you going?" Lynn asked.

"No . . . I didn't mean me. I'm holdin' out for a written guarantee I'll get a big house in heaven on a gold street."

"What time is it?" Joel asked. He could not seem to relax.

"You've got plenty of time," Lynn said. "I got ready early."

"You gonna give 'em hell, Joey?" Evita asked.

"No."

Evita put her cup away, took Joel's tie and walked to him. "I guess I can do this," she said.

Joel let her slip the tie around his neck. She looped it expertly, pulled it into a neat knot. Then she loosened it and slipped it over his head.

"There," she said. "All ready for you."

"Thank you."

Evita went to the door. "I hope you do good. You poor bastard."

Joel thanked her as she left.

"She's known you for years. I wonder why she won't come."

"Because she has known me so long. She could laugh at any other preacher, maybe even make fun of him. She wouldn't do that to me. If she went at all, she'd be pulling for me. I guess she doesn't want to take the chance that something I'd say would really hit home with her. We have an agreement. She

216

wouldn't make a prostitute out of me if I wouldn't try to make a Christian out of her."

"Maybe later," Lynn said.

"I hope so."

"Brogan . . . how do you feel?"

Joel went to the window and stared at the dingy window pane. At the bricks of the adjacent building.

"It's a go-for-broke deal. This is it."

"You shouldn't feel that way. This is a long, hard pull."

"I didn't mean this Sunday . . . it's just the beginning of the big thing. If I fail . . . Lynn, I've gone under twice. I feel that if I fail here . . . well . . . what's left?"

"Are you thinking about failure?"

"I shouldn't. But this is pretty important. It's not that I don't trust in God. It's just that this is so important. I want to succeed."

"Then you really don't have any worries."

"Okay. Let's talk about you. Let's forget this for a few minutes."

"You act like you're about to be executed."

"I'm not a good speaker . . . I've always known that. I know what to say, but my big worry is being able to say it. How's the book going?"

"It's not."

"Still taking notes?"

"No . . . these last few days I've been watching you. But you don't want me to write about you. I think you said you didn't want to be a character . . . to be immortalized in print."

"I don't."

"So I'm not taking notes. I'm watching you. Frankly I'm a little awed."

"Come on."

"Really . . . you fascinate me. You're like any other minister I've ever known, but the outside veneer, the polish is missing. Your human characteristics are clear. Besides loving the church, I can see your petty angers, weakness, strength, even your faith."

"Is that all, Lynn?"

She lighted a cigarette and spoke through the smoke. "No . . . I have seen your passion. I don't think many women have. All in all, you fascinate me. That's as close as I'll ever come to putting it into words."

"That's close enough," he said.

She smiled wistfully, a trifle sadly.

"Do you want to take me to lunch after the service?" she asked.

"Yes."

"Thanks. I accept." Lynn walked to the door. "I'll leave so you can put your preachin' pants on. I'll be downstairs." When she reached the door she stood with her back to him. "I know this means a lot to you. I feel for you."

"What does that mean?"

When she opened the door, she half turned. "It means I'm nervous, too." She left.

Joel let ten minutes go by. Then he dressed slowly. Thoughts cluttered his mind. Finally he was able to overcome the anxiety he had experienced before. When he left the room, he leaned against the door and prayed. It was eleven when he went downstairs and entered the church.

At first it was a shock. He stood motionless, trying to overcome the feelings that froze his footsteps.

He saw eight people. In a room designed for over a hundred, there were only eight. Rose was there, perhaps because she felt a debt. Old Viola was there because of loyalty to a dead man. The waitress from the

218

Poor Guy was there because she had given her word. Lynn was there. On the back pew a drunk sat, his head sagging against his chest. He was there because he had to get off the street to keep from being picked up by the police. The piano player from one of the bars was there because Joel had paid him five dollars to play the organ. And an old man and his wife were there. Strangely, Joel had never seen them before.

And that was all.

Joel checked his watch. At first he thought that he might be early. But the piano player, turned organist, began a hymn as Joel waited in the doorway. It was not a mistake. This was it. He had visited dozens and dozens of people. Up and down the street he had gone. He had offered his hand in invitation to this service. This was the result. A terrible sense of failure swept through his mind. He had known this feeling before. It seemed now that he had always known it.

His first thought was to leave, to run away, to go upstairs and lock the world out of his room so that he could pound his fist against the wall and demand of God an explanation.

He tried to understand why there were not more. Of course, he hadn't expected the church to be full, not the first Sunday. But these people . . . these were the only ones who had responded, and the reason they had responded was because in some way most of them felt a sense of obligation.

Joel walked slowly along the outside aisle, took his place behind the pulpit. Each face expressed an embarrassment for him, amplifying the first sense of defeat he had felt in the doorway.

Why?

His opening thoughts were pointless now. They would mean little to these people. The organist had finished the hymn with a loud chord which awoke the drunk, who had been asleep. Suddenly aware of his situation, the drunk got up hastily and staggered toward the door. He left. Which made seven.

Joel opened the hymn book and clumsily announced a hymn in the deathly quiet of the room. He could hear them turning the pages of the hymn books. The organist played the opening bars. Joel led the singing. He was painfully aware that his was the only real voice. Rose tried to sing along, but she did not know the hymn. Old Viola could not read the words on the page, and in all probability had never located the right number. But she stood staring toward the pulpit. Lynn was singing, a soft voice accompanying his own. At the end of the first verse, it was so pathetic that Joel ended the hymn at that point.

He began the Lord's prayer . . . and again he heard Lynn's voice joining his. Rose moved her lips, perhaps trying to follow his words, half a syllable behind. The man and his wife mumbled softly.

Several times Joel considered ending the service abruptly. The words were on his lips when Whitey McMillin paused at the entrance, a cigarette in his mouth. Whitey leaned against the door and smiled through the smoke.

"Hey, preacher," Whitey said, "you ain't exactly no Billy Graham." He waved his arm broadly, taking in the pews.

Joel spoke directly to him. "Will you join us?"

"I don't want to watch you play God. You got nuthin' for me."

The elderly man handed his hymn book to his wife, stood and turned to Whitey.

"He has something for us," the man said in a trembling voice. "And we'd like to hear him if you don't object."

The fervor of the voice sobered Whitey. He leaned away from the door. Without answering, he walked away.

The man sat down.

"All right, preacher," he said, "go on. We're listening."

Joel began his sermon. He was not conscious of his faltering delivery. At times he was not certain what he was saying. But he said it. Without using his notes. He did not preach. He talked conversationally. He told how the idea of this church came about. He quoted the verse from Matthew that Uncle Charlie had read over so many times, the one he had underlined and was reading when death came. He told them that Christ had not forsaken Reno Street. It was not an eloquent talk, and perhaps not inspiring. When he finished, he asked those who so desired to come forward, to join in the building of this church.

Rose did not come. She averted her eyes as the closing hymn was played. Lynn looked at him solemnly, but did not come forward. Viola let her head bend down. The waitress from the Poor Guy stared at her hymn book uncomfortably. Only one came. The old man walked down the aisle and stood at the foot of the altar while his wife remained in the pew.

"What is your name?" Joel asked.

"Oscar Francisco," the old man said. "I'll join."

Joel brought the man into the church. He shook his hand and closed the service with a brief prayer.

"I'll help the best I can, Reverend," Oscar Francisco said. When Francisco left with his wife, the church was already empty. Only the organist lingered out in front.

"You think you'll need me next week?" he asked, lighting a cigarette.

"Yes," Joel said.

"I'll take your money. You know I'm just in it for the money, but I didn't give you no five bucks' worth today."

Joel gripped his arm gently.

"We'll try again," he said.

Joel went up the flight of stairs, his legs heavy, a weariness in his body. He found the door to his room open. Rose was there, and Lynn.

"Look . . . I know you figured to help me and all, but I didn't join because . . ."

"Rose, don't tell me that. Think of what it was like with you before. You don't join to make a preacher feel better. You may never join. I'm glad you came, but I didn't help you because I expected you to join."

"I felt kinda bad . . . you know."

"Don't feel that way," he said.

"I better go. I got a little weak," she said.

When Rose was gone, Lynn lighted a cigarette, then put it out after a taste of the smoke.

"Hurt?" she asked softly.

Joel sat down on the bed beside her and sighed.

"Yes," he said. "These are my people. I thought I could reach some of them. It was a shock."

"You can't go by one Sunday."

"No . . . I know."

"How about lunch?"

Joel winced.

"Not hungry?"

"No . . ."

"I understand. It made me want to cry."

"It did me, too," he confessed, "but I think I'd just be feeling sorry for myself. That's no way to start out."

222

"I liked your sermon."

He ignored it. "Lynn . . . what did I do wrong?"

"Nothing . . . maybe you did the wrong people."

"What do you mean?"

"I was thinking down there. You went around and asked all the prostitutes and drunks. You concentrated on them."

"Of course."

"But maybe that wasn't right. What about the fringe people? Like the waitresses in the bars. Maybe they are on the fence. They aren't bitter yet . . . but some of them are slowly falling into prostitution. Maybe some of the men that work around the Street. The ones who aren't in organized vice yet. Did you ask many of them?"

"I concentrated on the worst, I guess. I had that idea in mind."

"But to get started . . . it seems as if the easiest to reach would be the most decent element. Catch them before they get thoroughly lost."

"Maybe . . ."

"About the prostitutes and that element . . . they didn't get that way overnight. Maybe it's not reasonable to expect to change them overnight. Look at Rose. She was new. She hadn't been around long enough to become hardened. She was easier to reach."

"If I've reached her."

"You have . . . give her a little time. She's coming out of it."

"Yeah."

"But Evita . . . Brogan, she's been at it so long it will be hard for her to change. She can't throw up her hands and shout glory to God."

"You might be right."

"I read a thing once. It said the best way to catch

an alcoholic is when he first gets into trouble. Or after he completely hits bottom. The ones in the middle are the hardest. They aren't yet ready to admit they've made a mess of their lives. They think they can stop any time. Does that make sense?"

Joel took the long stub of Lynn's cigarette and lighted it. "I suppose it does," he admitted.

"Then spend the next week working on those people. Get the hardened ones as you can. As soon as you get started, it will be easier."

"I wondered about you," he said. He had not intended to mention it, but he did anyway.

"Why I didn't join?"

"I don't know why. . . . I just thought you might."

"I would have except for one thing. I'm leaving."

He sat immobile for several seconds. He had known that it was coming, but it had always seemed to be a thing in the distant future. He inhaled smoke.

"You've finished the research?" he asked.

"No . . . I don't have a book. It's not for me. I don't want to sensationalize other people's misery. I knew that two weeks ago. Maybe before that. I should have gone before."

Joel pressed the cigarette into the tray. A thin line of smoke lingered, dying slowly.

"Where are you going?"

"I'm not sure," she said, but he knew that this was not entirely the truth.

"When?"

"In a couple of days."

A tone of desperation crept into his voice.

"Do you have to go?"

"You know I do," she said.

"Lynn . . . you said you could turn it off. I guess

for you that's not too hard. You've known a lot of men. Is it that easy?"

She touched his face with her fingertips. They were cool. "No . . . it's not that easy, Brogan."

Joel walked to the window, then away from it quickly.

"Lynn . . . I've never loved a woman. Perhaps there was never a chance before, I don't know. Maybe I just never found one. But I couldn't turn it off. It got all inside of me. All those years alone, and then you came. I don't even remember how it started or how I got lost in it." He felt his stomach tightening, twisting, trembling like the surface of the earth caught in the violence of a quake. "I love you," he said. Then their eyes met, neither able to speak.

A pair of English sparrows darted into view, perched on the window ledge. They fluttered and hopped about, then seeing Joel move, darted away.

"I didn't want it to be this way," she said.

"You cut it off. You really did that?" he asked.

Lynn did not answer.

"That night in the hallway. The jokes about knocking a hole in the wall between our rooms. All the things you said. The way you kidded about us making sparks." Joel sat down beside her. "I knew you didn't fit here. Sure, you had a life of your own in the writing game. But, Lynn, I didn't know how to keep from loving you. It just happened."

"I'm sorry . . . if you only knew how sorry."

And Joel stopped abruptly. His need was not for sympathy.

"Didn't you know what was happening to me?" he asked.

"Yes . . ." Lynn said. "I knew."

"Tell me, do people always love like this the first time?" he asked.

"I guess they do, Brogan." The words caught in her throat. She stood.

"Tell me more . . . how can they ever love again?"

She had gone to the door.

He heard her running down the hall to her room, heard the door close tightly. Joel fell back on the bed, no longer to control the emptiness that at last drowned him. This was complete defeat. He had no further strength. He pressed the pillow over his face so that she could not hear.

17

Painfully Sunday came again. Joel was still unable
to open his right eye. He reached up, touched it gently.
The area was tender, too tender to touch.

His left eye was swollen also, but he could now
open it slightly. His cheek bone on the right side was
aching. Even his lips were swollen, though he could
not remember anything that might have made his
mouth sore. Perhaps when he fell he struck his face.
The pain was worse than the first morning.

He remembered falling. Jimmy's frantic expression
those few moments before he died. Because then he
knew he was dying. For that short time he was aware.
The effort to hold the blood in his body with his hands
was futile, he knew. It was over. Like the snap of a
finger. Done.

During those fleeting instants, Jimmy had time to
see himself as he really was. While Joel prayed for
him. Was he listening? Was he asking for forgiveness?
Or did he just die? Reach the end and stop.

Joel heard footsteps in the hall.

"Joey . . . you got an hour. That's all."

"I'm getting up," he said. His words were not too
clear. The door opened. Evita glanced in.

"You look like hell," she said. "How can you get
up there and talk?"

He flipped his legs over the side of the bed, pressed

245

"I could call a cab," he suggested.

"One will be along." She seemed in no hurry.

No cab appeared. The minutes were long ones for both of them.

"When you write another book . . . you send me a copy. I'll say I knew you when." It sounded corny and stupid.

Lynn laughed. It was a difficult laugh.

"Brogah . . . it's awfully trite, but I hate good-bys."

He agreed, "I'll go back up."

"I'm proud of you," she said. "You'll help these people. It's a wonderful thing."

Joel started away, but Lynn extended her hand.

Although he had prepared himself, he found that he was not really ready for this moment. He released her hand and turned his back. He walked up the stairway, pausing only once to see her standing there.

"I'm sorry," Evita said. For once she was not bitching.

Joel straddled the chair, his chin resting heavily on the back.

"You really loved her," Evita said.

Downstairs he heard the trunk lid of the cab slam shut, the sound of the motor as the driver pulled away.

"Joey . . . if this church thing folds . . . where will you be now?"

He slipped his Bible under his arm.

"Where I was before," he said. "No place."

He started along the street. He went into the bars and the hotels. In the shine stands and the pawnshops. He kept moving. Driving himself along. Though he did not forget her that day, he did not allow himself to pause often for reflection. Until the sun was gone and he trudged back toward his room. A loneliness

228

came over him. It would not be the same with her gone. Joel did not think he could ever love this way again.

A fine mist covered the street. People moved as shadows in the darkness. Joel had not eaten, was not hungry. Yet he felt the weakness that is hunger's close companion.

The lights of the street, blinking red and blue and green became distorted in the fine mist. Automobile headlights were sparklers in the distance.

Joel neared the church, saw the several cars parked along the curbing. There were four of them parked closely together. Three or four boys sat in each car, smoking, talking softly. They turned to watch him as he passed.

They were waiting. Why?

He passed the lead car, then noticed the lights of the church. Joel frowned, quickened his step. He reached the door, opened it silently.

Their backs to him, a dozen strangers, both boys and girls, sat in the pews. Several boys had their feet propped up on the row of pews in front of them.

Facing him, gesturing from the pulpit, was Whitey McMillin, a can of beer resting on the pulpit. Looking around, Joel saw that all of the group were drinking.

Whitey waved the can of beer at him. "Come in, preacher," Whitey said. "I was just trying to teach these delinquents some morals. You want to hear the lesson?"

Joel did not answer. He fought terrible blinding anger. Until at last his anger became quiet inside him. Joel offered a silent prayer, a marvel in brevity and crispness. When he reached the nearest pew, he sat down, his mouth pulled tight. He did not answer

Whitey. He only watched as the handsome blond tipped his can of beer and swallowed.

"Now listen to me, you sinners. Listen to me and beware. God's up there and God knows about your sins. God is angry. You can hear His anger thundering in the heavens. The end of the world is near. He will reach down and in one moment destroy the world and all the people in it.

"God's not gonna stay up there and let you people sin. Put that beer down, Jimmy. Don't drink when I'm preachin' to you. You want to go to hell? Do you know what hell is?

"Let me tell you what hell is like. Hell is fire and brimstone and when you get down there, they don't have beer. You're going down there. You hear . . . you hear me? You're going down there." Whitey pounded the pulpit frantically with his fist. "There's only one way that you can be saved. Listen to me. There's only one way. You got to get down on your knees and give yourself to God. You got to say, God . . . God, I'm sorry. I ain't gonna be evil any more. And God will hear and wash away your sins.

"Do you believe in Jesus? Jesus Christ. Jeeeeeeeesus Christ!"

A few of the group giggled at the overemphasis of the Savior's name.

"Oh . . . I heard you." Whitey wagged his finger reproachfully. "I told you what will happen to you if you act like that. Now listen to me. You've got to give your heart to Jesus. You've got to confess your sins and be saved. How many here are saved? No . . . don't put your hands up now . . . think about it. You aren't saved. Think about all the evil things you've done."

Joel looked away from Whitey, opened the Bible in

230

his hands. He heard the voice of the boy . . . screaming and raving so passionately, resenting the existence of a God . . . a God he was not humble enough to worship. A God in whom he could not have faith, but could not entirely deny.

He found Matthew. . . . *Love your enemies, bless them that curse you, do good to them that hate you, and pray for them which despitefully use you, and persecute you;* Joel closed the book. He heard the words of the young man, but the words were empty words. This was the tantrum-like rebellion of a child. A man in body, a child in spirit.

It would have been easy to condemn him, but Joel knew that condemnation was not the answer.

Whitey paused for another drink from the can. "Now every week we have some miracles. You've seen it done on television by that guy in Tulsa. Well . . . we can cure people, too. I'll just up and cure the whole mess of you people. And you are a mess. You know that? Jimmy . . . I'm gonna cure you of having a hard head. Jimmy, you say, 'Thank you, Jesus,' seventeen thousand times and you'll be cured of your hard head. You won't even make sense after that.

"And, Sarah, you want to be taller. You just get up every morning and say a little prayer and you'll grow an inch a day. Boy . . . I'm better than that clown in Tulsa. Then Jackie is always bawling because she's got a flat chest. Jackie . . . you just have faith and massage yourself and you'll look like Marilyn Monroe. And if you get tired, Mark will help you massage. He's always interested in helping others.

"That just about takes care of everything. Now we're all saved, you hear? You don't need to be afraid of hell any more. I'll get you into heaven. The back

231

door, maybe, but I'll get you in. Now we got one more thing to do.

"Squirrely . . . come up here, Squirrely."

A very thin awkward youth stood and moved self-consciously to the altar.

"Squirrely . . . you ain't been baptized. Now I can't get nobody into heaven if they ain't baptized. You want to get to heaven, don't you?"

Squirrely shrugged and glanced out at the congregation foolishly.

"Okay," Whitey said, "lean over, kid. I now baptize you so that you can get to heaven."

Whitey poured part of the beer on Squirrely's head. Squirrely pulled away when the cold beer touched his neck, and ran insanely back to his pew. This was considered very amusing by the others. Joel remained expressionless.

"I guess that's all," Whitey said. "Church is adjourned. How'd I do, preacher? I'm practically a pro."

"You forgot one thing," Joel said, walking toward the pulpit.

"Yeah . . . well, I wouldn't want to have a service and forget anything. How 'bout that? What'd I forget, preacher?"

"We always close the service with a prayer. Why don't you lead us in the Lord's prayer?"

"Yeah . . . sure . . . I forgot. Okay. All you sinners bow your heads out there."

Joel bowed his head. An intense silence followed.

"Our Father, which is in heaven. Hallowed be thy name. . . . Thy kingdom come. . . ." Whitey's voice trembled slightly. "Thy will be done on earth as it is in heaven." He paused, the room was silent except for his heavy breathing. Joel prayed ahead of him silently.

232

"Give us this day . . ." Whitey's voice ended. "Okay . . . that's enough prayin' for one time. No sense in gettin' all prayed out, is there?"

Joel raised his head. Whitey was coming down from the pulpit, his face and neck flushed. Joel moved aside, let him pass. The others followed him, strangely silent, leaving behind the empty beer cans. . Joel gathered them up.

He looked under the pews. It wouldn't do to miss one of the cans, only to have it discovered the morning of the service. He had collected them when he heard the scream, followed by boiling shouts of rage, of pain.

Joel ran to the door and looked down the street. A large group of teen-agers were gathered in one great heaving mass, struggling, shouting, screaming. Fists flew wildly, a blackjack fell to the sidewalk. A hand was smashed under a heavy heel, and from the hand a zip gun, ready to fire, fell to the edge of the mass. Boys and girls were equally engaged in the struggle, the girls aiming their knees for the groin.

Joel ran toward them. "Help," he screamed, "call the police, somebody!" He reached the struggling group, grabbed a boy and jerked him aside. "Police!" he shouted again. "Somebody call the police."

Cars began to stop in the street. Joel was pulling another boy from the tight group when he felt the sudden blinding impact against his face. His stomach turned suddenly. Joel staggered backward holding his face, seeing the red and blue and green neon lights swimming dizzily until he saw only the misty concrete sidewalk. The second blow fell, smashing across his nose. He dropped, blind now, to the sidewalk.

The world was silent around him. Then the cries

233

began, to reach him. He heard tires burning rubber on the concrete, heard the sound of fleeing footsteps move past him on the sidewalk. He pulled his chest up with his arms and stared into the blurred darkness until he was able to see.

The last car screeched away from the curbing. They had all fled. All except two. Joel reeled forward, trying to establish his footing. He knelt over Jimmy's crumpled form. The boy was struggling for breath, holding his hand over his chest. Joel's eyes cleared and he saw the gaping wound, the throbbing flow of blood, the white, white face. When the boy breathed, blood bubbled from his lips.

"Jimmy . . . do you hear me . . . do you?"

The boy gasped.

"Jimmy . . . Take Jesus Christ as your personal Savior."

The boy searched for breath.

"Can you hear me? Jimmy . . . please . . . ask forgiveness for your sins. If you can't speak, think it. Give yourself to God. Listen to me. I believe in God the Father, maker of heaven and earth, and in Jesus Christ His only son . . ." Joel kissed his scarred face. It was too late. God . . . oh, God, have mercy. . . .

He let the body of the boy fall back against the blood-soaked sidewalk. As he did, Jimmy's hand fell limply away, exposing the terrible wound. His chest ruined by a plunging knife.

Joel pulled himself to his feet and turned to the other. Blood was flowing from the boy's neck, down across the sidewalk in a steadily widening circle. The boy's face was also pale, just as Jimmy's face had been. Joel examined the wound. The knife had slashed the throat severely. The long blond hair was matted in blood. Whitey opened his eyes.

"They were laying for us," he said with effort. As he spoke, fresh blood spurted from the gash.

"Don't talk," Joel said. He searched the street. A few people had gathered. He looked through them. Then he saw a cab cruising along the street.

"Get that cab," he shouted. He lifted Whitey from the street, his foot slipping in the blood, and carried Whitey to the curbing. A woman opened the cab door and Joel slid Whitey across the seat. He climbed inside and slammed the door.

"St. Anthony's Hospital," he shouted to the startled cabbie. "This boy will die if we don't hurry."

The cabbie executed a sudden U-turn and headed toward the hospital, keeping his forearm on the horn.

Joel placed his hands against Whitey's neck and pressed gently but firmly. The flow of blood slowed. He did not stop the flow entirely.

Whitey was semi-conscious.

"Whitey, can you hear me?"

Whitey moved his lips, but no sound came.

"Jimmy is dead. Do you hear?"

Whitey opened his eyes.

"Whitey . . . I asked him to give himself to God and he died in my arms. Listen to me. Whitey, ask for forgiveness. Say that you believe in God, in Christ. Think it. Do you understand? Pray to Him."

Whitey did not move. He stared ahead, as if blind.

"Whitey . . . do you hear me? Let me know."

Whitey's lips moved, and though no sound came, Joel knew he had reached him.

"Just listen to me. . . . I believe in God the Father, maker of heaven and earth, and in Jesus Christ His only son . . ." Joel went on. When he finished, he shouted above the sound of the cab horn.

"Did you hear that? Let me know."

235

Whitey sighed deeply, causing the blood to flow in a sudden spurt. But he managed to move his lips.

"Then do you believe those things? Say that you believe them if you do."

Whitey made the effort.

Joel felt blood running over his fingers, down his arms. "Pray to yourself, Whitey . . . don't think anything else. Just pray. Ask God to forgive you for everything. Think it in your mind. God will forgive you."

"I'm takin' you to the emergency entrance," the cabbie shouted. "We're only a block and a half away."

Joel closed his eyes and prayed for the boy whose lifeless body lay on the sidewalk a few steps from the entrance of the church. Almost within view of the outstretched arms of Christ on the glass. The cab stopped abruptly.

"I'll get a stretcher," the cabbie yelled.

He jumped out of the cab, running inside. Two white clad interns appeared, pulling a rolling stretcher table. They saw the way Joel was holding the open gash at Whitey's neck.

"All right," one of them said, "you keep your hands where they are. We will lift him out. Try not to move your hands. You've slowed the flow."

Joel slid across the blood-wet seat, holding his hands firmly as they lowered Whitey to the stretcher.

"Inside now," the intern said. Joel walked beside the moving stretcher, trying to seal the life inside of this boy. They reached the emergency room. A doctor was thrusting his hands into rubber gloves. He studied the patient briefly.

"Do you want him on the table, Doctor?"

"No . . . don't move him."

A nurse in gown and mask and gloves opened a

236

towel-wrapped package of instruments and placed them on a tray. She pushed the tray near the doctor with her foot. "Ready, Doctor," she said.

"Plasma. Quickly," the doctor said.

The intern cut away Whitey's shirt and rubbed the arm with alcohol. He fastened a needle to a long tube extending from a bottle, then inserted it into the vein at Whitey's elbow.

"Take a sample of that blood. Let's get some whole blood ready. Hurry . . . I want that typed in record time."

The intern drew some of the blood into a syringe and rushed to the laboratory.

"Just hold your hands steady," the doctor said to Joel. "How did it happen?"

"A knife."

"Good."

Joel frowned.

The doctor, seeing his expression, shrugged. "We don't have to worry about foreign matter. If it happened by glass, we'd have to search for it. There may not be time for that. A knife is clean. It just cuts."

Joel's hands were trembling now. He tried to control them. "I don't know his type," Joel said, "but my type is A positive."

"You can't give blood. You may need some yourself."

Whitey was staring at the bright lights above him.

"Step up the flow of plasma," the doctor instructed. The intern returned with bottles of blood.

"Type O positive," he said.

"Get it in him," the doctor said. Then to the nurse, "Clamp."

The nurse slapped the instrument into his hand.

"Take your hands away," he instructed Joel.

Joel removed his hands, the flow of blood increasing instantly.

"If he lives, you saved him," the doctor said indifferently.

The intern wheeled a table into the room. "Get on this," he said to Joel.

Joel lay down and the intern rolled his sleeve up past the elbow. He was given a shot.

The doctor was busy, yet seemingly aware of the intern's progress. Joel lay motionless, breathing rhythmically, his eyes resting on Whitey. Joel started to sit up.

"Just stay there for a while. We'll get to you in a minute."

"I'm all right," Joel said.

"With about ten stitches you will be," the doctor said without looking away from his field of operation.

Joel touched his face. He was bleeding from a cut over his left eye. He had not even known.

The intern rubbed a salve on Joel's left eye and cheek.

"Sew him up," the staff doctor said.

Joel did not feel the needle. In ten minutes the intern had finished.

The blood transfusions were doing the job on Whitey. His face had more color, his breathing easier. The doctor had stopped the flow of blood, was busy suturing the gash.

"You'll have a scar, son. But not much. Are you leaving?" he asked Joel.

"Yes."

"Does this boy have relatives?"

"I've heard of his mother."

"You'll tell her? Stop at the desk."

"I imagine she knows," Joel said. "The word spreads fast."

"Then just leave the information about him at the desk, will you?"

"Yes . . ."

Joel went to the door, aware of the ghastly blood-stains on his shirt. His head was throbbing painfully. When he opened the door, a man in a brown gabardine suit stepped forward. "You're Brogan, the preacher at that church where it happened?"

"Yes."

"Detective Hazlett. Will you come down and tell us about this?"

"Yes . . . I've got to stop at the desk."

"All right."

A small, agile man crouched in front of Joel. Joel was blinded by the light of a flash bulb. "How about the story, Brogan?"

"All right."

"Later," the detective said.

There was obvious friction between the reporter and the detective.

"I left my hat in there. I'll get it."

"Hurry, Brogan," Hazlett said.

Joel went back into the emergency room. He walked around Whitey.

"Whitey . . . are you awake?"

"Don't ask him questions. I'm trying to sew him up," the doctor snapped.

"Sorry," Joel said. "Whitey . . . a reporter is outside. And a detective. I'm going to tell him the truth. I'm telling him that you and your group were having a youth service in the church. And after it was over, this group of boys jumped you and your friends. I'll tell

239

them you led the service. I'll also tell them that you don't have any idea who jumped you."

"What are you up to?" the doctor asked. "Are you a minister?"

"Yes, Doctor," Joel said. "Will the detectives quiz him tonight?"

"Nobody will quiz him tonight. He'll be under morphine. You'd better find a bed yourself. We gave you a shot."

"Thank you, Doctor. Good-by, Whitey."

Joel went outside the door.

"I guess I lost the hat on the way," he explained.

"Let's go," Detective Hazlett said, taking Joel's arm firmly.

"How about the story, Brogan?" the reporter said.

"I guess we have time for that." Joel resisted the pressure of the detective's hand.

"Brogan . . . let's go."

"Mr. Hazlett, are you asking me to help you, or are you arresting me?"

Before the detective could answer, Joel turned to the reporter. "The boys and girls had a youth meeting in our church. Whitey McMillin, the boy inside, led the service. When it was over, they went outside. A group of cars were parked there and boys started getting out. They had been waiting until the service closed. They killed one boy. Nearly killed another."

"What is the name of your church?" the reporter asked, writing hurriedly.

"The Reno Street Church."

The reporter paused. "Is that a mission sponsored by . . ."

"It is not a mission. It is a church. Just like the one you attend."

240

"I see."

"Is that enough?" Joel asked.

"The cab driver said you held the boy's throat to keep him from bleeding to death. Is that right?"

"I tried to apply pressure," Joel said.

"How is the boy?"

"You'll have to ask the doctor. He's going to live. That much I know."

"What happened to your head?"

"I tried to stop the fight. Somebody clobbered me."

"Thanks, Reverend. Thanks for taking the time."

"Not at all," Joel said and turned to Detective Hazlett.

"As soon as we stop at the desk, we can go downtown."

At headquarters, Joel was seated in a comfortable chair. The detective popped questions at him. "Do you think Whitey had this rigged?"

"That's what you've been trying to figure. It shows all over your face," Joel answered.

"You don't think I believe that nonsense about Whitey's leading a service in the church, do you?"

"That's your business."

"I've given that kid two warnings. If he was the cause of this one, I'll send him up."

"You think so, with me as his witness?" Joel asked.

"I suppose he led the group in prayer, too?"

"The Lord's Prayer," Joel detailed.

"You don't like police, do you, Brogan?"

"No. Not much."

"Why?"

"Because I know a fat slovenly cop who pads along Reno collecting from the prostitutes. He's from the vice squad. I can have his name for you in five minutes

241

if you want it. I can also give it to the reporter. And I don't like that kind of cop. Did his collections help buy that gabardine suit of yours?"

"I don't appreciate that crack," Detective Hazlett snapped.

"Okay!" Joel shouted. "Give me the phone. It's there on your desk. Hand it to me. You want to know the name of the payoff man? Do you, cop?"

The detective sighed. "Don't get excited, Brogan."

"Lay off those kids. They were jumped tonight and you know it. But it's good business to send Reno Street kids to jail. A few months ago a bunch of kids from some of the most prominent families, one even from Nichols Hills, stole some dynamite and were planning to blow up a bridge for kicks. That one got hushed up pretty fast. But you can have a field day down on Reno. Nobody cares. But before you send Whitey to jail, you'd better be ready to clean your own house, because I'll talk like a parrot. I grew up on that street."

"You can go, Brogan," the detective said and flipped his hand toward the door.

"Thanks. Tell the fat man I'll be watching him."

"Brogan," the officer said, standing, "that kind of thing happens from time to time. The officers are usually caught and fired. This isn't the only city where an underpaid cop takes a payoff. Sure, it can happen. But that doesn't mean we're all a bunch of hoods with badges."

"I hit where it hurt, didn't I?"

"Yeah."

"I just want my kids to get a fair break."

"They will. I give you my word. Maybe you'll help Whitey. I hope so. I'll have a car take you home."

"Thanks."

When he was back on Reno Street, the squad car

242

stopped. Joel got out, becoming dizzy as his feet touched the pavement.

"You okay?" the officer asked.

"Yes," Joel said. He closed the door of the squad car. Several people were still standing around the spot where Jimmy and Whitey had fallen. They made way as Joel came through. It was raining now and the blood had been washed from the sidewalk, carried away by small currents through a drain, disappearing in a sewer.

Joel started upstairs.

"Reverend Brogan."

Joel turned. He was dizzy and sick at his stomach. "I'm Harry Byrd from the television news staff. We'd like to interview you."

"There isn't much to say."

"I can't tell my manager that. Why don't you let us ask you a few questions and take some film? Do you want to go upstairs?"

"I'm a little shaky," Joel said wearily.

Harry Byrd jerked his thumb to the camera boys. They followed Joel up the stairway, into his room.

"Why don't you sit down in the chair," Byrd said. He gestured the cameraman into position. "Suppose I just ask you about what happened?"

"All right." Joel touched his eye. It was becoming painful.

The newsman asked Joel the same general questions he had been asked by the reporter at the hospital. It did not take over five minutes. Harry Byrd thanked him and explained that the film would make the late news show at midnight and would be picked up for the morning newscast in case he wanted to see it. He picked up his hat and followed the cameraman out.

Joel took off the shirt, filled the sink with cool

243

water, and put it in to soak. The hypodermic was taking effect, but it did not stop the throbbing in his head. Neither did it stop the recurring vision of Jimmy's body on the sidewalk, his hand futilely pressed over the wound in his chest. Of Whitey's willingness to accept God in the taxi. Of the sudden blinding impact against his face. At last Joel relaxed and finally the drug blotted out the ugly sight.

17

Painfully Sunday came again. Joel was still unable to open his right eye. He reached up, touched it gently. The area was tender, too tender to touch.

His left eye was swollen also, but he could now open it slightly. His cheek bone on the right side was aching. Even his lips were swollen, though he could not remember anything that might have made his mouth sore. Perhaps when he fell he struck his face. The pain was worse than the first morning.

He remembered falling. Jimmy's frantic expression those few moments before he died. Because then he knew he was dying. For that short time he was aware. The effort to hold the blood in his body with his hands was futile, he knew. It was over. Like the snap of a finger. Done.

During those fleeting instants, Jimmy had time to see himself as he really was. While Joel prayed for him. Was he listening? Was he asking for forgiveness? Or did he just die? Reach the end and stop.

Joel heard footsteps in the hall.

"Joey . . . you got an hour. That's all."

"I'm getting up," he said. His words were not too clear. The door opened. Evita glanced in.

"You look like hell," she said. "How can you get up there and talk?"

He flipped his legs over the side of the bed, pressed

245

his hands against his temples and sat up. It hurt. But soon his head was clear.

"You need anything?" she asked.

"No . . . thanks, though."

"How can you talk? Your lips . . ."

"I'll talk," he said, making an effort to speak clearly.

Evita came on into the room, filled the pan with water and put it on the hotplate.

"You want coffee?" she asked irritably.

He sat on the edge of the bed. "Yes."

She fixed coffee water, put it on to heat.

"Which suit?" she asked.

"Blue," he said.

She got out his blue suit. Put his shoes in place. Selected socks to match and tied his tie. She handed him a cup of coffee.

"That's all except to put on your pants," she said.

"I think I can manage," Joel said, grinning painfully. "I feel better. I'll take an aspirin. Are you coming?"

"No . . . I'm not having any."

"I understand," he said. "And thanks for the help." Evita left. Joel got up, went to the sink. He looked into the mirror. His face was bad. Bruised and swollen. Discolored. It did not seem possible that two blows from a rubber hose filled with lead could do this much damage. His mouth was not as swollen as he had first imagined. Very carefully he began to wash around his chin and the areas he could shave. He sipped his coffee from time to time and remembered yesterday, Saturday.

It had begun when the strange woman had come to see him. She opened the door, stood nervously before him. Her eyes were drawn, a darkness beneath the

246

lashes suggesting fatigue. Her face was square-shaped, homely. She twisted her hands nervously, wrinkled hands, ugly hands. She wore a work dress of plain cotton. If it were not for the expression in her eyes, she would have appeared a completely drab, miserable woman.

But the eyes expressed a hopefulness, a faith that Joel instantly knew had carried her through years of toil and sadness.

"Yes?" Joel asked. Strangely his head had not been too painful.

"You are Reverend Brogan?"

"I am."

"I'm Whitey McMillin's mother."

"Sit down, Mrs. McMillin," Joel said. He glanced about the room quickly to see if he had left the blood-soaked shirt in sight. He remembered placing it in the sink Friday night.

"I came to thank you for saving my son."

"I didn't save your son, Mrs. McMillin," he said quickly.

"I know what you mean. You mean God willed it, don't you?"

"Yes . . . it's almost that simple."

"But I wasn't talking about his life. I was talking about what you told the reporter and the police. It's here in the newspaper."

She placed a folded newspaper on the table.

"Well . . . that was not far from the truth," Joel said.

"I left Whitey a few minutes ago. He told me the truth. He said that he was drunk and saying things about Jesus in the church."

She frowned, gripped her purse nervously. Then with a sigh she went on.

"I want to thank you . . . you probably saved my

247

boy from prison. If he ever went there, he'd be lost."

"But he won't go. So we won't entertain thoughts like that."

The woman smiled. "You're different than I expected. He told me that you talked to him on the way to the hospital, when he might have died."

"He said that this morning?"

"Yes."

"I'm glad to hear that, Mrs. McMillin. I really am."

"He couldn't understand how you could be so worried about him, after he said all those terrible things in the church. I think that really made him understand."

"Your boy has a lot of ability." It was a charitable statement.

Mrs. McMillin smiled. "I'd better go. I'm due at the laundry. Whitey asked me to tell you he wants to see you if you can come visit him. He wanted to see you today. Maybe you don't have time today?"

"I'll have time, Mrs. McMillin."

"Thank you . . . and you'd better let them look at your face. You took a mighty blow yourself."

"I'll do that."

"Good-by, Reverend Brogan."

"Did Whitey mention that the church will open tomorrow?"

"Yes . . . I'll be there. You can depend on that."

"Good . . . and I'll see Whitey today."

She was gone. Joel had opened the newspaper and caught his breath. His picture was two columns wide on the front page, taken just as he had left the emergency room, the blood-soaked shirt displayed grotesquely. Joel read the story. He went downstairs, crossed the street and entered the Poor Guy Café. Heads turned as he sat on a stool.

248

"Good morning, Joey," the waitress said. "How would eggs taste to you?"

"Just fine," he said.

"Did you see the TV news?" she asked.

"No."

"You was on it. Boy, live, right there. It was on at seven-thirty. Imagine that. You was on practically every set in the city. Actually, you're famous now. The guy said you saved Whitey's life."

A man with a soiled shirt and greasy carpenter's overalls leaned toward him.

"It was on the late news last night. I seen it in a bar. Say, pal, you really got clobbered."

Joel flushed, picked up his water glass.

"Not speakin' unkindly about the dead, Joey," the waitress said, "but everybody knows that Whitey and that Jimmy kid had been givin' you a hard time. You went all out for that kid."

Joel had never done anything newsworthy before, if this could be considered outstanding. It seemed to him that anybody would have done the same. There was simply no other way to react to what he saw. But now they were making a big thing out of it. He didn't know how he was supposed to act. It was an odd situation for him.

Everywhere he went they had recognized him. At the hospital they greeted him warmly. The Sister insisted that he follow her downstairs to have his bandage changed. The doctor, knowing he was a minister, purposely told a dirty joke for his benefit as he changed the bandage, and enjoyed it tremendously when Joel laughed. And he had seen Whitey.

Whitey had his head between two blocks so that he would not turn suddenly in his sleep. His neck was heavily bandaged. He appeared slightly paler than before, but seemed to be feeling strong.

"You really took one," Whitey said slowly.

"Well, you haven't been watching any pingpong matches this morning, I guess." Joel gestured to the blocks.

"No."

"Your mother said you wanted to see me," Joel said.

"To tell you this thing. I owe you favors. You lied for me. For you that wasn't easy, I guess." Whitey was more cocky than Joel had expected.

"I didn't exactly lie. Anyway don't noise that around. I had cops in my hair last night."

"I told 'em about Jimmy. His folks are in Dallas. They'll take him home, won't they?"

"I'm sure they will."

"Did Jimmy say anything before he cut out?"

"No . . . not a word."

"It was my idea to go mess around the church. He wanted to sneak into a movie. I had to be smart."

"Don't think of it that way. They'd have tangled with you sooner or later. It was bound to come."

"Mom said it was on TV. And in the papers. They won't show 'em to me."

"Why would you want to see them? You were there."

Whitey grinned. "Yeah . . . I was!"

"I'd better go," Joel said. "They told me just to say hello and leave. When you feel better I want to talk to you about the church. You lead that bunch of characters. You could help."

"I never figured myself for Sunday School," Whitey said quickly. He was not dying now. His willingness to accept God lessened as his physical condition improved.

"No . . . I don't imagine you'll be much help."

The boy's face contorted. "I didn't mean that. After what happened, I owe you. I mean . . . it's a debt."

"God doesn't want you to do any favors. And let me tell you, kid, neither do I. If you come into this thing owing me, you'll be back in court in two months. Oh, wouldn't I love getting my head cracked to have you turn up in a lousy court. Listen, boy, I told you once and I'm telling you again. I've done all you've done, but I did it better. A man died trying to get me to understand God, and he wasn't asking or expecting favors for himself. He said it was for me. The idea was I'd be a better man. That's what it is. If you want to go on until some bastard cuts your intestines out, that's your business. If you need God, you need Him for yourself. You make me sick with your debts."

Whitey stared somewhat sullenly. He did not speak.

"Remember your cheap talk about my buddy Jesus? You haven't such a short memory you can't remember that. You were pretty cocksure of yourself then. Jesus was a very funny joke. You were real sharp up in that pulpit, too. Big man. Baptize a boy with a can of beer. Oh, you were great, Whitey. Real great."

"Look . . . I said I wanted to make it up."

"No," Joel shouted. "Not to me. I just wish that when you were dying you could have seen yourself up there in that sacred pulpit making sleazy jokes about God." Joel drew a deep breath. His jaws set tightly.

"I'm sorry," Whitey said. "I'll do what you want."

"No . . ." Joel's voice dropped into a deep register and he was remembering his own terrible hours of doubt. "I need you, boy. You don't know how much.

251

But I want all of you. I don't want a paid obligation. You know the life you've had. A year in a correctional institution. If I hadn't lied, you'd be on the way to the state penitentiary. Don't bribe me with talk about a few sessions in my church. If you come to me, and I hope you do, it's because you know you need help. The whole bunch of you needs help. I don't want an answer now. Anyway you aren't ready to give one. But if you come, boy . . . I'll use you."

Joel went to the door. He opened it and paused.

"Just be concerned with Whitey McMillin and God. You're lucky. Jimmy didn't have that chance. He died on a dirty street. You think about it. I'll see you later."

Joel had closed the door. He had stood outside quietly for several moments. Then he had gone back to Reno.

He found Rose on the telephone and Evita was standing near by, smoking.

"Here he is now," Rose said. She handed him the phone.

"Hello . . ."

"Reverend Brogan," the voice tinkled, "I'm Mrs. T. H. Horton. I saw you on television this morning and I want to send a donation to your church."

Joel recalled Saul Bernstein's advice.

"That would be nice," he said. His head was aching.

"Perhaps we could get you to speak at our club sometime."

"Speak?"

"About your work with *those* people."

Joel sighed at her inflection. "Perhaps," he said.

He got rid of her, then turned to face Rose and Evita.

252

"What is this?"

"Do-gooders," Evita said. "They been callin'. Every-time I think I got a trick, it's a do-gooder. They just want to grab onto your coattails. The bitches."

"Some of them are nice," Rose defended.

"Cat crap!" Evita snapped.

"Rose . . . tell them I'm out. This isn't my meat."

"Sure . . ."

"But don't turn down any money. Do-gooders or not, we need it to run the church. We went in the hole last Sunday."

Evita started down the stairway. "If one of them calls is for me," she sassed, "do-gooders or not, tell 'em to send money. I'm in the hole today myself."

Joel went to his room. Occasionally the phone rang. It did not ring nearly as often as Rose and Evita had imagined. He sat down and started on his sermon. He heard it ring again.

"He's out," Rose said.

A pause.

"I don't know when he'll be back."

Another pause.

"Okay . . . I'll ask."

Rose appeared at the door.

"It's an operator in St. Louis. They want you."

"St. Louis?"

"What should I say?"

"I'd better take it. Long distance . . . I don't know anybody in St. Louis." He picked up the phone. "This is Joel Brogan," he said.

"One moment for St. Louis." Then, "I have your party. Go ahead."

"Brogan . . . are you all right?" Lynn said.

He could not respond. His pulse hammered pain-fully behind his bruised eyes.

"Brogan . . . hello . . ."

"Yes . . . I'm all right," he said finally.

"I saw a wirephoto of you. You were smeared with blood and you . . . Brogan, it scared me. Are you sure you're all right?"

"Yes . . . just bruised," he said. His fingers were moist. He was trembling. He could hear her breathing into the phone, so close. "I'm glad you called, Lynn. I mean, I'm sorry you were worried and . . ." He stopped. He was making no sense at all.

She did not speak for several moments. Her voice became soft and deep. "Brogan . . . I've got to finish up some loose ends here. It may take two or three days. Has anything changed with us?"

"No, Lynn."

"I can't help it. I don't think I could get any more miserable."

"Lynn . . . what are you trying to say?" Joel's throat constricted painfully.

"I want to knock a hole between those rooms, Joey. I want you. Marry me, Brogan. . . . I love you."

His grip tightened on the phone. "Lynn, can you take Reno?"

"Oh, Joey . . . you crazy fool!" She was crying now.

"Come on back," he said. It was all he could manage.

"I'm coming, Joey . . . I love you. I'm coming."

When he had left the phone he was exhausted.

And now it was Sunday. Joel looked into the mirror and examined his shave again. He put on his shirt and slipped the tie under the collar. In a few minutes he opened the door. Rose was coming up the stairs. "It's time," she said. "The people are waiting."

Joel nodded. "I'm ready."

254

But this was his place. Reno Street. These were his people. He understood them. He loved them.

Joel Brogan listened to the throbbing organ. His heart grew full. Then he took the final step and swung into the Reno Street Church.

He said good morning to God.